# Reawakening

## the

# *Dragon*

## Jessie Donovan

*Reawakening the Dragon*
Copyright © 2015 Laura Hoak-Kagey
Mythical Lake Press, LLC
First Edition

Cover Art by Clarissa Yeo of Yocla Designs.

ISBN 13: 978-1942211303

*To My Family*

*They continue to support me even if I don't get to see them for months because I'm under a tight deadline. I love them all and am grateful to have them.*

# Books by Jessie Donovan

## Stonefire Dragons
*Sacrificed to the Dragon*
*Seducing the Dragon*
*Revealing the Dragons*
*Healed by the Dragon*
*Reawakening the Dragon*
*Loved by the Dragon*
*Surrendering to the Dragon*
*Cured by the Dragon*

## Lochguard Highland Dragons
*The Dragon's Dilemma*
*The Dragon Guardian*
*The Dragon's Heart*
*The Dragon Warrior* (Feb 2017)

## Asylums for Magical Threats
*Blaze of Secrets*
*Frozen Desires*
*Shadow of Temptation*
*Flare of Promise*

## Cascade Shifters
*Convincing the Cougar*
*Reclaiming the Wolf*
*Cougar's First Christmas*
*Resisting the Cougar*

# CHAPTER ONE

Jane Hartley plumped up her breasts in the low-cut dress and decided it was time to quit stalling. She had a job to do.

As she walked into the Fox and Stag pub, she gave a cursory glance around the crowded room. The bar was wooden and worn. The nicks spoke of more than one pub fight.

A billiards table was at the far back and the rest of the space was dotted with tables and patrons. Most of them were men, although there were a few other women here and there. All of them were dressed in more casual clothes than Jane's tight dress, which was already attracting notice. One or two men gave her lewd glances, but she merely smiled and headed for an empty seat near the bar.

Despite the heavy make-up, tight dress, wig, and heels, Jane wasn't there to pick up a man. According to one of her contacts in Manchester, some of the former Carlisle-based dragon hunters liked to have a few pints there on Fridays. Since the pub was full of somewhat shady-looking men, the hunters should fit right in.

She hoped to find out something useful or she'd have to reevaluate her strategy. She'd already wasted two days of her vacation tracking down the Fox and Stag in Newcastle. The former hunters' hangout in Carlisle had been abandoned after their loss to the Stonefire dragons earlier in the year. Who knew how long they'd use Newcastle and its surroundings as their new base. If she couldn't find the hunters, she couldn't write the story that could change the course of her career. Jane wanted to be more than a pretty face on camera, interviewing passersby. She wanted to be a true journalist.

The thought of never reporting stories that could make a difference in the world made Jane clutch her purse strap tighter. Working with the Stonefire dragon-shifters had reignited her drive to find out the truth and she would find her story even if it killed her. After all, no human had ever revealed the inner workings of the dragon hunters.

If Jane could do it, not only would she have the story of the year, she could also help sway public opinion even more in favor of the dragon-shifters. She knew firsthand from her interactions with Clan Stonefire that they weren't monsters. The trick was proving it with facts and a narrative that would tug at the public's heartstrings and make a lasting impression.

Reaching the bar, Jane slid into an empty seat and smiled at the bartender. It was time to get to work.

After asking for a pint, Jane casually staked out the room from the corners of her eyes. The largest group of men was seated behind her and to the left. Inspecting her nails as she waited for her drink, she listened to the group.

One of the men said, "Check out that bird. She's well fit. I'm going to chat her up."

The man didn't speak with a Geordie accent, but rather a Scouse one, which meant he was from Liverpool. Since Liverpool didn't have a dragon hunter branch, the man could be from the Carlisle group. One of the trademarks of the Carlisle branch was that they recruited from all over Great Britain.

# REAWAKENING THE DRAGON

She needed to talk with the men behind her and find out if her hunch was correct.

Jane's lager arrived. Taking a sip, she waited to see if any of the men would approach her. If not, she'd have to take matters into her own hands.

She didn't have to wait long. Less than a minute later, a man of average height, wearing jeans and a button-up shirt with the tails hanging out appeared on her left. His voice matched the Scouser from before. "Hey, beautiful, did you fall from heaven?"

Resisting the urge to roll her eyes, Jane forced herself to smile and change her voice into a flat American accent. "I guess that line works on either side of the pond."

The man smiled. "You're American."

"Yes, I'm here on a little vacation." She leaned forward a fraction and the man's eyes darted to her cleavage. "It's been awesome so far. Everywhere I turn, the men have such sexy accents. I can never get enough."

He met her eyes again and his smile grew wider. "Well, love, this is your lucky day. Me and my mates would love to have you over at our table. We'll say whatever you like."

The glint of desire in the man's blue eyes made her stomach churn. But Jane was prepared. If anything went wrong, she had an illegal can of pepper spray in her purse. Not to mention that ever since the dragon hunter attack on Stonefire earlier in the year, she'd been taking advanced self-defense classes, which would come in handy if needed.

With a nod, she answered, "I'd love to meet your friends. Maybe you can teach me how to sound British."

"Then come with me. My name's Jason."

Jane had long ago picked a fake name similar to her own. "I'm Jenn."

As the man guided her toward a table with about eight blokes, Jane catalogued their faces. While she didn't have an eidetic memory, she had always been good with faces. Even if she didn't find out any information about the dragon hunters from these men, she could later cross-check them with known dragon hunter associates and see if she was on the right track.

Of course, Jane was getting ahead of herself. She had to survive chatting with the slimy men at the table first.

The stench of beer, cigarettes, and stale male sweat hit her as she stopped next to the long table with Jason. This was going to be a long ten or twenty minutes with these men.

*Remember, these men can lead me to my next clue.* Even as they leered at her breasts before looking back to her face, Jane never stopped smiling. She waved. "Hello."

One of the men whistled. Since she'd spent the last decade focusing on her career, it'd been a long time since she had interacted with men in a pub. If whistling was the way to win a woman these days, Jane would remain single for the rest of her life.

Under normal circumstances, she would probably glare and give him the double finger salute.

However, these weren't normal circumstances, so the mental image of kicking each of the men in the balls would have to do for the present.

Jason placed his hand on her lower back. His touch made her want to take a long, hot shower. "This here is Jenn. She's an American looking for sexy accents. I told her we were it."

A dark-skinned man with black hair and brown eyes spoke up first. "Is that so? Then mine is the best."

A Birmingham accent.

A man with brown eyes and a pale, bald head spoke next. "Don't listen to him. Yorkshire is better. After all, we're the Texas of England."

With three accents identified, Jane's gut said this group of blokes might be the right one.

Keeping up her act as an American, she put her hands up and shrugged. "They all sound the same to me."

"Oi," the bald man said, "sit yourself down and we'll teach you properly. Next thing you know, you'll say we sound Australian."

Putting a finger to her mouth, she tried to look coy. "Well, you kind of do."

The man at her side motioned to some of his friends. "Move your arses and let the lady sit down. I think it's time we teach her the difference between us and the criminals."

Jane's mother was Australian, so she was familiar with how some Brits called Australians criminals—after all, the British had sent a lot of their convicted criminals to Australia and America back in the day.

She couldn't defend her mother, though, so she bit the inside of her cheek to prevent her from saying something out of turn. Playing the part of a clueless American was going to take more concentration than she'd thought.

Once Jane scooted into the booth and Jason slid in next to her, Jane was trapped between two possibly dangerous men. The reminder of exactly where she was and who these men could be calmed her mind. If she fucked up, more than her story would be on the line.

Her life could be, too.

Jane upped her charm and went to work.

~~~

Kai Sutherland tugged the sleeves of his new jumper and exposed his forearms. Unlike most dragon-shifters, Kai had tattoos on both arms. His jagged flame one in black ink helped him to better blend in with the humans and he needed all the blending in he could do given his height and tendency to growl.

Or, at least, that's what the human females of his clan had told him—that he growled too much.

Eyeing the pub across the street, Kai pushed aside thoughts of his growling and focused on his task. Newcastle was a dangerous city for dragon-shifters. While no one remembered the reasons, the Geordies were the most afraid of his kind in the entire United Kingdom and they did everything in their power to keep their cities clean of dragon-shifters. He couldn't fuck up or he could end up in the hands of the DDA, or worse.

However, their hatred was why Kai was here.

Because of it, the city welcomed dragon hunters without a second glance, believing the hunters could help protect them. According to his contacts, the pub across the street should be one of the usual hangouts for the hunters in the area.

Kai's dragon grunted. *Lure them out and we can eat them.*

*No eating humans. That's one of the rules.*

*But rules are meant to be broken.*

*Not this time. Remember what they did to Charlie? Eating one or two isn't enough; we need to bring the bastards down.*

Charlie had been Stonefire's first female Protector. Seven months ago, she'd been captured and drained of blood.

Clenching his fingers, Kai forced his anger to the back of his mind. Strong emotions would cloud his judgement and risk

12

what might be the only chance he had to try to capture and interrogate one or two hunters at his leisure. To protect his clan, he needed to take down Simon Bourne, Carlisle's leader. But he couldn't do that without more information.

His dragon replied, *The DDA will punish you if they find out what you're doing.*

*Fuck the DDA. They always let us down.*

*Except Evie.*

Evie Marshall was the human female mated to Kai's clan leader. *Of course, not Evie. That female proved herself.*

*Just hurry up. I hate being in the crowded streets of cities.*

In this, Kai agreed. *Then stay quiet and let me do my job.*

*Fine, but you owe me a hunt later.*

With that, his dragon retreated to the back of his mind and Kai crossed the street to the pub.

Upon entering, he took in his surroundings as he made it to the bar. Most of the patrons were working class males celebrating the end of the work week. A few human females drank with them or watched as some men played billiards on the far side of the room.

Then he looked toward the left and saw the back of a dark blonde-haired female sitting with a group of males. Her hair was swept up, exposing the delicate skin of her neck.

His beast growled out, *Ours.*

*Don't be daft. No one is ours.*

*She is. Get her away from those humans.*

*Her biceps are bare, free of material and tattoos. She's human too.*

*That doesn't matter. Those human males aren't worthy.*

Kai wanted to sigh. His dragon had always been a little dramatic. *You're not being quiet, so I will make you quiet.*

Wrestling his dragon into a mental prison before he could reply, Kai took the last few steps to the bar. While he waited for the bartender, he looked over his shoulder so he could see the woman's face.

The second he saw the blue eyes, long face, and bright smile, he felt as if he'd been punched in the gut.

The woman might be wearing too much make-up and had blonde hair instead of black, but it was Jane Hartley, the BBC reporter who'd been working with Stonefire over the last few months.

He wondered why the hell she was in Newcastle. He highly doubted it was a coincidence.

His dragon banged against his mental cage. Since Kai had lots of experience dealing with his temperamental beast, the cage held. However, if he stayed in the same room as Jane for longer than five minutes, his dragon might find a way out.

After all, his bloody beast believed the human was their second chance.

Rather than allow his thoughts to go down that path, Kai clenched his jaw. He needed to get the human female out of the pub and send her on her way.

The bartender approached, but Kai merely waved him off and headed toward the table. He had an idea.

The sight of Jane smiling and flirting with the human bastards sent a flash of anger through his body. They shouldn't be anywhere near her. All Kai wanted to do was toss the hunter bastards against a wall and whisk the human female away to safety.

The thought made him pause. He wasn't here to protect the female. She could fend for herself.

Kai's dragon broke free. *No, we must protect her.*

14

# Reawakening the Dragon

*And risk the mission? I think not.*

His beast growled. *We'll do both.*

*I don't take orders from you.*

*In this, you will listen. She is ours.*

Tired of arguing, Kai decided to placate his beast temporarily. *Give me some credit. I can send her away and best the hunters. Have faith in me.*

His dragon huffed. *For now, but I'll be watching.*

Kai resisted shaking his head and approached the table. On closer inspection, he noticed that the man to Jane's right was one of the Carlisle hunters. Kai had seen him while in dragon-form on a rescue mission earlier in the year.

His dragon spoke up again. *Get Jane away from him, but don't let him escape.*

Ignoring his dragon, Kai stopped next the table where Jane was sitting with the men and kicked the outer table leg. All eyes were on him, and he caught the flash of surprise in Jane's gaze. He growled, "There you are, Janey."

To her credit, Jane quickly replaced her surprise with confusion. "Do I know you?"

"Of course you bloody well know me. I'm your man."

The male he'd seen on his previous mission reached under the table, no doubt to retrieve a stolen gun. The bald man asked, "Who the hell do you think you are, mate? This lady right here is having a good time and doesn't recognize you. So, sod off and leave her be."

"No," Kai stated.

The male on Jane's other side raised his brows. "You'd best listen to my friend, arsehole, or we'll take you outside and teach you a lesson."

Since that was what Kai wanted he took one of the pints of lager on the table and tossed it to the side. The glass shattered and the two closest men stood up. The bald one spoke again, clutching something under his shirt. "Last chance. Leave or we'll make you leave."

The bartender and one of the bouncers headed toward them. Kai needed to move this outside where he could better control the situation and avoid too many human eyes. "How about a fight? If you win, you can keep the tart. If I win, you let me take her and I'll allow you to escape alive."

Everyone looked at the bald man, who appeared to be their leader. The urge to look at Jane was strong, but he kept his focus on the men. He'd deal with the human female after the fight.

The bald man gave a slight motion toward the door and his men started to file out. Two of them grabbed Jane's biceps and Kai's dragon roared inside his head and then added, *They shouldn't touch her. They aren't worthy and might hurt her.*

Kai quickly stated, *She'll be fine. No one is going to hurt her in front of me. If they try, they will regret it.*

His beast grunted. *I will trust you for now. But you know what will happen if you fail.*

If Kai failed, there'd be hell to pay; his beast didn't tolerate failure. *Yes, yes. Now, leave me alone so I can concentrate.*

With a huff, his dragon fell silent.

Only the bald man remained at the table and he motioned toward the door. "After you."

"We walk out together. I don't trust you at my back," Kai answered.

"Clever man."

Kai merely raised an eyebrow and the bald man started walking.

16

# Reawakening the Dragon

All he needed to do was knock the bald man out and toss him over his shoulder so he could question him later. Then Kai could take the reporter far away from there and persuade her to stay clear of the dragon hunters. A single human female didn't stand a chance against them, especially one as pretty as Jane. There was no telling what the hunters would do to her if they found out she was a reporter.

His dragon whispered, *Protect her at all costs.*

*I will, but only so I can finish my mission, nothing more.*

*One day you will stop lying.*

Kai didn't like the confidence of his dragon's words.

However, Kai reached outside the pub and focused on the situation at hand.

The bald man went around the back to the alley. As soon as Kai turned the corner, he saw Jane being held between two men at the end of the street. He resisted the urge to shift into a dragon and take them all out in one fell swoop.

But doing so would land him in trouble with the DDA. Any dragon that shifted inside a major city would be charged and serve out a jail sentence. As hard as it was to resist, Newcastle wasn't his land. Being thrown inside a DDA prison would prevent him from finishing his task.

And once Kai set his mind on something, he always followed through. Always.

The bald man motioned for Kai to approach. "Come on, mate. It's time to put you in your place."

~ ~ ~

Jane was seething on the inside. The bloody dragonman was going to ruin her investigation and get himself killed. The bald man, Joe, had a gun under his shirt. She'd seen the butt poking out several times over the last quarter of an hour.

Joe and his men had just started talking about how far away they lived from their favorite pub when Kai had shown up. How dare he call her his woman. No doubt, he thought she needed rescuing.

Bloody daft dragonman.

When this was finished, she would give Stonefire's head Protector a piece of her mind. While she rarely interacted with him, the quiet dragonman always managed to get what he wanted. She had no fucking idea why he was here, but if he was also after the hunters, he would have a wakeup call. Jane Hartley didn't give up a lead for anyone, not even a growly, hot muscled man who could shift into a giant gold dragon.

Kai's voice echoed down the alley and answered Joe's taunting. Since Jane was taller than most of the men, she turned her head to watch.

"No weapons. That's my only rule," Kai stated.

Joe answered, "Who says you get to the make the rules? I'm only agreeing to fight because you might actually be a challenge and it's been a while since I've had one. If you weren't, me and my men would've taken you out by now."

Jason at her side murmured in agreement and Jane wondered if all of the dragon hunters had guns.

"No weapons," Kai repeated.

Despite how angry she was with Kai Sutherland, the steel in his voice made her want to obey.

And if she were honest, every time she heard it, his voice made her shiver in a good way.

Not that she was going to waste time thinking about Kai's deep, sexy voice. She was more concerned about the hunters figuring out he was a dragonman. Kai's jumper and trousers did a good job of helping him blend in with the humans in the area, but very few humans could thread so much dominance into their voices.

Joe moved his hand away from under his shirt. "I like a challenge. You look ex-army, am I right?" Kai merely nodded and Joe continued, "Then let's see if what they teach you nancy boys stands up to what we learn on the streets."

In the blink of an eye, Joe moved to the side and swung a fist.

Jane held her breath, but then Kai stepped out of the way. Even in the half-darkness, Kai was graceful as he moved. It was almost as if he were dancing.

Blinking, Jane pushed the ridiculous thought out of her head. The dragonman had ruined everything. She would not think positive thoughts about him, and certainly not wonder if Kai was just as graceful out of his clothes as he was in them.

*Stop it, Jane.* She'd wondered too many times over the last few months what Kai would look like naked. But she couldn't afford to see any man naked. At least, not until she'd finished her story and secured her reputation as a true investigative journalist.

The hunter at her side, Jason, murmured, "Tell me you want the bastard to lose." He caressed her upper arm with a finger and she barely resisted punching him in the jaw. "We were getting along so well before. I'd like to take you back to my place and show you what a real man is like."

*Must. Not. Roll. Eyes.* Jane flashed a coy smile and looked down at Jason, who was a few inches shorter than her. "That sounds nice. I've always wondered what a British man would be like."

Desire flashed in the man's eyes. He moved toward her as if he were going to kiss her, so she added, "But I want to watch the fight first, okay, sweetie? I want the stranger who claimed to be my man to be punished for his lie."

"Don't worry, Joe will take care of him." He caressed her arm some more and her stomach rolled. "But we'll stay. Watching a fight will only make me harder."

*Ew.* Pushing aside thoughts of the man naked and hard, Jane bobbed her head. "I can hardly wait."

"Then watch the fight, love. If you're like me, and I think you are, it'll make you wet."

Only her stubbornness kept the smile on her face. Someone really needed to smack this man once in a while. That was definitely not the way to win a woman. "Maybe."

Before he could spout out any more crude comments, Jane looked back to Kai. He and Joe were circling each other. Neither one appeared winded, nor did they have any visible injuries on their faces.

She wondered what Kai's strategy was. He needed to hurry the hell up so she could ditch the pervert at her side.

Yet Kai took his time circling his partner and dodging one punch and then another. He acted as if he had all the time in the world.

Joe went for an uppercut, but Kai sidestepped and punched him in the kidney. In the next second, Kai turned around and clocked him on the jaw. Joe went down with a thud.

Everyone held their breath, Jane included, but Joe didn't get up again.

Kai's eyes sought out hers and she shivered at the mixture of heat and triumph in his eyes. That look made her want to strip naked and offer herself up as a sacrifice.

# Reawakening the Dragon

Blinking, Jane nearly frowned. That was twice now she'd fantasized about Kai being naked in the span of a few minutes. If she wanted to find her story and advance her career, she couldn't afford to sleep with any dragon-shifter. The second she did, her opinion would be deemed biased.

She'd had to repeat that mantra over and over again the last few months. Being surrounded by a clan of hot dragonmen had been temptation itself. And who the bloody hell knew why, but she'd always had the strongest pull toward Kai, although she'd managed to stay clear.

Luckily, Mr. Tactless at her side spoke up. "Did you want me to get rid of him for you, love?" He reached down and took hold of what she assumed was a gun. "His fist can't hurt us this far away."

She was trying to think of how to respond when Kai bent over and took Joe's gun. His supersensitive dragon-shifter hearing must've picked up Jason's words.

Flicking off the safety, Kai pointed the gun at Jason. "The woman is mine. Let her go."

The men stared at one another and Jane decided to fuck it. These men would never talk to her again anyway.

Turning, she kneed Jason in the balls and took his gun. Before the other men could draw theirs, she pressed the muzzle against Jason's temple and flicked off the safety. Not wanting to completely break her cover, she kept up her American accent. "I don't think so, guys. I'm not a prize to be fought after. Besides, I'm American and we love our guns. You won't win against me. I suggest you run far, far away before I show you my skills."

Jane was careful to keep her face stony. In truth, she was horrible with firearms. She only knew the basics because of her older brother, who had all but forced her to learn them a few years earlier. But the hunters didn't need to know that.

Pressing the muzzle harder against Jason's forehead, the man's strangled voice ordered, "Do as she says."

One of the men spoke up. "What about Joe?"

Kai's voice drifted from behind her. "Leave him."

Jane nearly turned her head and frowned at the dragonman. If he wanted to help her, he could surely muster more than two words.

As the men waited for Jason's confirmation, Jane murmured, "Tell them to leave or I won't be so gentle with your balls next time."

Jason yelled to the others, "Go. Joe can take care of himself."

Not waiting for another word, the group of men left, except for Jason, whom she still had under the gun. Before she could tell the man to flee, Kai was next to her. After hitting the man on the back of the head with his gun, Jason fell to the ground.

She hated the fact she had to look up to meet his eyes, but she did it. "Why the bloody hell did you do that?"

"Good to hear you're British again."

She frowned. "That is probably one of the least important things you could say right now. How about telling me why you're here? You ruined everything."

"All of that can wait."

Kai kneeled, flipped Jason over, and tied his hands with plastic zip ties from his pocket. Putting the safety back on her gun, Jane asked, "Care to explain a bit more?" She lowered her voice. "I can't read minds, dragonman. You sure as hell shouldn't be here."

Rather than answer her, Kai took out his mobile and sent a text. Jane was tempted to pluck the phone from his hands and toss it onto the roof of the pub.

Sadly, before she could execute her plan, Kai tucked his phone into his pocket as he stood up. His expression was as unreadable as always as he answered, "Stop demanding and just listen. Let's go somewhere safe before the hunters come back with reinforcements."

Jane's curiosity won out over her irritation. "How do you know they're hunters?" When Kai merely stared, she put a hand on her hip. "In the amount of time you've stared so far you could've explained half a dozen sentences about what's going on. I get it, you're the big, bad head Protector. But you can let that image slip with me. I won't tell anyone."

"Says the reporter."

If she were on official business for work, she'd have to smile and say nothing. But she wasn't, so she narrowed her eyes. "You know what? Fuck you. I don't need to put up with this. I'm leaving."

Jane walked two steps before Kai came up behind her and trapped her against his chest. For a split second, all she could think about were the hard muscles and broad chest at her back. It had been a long time since she last had a man's arms around her in a non-slimy way. Being a female reporter wasn't glamorous most of the time; too many men liked to cop a feel. Kai's arms around her, on the other hand, actually made her skin hot and tight, which rarely happened.

His heat at her back was better than any dream she'd had of him over the last few months.

Realizing she was going off on a tangent, she forced her brain to focus. "A scream from me and the pub patrons will spill into the street." She tilted her head up until she could see Kai's blue eyes. "If I tell them a dragon-shifter is causing trouble on the streets of Newcastle, that would definitely be a big enough distraction to allow me to slip away."

Kai remained silent. The second she opened her mouth to scream, Kai released her and she swore she saw a flash of irritation in the unshakeable dragonman's eyes.

However, the look was gone in the next breath. Kai merely shrugged. "Do what you wish. But does your boss know you're out here wielding a gun and rubbing elbows with the hunters? You should be behind a desk."

"I'm a journalist."

He shrugged. "If you say so." He turned toward Joe. "I have a job to do. Go home and let me handle the hunters."

Jane clenched her fingers. "I found them first. This is my story and I won't let you brush me off."

Kai met her eyes again. "Go home or I will send you home."

A million ideas raced through her head. Given what little she knew of Kai Sutherland, he could be carrying chloroform or who the hell knew what that could knock her unconscious. And he would use it, too.

Before he had a chance to do any of that, Jane would play her only card. "You can send me home and waste your time interrogating the hunters for information, or you can work with me. The men were quite chatty before you rudely interrupted. Give me access to a computer with internet and I can point out the possible new living quarters of the former Carlisle gang."

Kai studied her, but despite the butterflies banging around in her stomach, she didn't so much as fidget as she waited for his response.

# CHAPTER TWO

Kai knew it was only a matter of time before the hunters sent reinforcements. He needed to get the hell out of the alley and back to his temporary safe house on the outskirts of Newcastle.

The easiest way to accomplish that was to drug Jane Hartley and drop her off somewhere safe. The damn female had already complicated his investigation. Hell, her actions might cause the hunters to move bases again. If that happened, he'd have to start from scratch.

She was definitely a pain in his arse.

Yet as she stood up to him with fire in her eyes, his dragon roared and clawed at his mental prison to get out. His dragon wanted her.

Not in the way his dragon had lusted after their true mate all those years ago, but it was pretty fucking close. Even without a mate-claim frenzy, his dragon wanted the human naked and under them as soon as possible.

And a small part of Kai agreed. His cock was still hard from holding the human female in his arms, with her tall, soft body against his chest.

*No.* He wouldn't let his dick control his brain. His entire clan's safety was riding on his actions. Until he took down Simon Bourne, Clan Stonefire would always be a target. Even with heightened security, it wouldn't be long before more of his Protectors would die.

Jane raised an eyebrow and asked, "Well? Are you going to just stand there or are you going to reply?"

His mobile phone vibrated in his pocket with a text message, which meant his ride would be here in two minutes.

Kai needed to make a decision.

His dragon finally broke free. *She comes with us.*

*Not if you're going to lust after her constantly.*

*She has information. Once we plot our next move, then we can fuck her.*

*No fucking the human. End of discussion.*

*When you stop lying to yourself, I'll be ready.*

His beast fell silent and Kai mentally cursed. Being near Jane Hartley was a bad idea, yet he couldn't resist finding out what she knew. Her intel could save him a few days if the hunter bastards proved resilient, and that could make all the difference in the world. "Come with me, but no more talking until we're some place safe." She opened her mouth and he cut her off. "That's the rule and it's non-negotiable. Nod if you agree."

Anger flared in her eyes, but for whatever reason, Jane nodded.

At the gesture, his dragon preened. *Good. I can't wait until the anger in her eyes turns to desire. Then I will make her scream.*

Ignoring his dragon, Kai moved to Joe, pulled out one of the pre-filled needles inside a case in his pocket, and pumped the sedative into the dragon hunter. Hefting the unconscious man over his shoulder, an SUV stopped at the opposite end of the alley. Nikki Gray, one of his junior Protectors, waved from the driver's side and exited the car.

Kai motioned his head and looked to Jane. "Get in the car."

# Reawakening the Dragon

Jane clenched her jaw and moved toward the car. His dragon spoke up. *I don't like her so quiet. Hurry up so I can hear her voice again.*

*Now you only want her voice? I think you're planning something else.*

*Maybe. But admit it—you love her voice, too.*

As Kai loaded Joe into the back seat, he replied, *Why do you bring it up? You already know the answer.*

*Because I want to remind you of how much you want her, too.*

True, Kai had listened to every report of Jane's he could find over the last few months. The rise and fall of her voice had relaxed him. For the first time in eleven years, Kai had been able to temporarily forget about the female who should've been his mate.

But he didn't have time for a female. Jane's voice was all he could allow himself to have.

Shutting the car door, Kai moved to the passenger seat and retrieved a long, black scarf from the glove box. Turning to Jane, he held it out to her. "Put it on." She shook her head. Bloody stubborn female. "You agreed to remain silent until we arrived someplace safe. Arguing with your eyes isn't going to change my mind."

She glared and stuck out her tongue before swiping the cloth from his hand. His dragon whined, *Why didn't she touch our skin? I want to feel her warm, soft skin again.*

Not replying, he watched as Jane tugged off her wig and tied the scarf at the back of her head. When she finished, she put out her hands with a flourish and Kai couldn't help but smile.

Nikki finished loading the other human into the back and climbed into the car. "Why are you smiling? You never smile."

With a grunt, Kai answered, "Drive."

Nikki turned on the car and changed gear. As she moved the car down the narrow streets, she added, "So much for a thank

27

you, boss. One of the men who guarded me during my time with the hunters is in the back seat. Being in the same car as him isn't exactly easy."

Kai snapped his fingers and pointed toward Jane. Nikki sighed. "Right, the reporter. I'll keep quiet for now."

Stonefire's clan leader, Bram, had suggested Kai bring someone else to help him with his mission since Nikki was young and inexperienced. But ultimately, Kai's argument had won. After all, Nikki had seen a large number of dragon hunters while she'd been imprisoned by them earlier in the year. She had details Kai would need. Not only that, she could identify members by sight.

Helping to bring them down should also bring a sense of closure to the young dragonwoman.

However, Nikki would serve another purpose now that the human was with them. As long as one of his subordinates was around, Kai should be able to keep his emotions under control. And more importantly, he could keep his hands to himself.

His dragon chimed in. *That's what you think.*

Kai didn't like his beast's smug tone.

Glancing back at Jane, he decided he would get rid of her once she gave him the information he needed. Considering he had kept his distance from his true mate for years without touching her, he could spend a few hours with Jane Hartley and act normal.

~~~

The silence in the car rubbed Jane the wrong way. Since she'd watched Kai inject Joe with some kind of drug, and had a feeling the young dragonwoman had done the same with Jason, Jane was fairly certain they would be unconscious for a while yet.

28

Not only that, but over the last few months she'd learned how cautious Stonefire could be about sweeping for bugs or any other sort of anomalies. She'd bet her life savings that the car was clean.

There was no bloody reason to waste time in silence. She should ask a question, but her gut told her Kai would carry out his threat and discard her somewhere. And she needed to stay on his good side long enough to find out what he knew.

Then she could slip away and continue her investigation on her own. A tall, brooding dragonman constantly looking over her shoulder would only bring suspicion and scare away the locals.

She could pretend that was the only reason to send him away. In truth, constantly having his heat nearby might addle her brain.

Tapping her fingers against her thigh, Jane pushed aside the memory of Kai's hard chest at her back. The more pressing problem was that the hunters would run before she had a chance to pinpoint their location.

The car made a turn and soon stopped. Kai's voice filled the car. "Take off the blindfold and follow me." She opened her mouth, but he cut her off. "No talking until we step inside the safe house. That's the rule."

She wanted to tell him where he could stuff his rules.

*Just a little longer, Jane. Then speak your mind.* Taking a deep breath, she followed Kai out of the car. He gave the other dragon-shifter some directions and then motioned toward the front door. "This way."

The second they stepped inside the house, Jane stopped in her tracks. "I've followed your daft rules. Now, tell me what you know and what you plan to do."

Kai frowned. "I never agreed to tell you everything, only that I wouldn't send you home."

Closing the distance between them, she poked his chest. "If you think I'm just going to tell you everything I know for free, you're out of your bloody mind." She poked again. "As I mentioned, I was in the pub first. This is my story and you're not going to take it away from me."

"Stop with the 'my story' bullshit. While you're aiming for glory, I'm trying to ensure the safety of my clan."

"Don't make me sound self-centered. I've done more than you will ever admit to help your clan. It's my reports that have helped reveal how the dragon-shifters are more human than beast."

Kai leaned forward. "Don't sugar coat a pile of shit to make it taste better. You report to help your station and yourself. You have yet to prove you care about the dragon-shifters."

Jane moved an inch closer, tilting her head up to Kai's. "Listen, Mr. High-and-Mighty, just because I'm human doesn't mean I don't understand the animosity some feel toward dragon-shifters. From the second my interview with Melanie Hall ended, I've received death threats. People have also broken into my flat so many times that I moved not once, but three times. Not to mention the colorful insults people shout at me on the street on a daily basis." She shoved against his chest. "If I were truly only looking out for myself, I wouldn't put up with that shit. I'd find a nicer, safer position. But I don't. I stick it out. So don't pull your judgmental crap with me. I won't put up with it."

When all Kai did was stare, she pushed against his chest again. This time, however, he trapped her hands against his chest and his touch sent a shock of heat through her body.

It took everything she had to focus when he replied, "Tell me the truth of why you want this story. Give me an excuse, and I'll send you packing."

# Reawakening the Dragon

The way his gaze burned into hers turned her mouth dry. Kai might be a quiet man who liked to be in control, but she wondered what would happen when he lost that control.

Then he squeezed her hands and she pushed that thought aside. She definitely wouldn't stick around long enough to find out.

He spoke again. "Tell me, Jane. And if you lie, I'll know."

Fighting him hadn't worked very well, so she decided what the hell; she'd tell him. The worst he could do was throw her out on her arse, which he'd do anyway if she remained quiet.

Still, she wouldn't let him be in complete control. "Release my hands first."

His pupils flashed to slits and back. She wondered why he'd be talking to his dragon at this second. For all the reporting she'd done on Stonefire, she still had yet to truly understand how both man and beast worked together in one mind.

Releasing her hands, Kai stepped away. "Now talk."

She raised her brows. "I'll ignore your tone for once. As for the truth, well, of course this story would help my career. My boss sees me as a pretty face people want to see on TV rather than a serious journalist. I want to prove that I am one." Kai remained silent, so Jane continued, "The other reason is that the dragon hunters are bastards who fly under the radar. They kill humans and dragon-shifters. All they care about is money. And as you know firsthand, the DDA doesn't always do what it promises. A good exposé might be the final thing we need to convince the public that the dragon hunters are much more than troublesome gangs we just shake our heads at. The dragon hunters are murderers and criminals that we should all demand be thrown into prison for life."

She waited to see if Kai believed her. As far as she knew, dragon-shifters weren't walking lie detectors, but given his military training, he probably could tell she wasn't lying.

After another few seconds, Kai finally nodded. "I'll believe you for the time being. However, the second you start lying to me, I will have you removed and kept out of trouble. Are we clear?"

She raised an eyebrow. "If you're expecting me to salute you as I say 'Yes, sir,' then you'll be waiting a long time. You're not my commanding officer or boss. We stand as equals. That's my condition."

Kai crossed his arms over his chest, which made his biceps bulge. Jane forced herself to move her gaze back to Kai's face as he answered, "I'll consider it. But first, I need something to merit keeping you around."

"Keep me? Does anyone ever question you or tell you to stuff it?"

He shrugged. "Patience ultimately wins. Those who let their emotions cloud their judgement and reactions always make mistakes. I simply pounce on the opening."

His words were a poorly veiled hint that Jane let her emotions get the better of her.

It was on the tip of her tongue to throw a quip back, but her curiosity and drive to find the truth of the dragon hunters won out. "Fine. Fetch me a map of the area and I'll give you something worth keeping me around for."

"Just tell me the location."

"I need a map."

After a beat of silence, Kai uncrossed his arms. "Follow me."

# REAWAKENING THE DRAGON

As he walked down the hallway, Jane let out the breath she'd been holding. Dealing with the dragonman was exhausting. She wondered if he ever relaxed.

Since she wasn't about to ask that question, Jane's eyes fell to Kai's shoulders. Even for a dragon-shifter, they were broad and powerful. As she had many times before, she could just imagine the muscles hidden beneath his shirt. How she'd love to trace his spine and make the alpha dragonman weak.

Then she looked down to his round arse, an image of her gripping the firm mounds as he fucked her flashed into her mind. All of that power and reserve focused on her only made wetness rush between her legs.

Kai turned into a room and Jane took a few deep breaths. *Stop it, Jane.* Dragon-shifters had a sensitive sense of smell. She couldn't allow him to scent how attracted she was or he'd lord it over her. It wasn't as if she would ever have the chance to see him naked anyway.

So Jane thought of a past assignment, when she'd had to report on abuse in nursing homes, and her arousal cooled.

Ready to face Kai again, she walked into the room. Kai was already unfolding a map on a table off to the side. Jane stopped and Kai tapped the map. "Point it out."

"You don't say more than the absolute minimum, do you?"

"No." Kai tapped the map again. "Show me where the hunters are."

Jane shook her head and leaned forward. Without her glasses, she couldn't read tiny print close-up very well.

As she searched out the legend, she felt Kai's eyes on her breasts. Unlike with the hunters back in the pub, her body warmed at the feeling and her nipples hardened.

While the bloody dragonman had probably already noticed her body's reactions, she would distract him with something else.

Jane looked up to meet his unreadable eyes. "The blokes asked me back to their place. When I inquired about how long it would take to get there, they said about half an hour by car." Jane looked down at the map and made a circle with her hand. "I calculated inside my head the distance and the time it takes to drive, which means they should be somewhere inside this area."

"That's still a wide area."

Looking back up, she raised her eyebrow. "It's a matter of deduction. As a head Protector, I figured you would know that."

"It's a lot harder to deduce and sort out the best choices when it's a different species."

He had a point, but it gave her an opening. Even if it meant sticking around longer than she'd anticipated, she would jump on it. "Which is why you need me. Promise you'll allow me to stay on and help until I have my story, and I'll tell you which areas to start with. Then I'll dust off my investigative skills and get to work."

~~~

Kai studied the human female.

He was honest enough with himself to admit he'd been focusing too much on her full breasts, the curve of her neck, or the rogue tendril of black hair that curled around her cheek and not on the map in front of him.

Allowing himself to be so easily distracted was unacceptable.

His dragon spoke up. *The sooner we get her naked, the sooner we can fuck her and you can focus again.*

Not dignifying his beast's words with a response, Kai studied the map.

# REAWAKENING THE DRAGON

The human had pointed out a fifteen-mile radius from Newcastle's city center. Since Kai rarely drove a car, he would have to take her guesstimate.

During his time in the army, he'd become quite accomplished at eliminating unlikely targets until he had a shortlist. The only difference in this situation was Kai didn't know the area around Newcastle. He had a few guesses as to where the hunters would hide based upon their history, but it would be much easier to have Jane ask the locals about any unusual activity and further pinpoint the possible targets from there.

True, he had two prisoners who would be interrogated the instant his best interrogator, a Stonefire Protector named Zain, arrived. But each second he wasted waiting around for information was a second the hunters could move their location. The men from the pub might not have guessed Kai was a dragon-shifter, but kidnapping two of their men could lead to trouble.

No doubt, the hunters' leader Simon Bourne knew this.

He would use any timesaver he could find, even if it came in the form of a delectable human female with dark hair and blue eyes.

His dragon hummed. *Yes, she is delectable. She will taste good.*

*Why are you this insistent? You haven't act this way around a human before.*

*They weren't this human*, his dragon stated.

Looking up at the female in question, Kai answered, "As long as you don't become a liability, we'll work together."

Jane stood up and crossed her arms under her breasts. "As equals?"

"For now." She opened her mouth, but he cut her off. "Trust takes time. I'm sure you'd agree."

She studied him a second before tilting her head. "Considering how much you like to be in charge and give orders, that compromise must've killed you." He frowned, which made Jane smile. "I'll take it."

"Good, now—"

"But if I find out you've been holding out any information from me, then I'll leave. Understood?"

His dragon chuckled. *She doesn't have to take orders from you. I like her fire.*

*Shut it, dragon.*

Kai put on his toughest looking expression. "As long as you don't hold out on me. Cross me and see what happens."

Jane rolled her eyes. "You sound like a bad movie hero. It's not as if you'll kill me. I know most of the major DDA rules by now, mister. Remember that."

Instead of answering, Kai let out a high-pitched whistle. Then he asked, "Are you done with your threats?"

She raised her brows. "Are you done with yours?"

It took everything he had not to smile at the sight of Jane dismissing him in her skimpy dress, heels, and too much make-up. Buried beneath her beauty was a steel core.

His dragon chimed in. *You always wanted a strong female. She can be ours. Are you sure you don't want to coax her out of her dress?*

*No sex with the human. It's—*

*I know, a rule. Maybe I should take control and go after the human myself.*

*Try it, dragon. You know what happened the last time you tried to take control.*

His beast huffed. *I wasn't feeling well that day.*

*No, you were fine. You lost. Accept it.*

*Says the dragonman who won't accept the possibility of a second chance.*

*Enough.*

# Reawakening the Dragon

Kai shoved his dragon to the back of his mind and met Jane's blue eyes. Rather than answer her question, he changed the subject. "Nikki will take you to the room you'll be sharing with her. She'll give you resources, although I'll have one of my people monitor your internet activity. Don't screw up."

"Wow, you said more than one sentence. I'm impressed."

Kai ignored her. "We'll meet in the morning. Be ready to give me a report and to receive your assignment."

"I'll be the one to decide whether I take it or not."

Since she already knew what he'd do if she refused, he let the comment pass.

After a brief knock on the door, Kai replied, "Come in."

Nikki's dark-haired head popped in. Her dark brown eyes looked to him as she raised her brows. "You called?"

Jane beat him to a reply. "I can't believe you call her with a whistle like a dog."

Nikki moved her gaze to Jane and shrugged. "With our hearing, it's easier than using a cell phone."

Kai interrupted, "Take Jane to your room and find her some clothes. Give her reasonable resources and then report back to me."

Nikki walked up to where Kai and Jane were standing. The young dragonwoman turned to Jane. "Hi, I'm Nikki."

Jane smiled at Nikki and a thread of jealousy spiked through Kai's body. Jane had never smiled at him.

Even trapped in the back of his mind, Kai's dragon was smug.

Jane answered, "Hi, Nikki. I'm Jane. Nice to meet someone who has some manners."

Kai ignored her comment and focused on Nikki. "Once Jane is secure, I want to hear your updates."

Nikki bobbed her head.

Kai looked to Jane. "We have lots of work to do, so we'll start early. Be ready at seven a.m."

Before Jane could answer, Kai left and headed toward the room he used as both his bedroom and his office. He would contact Stonefire and check up on things. Focusing on his work would help him forget about the human female.

Especially the fact that she'd be two doors down the hall from him.

# CHAPTER THREE

The next morning, Jane rubbed her eyes and willed for a cup of tea to magically appear before her. The protein bar and a bottle of water she'd been given for breakfast wasn't cutting it. Surely some dragon-shifters also relied on caffeine to kick-start their mornings.

Well, except maybe for Kai. He probably went swimming in a cold lake to start his morning or some other such extreme.

Not that she'd complain about water trickling down his body, leading to the hair trail on his lower stomach, before dripping off his cock. After all, she'd seen something similar in her dreams the previous night, except in her dreams, she'd been licking him dry.

*Damn him.* Jane had hoped a night's sleep would clear her head, but even her subconscious was a little obsessed with a certain dragonman.

Taking a bite of her protein bar, she made a face at the tasteless muck that passed for food. She'd almost think Kai was treating her as a prisoner on purpose, but Nikki had the same food laid out on her bed, telling Jane it was the norm.

Kai took efficiencies to new heights.

Taking another bite of her breakfast, Jane picked up her notebook and tried to focus on something other than the quiet dragonman.

Scanning the list she'd made last night, the five possible locations were still too many. As much as it pained her to admit it, she would need Kai's help to narrow it down to a more manageable number before she could start interviewing the locals and pinpointing the location of the hunters' base.

Nikki stepped out of the en suite bathroom. Jane looked up to see the dragonwoman smile. Nikki looked to the protein bar and back to Jane's eyes. "Enjoying the breakfast of champions?"

Jane made a face. "Are you sure you can't allow me downstairs to make a cup of tea? If I'm to put on my charm today, I'm going to need caffeine."

Nikki went to a locked drawer next to her bed, inserted a key, and opened it. The action was a stark reminder that Nikki might be polite, but she was still Jane's guard. "You'll need to talk to Kai."

"Then that means no."

Nikki glanced at her. "He can be persuaded. Prove yourself and you might be surprised at the lengths he'd go to help you."

"Isn't telling me that violating some sort of enforced silence?"

The corner of Nikki's mouth ticked up. "He never ordered me to be silent." The dragonwoman's face became serious again. "However, I'd never tell you anything that could hurt my clan. Besides, proving yourself works with just about any profession. As I understand it, you're trying to prove yourself to your boss as well."

Kai must've told her. "Yes, but my boss would never force me into a room and post a guard."

Nikki shrugged. "Hey, I'm pretty brilliant as far as guards go."

During her time reporting on Stonefire, Jane had learned bits and pieces about what had happened to Nikki with the dragon hunters. She wondered how much the young dragonwoman's smile and cheery manner hid her true self.

*Not now, Hartley.* She wasn't there to find out Nikki's story. Not that it wouldn't be a great story, but she wouldn't expose someone's pain just for recognition. It was the one thing Jane had vowed early, after one particular assignment at the start of her career.

Pushing aside her past, Jane stood. "You'd be even more brilliant if you could find me some clothes in my size. I'm grateful that you're lending me some things to wear, but I'm two inches taller than you and you can see my socks."

Nikki grinned. "Maybe you're bringing the look back." Jane shook her head and Nikki continued, "Someone is bringing some clothes and other things later today. You'll just have to make do until then."

"Then I hope I don't have to go out and talk to people today. If the hunters are in one of the locations I think they're in, the locals won't talk to the likes of a high-water jeans wearing mum figure."

Nikki finished strapping and attaching things to her body. Closing the nightstand's drawer, she faced Jane. "That kind of logic will convince Kai to get you clothes on the way. If there's one more piece of advice I can offer, appeal to his logic. Emotions only irritate him."

Interesting, considering Kai had come close to showing his own emotions yesterday and Jane had barely tried to provoke him. "I'll take that to heart."

"Right." Nikki motioned a hand toward the door. "Let's go or we'll be late. And believe me, you'll never get your cup of tea if we're late. Kai's probably been waiting fifteen minutes for us already."

Nikki exited the door and Jane followed. "Is he always one step ahead?"

A male voice boomed behind her. "Three steps, actually."

Jane took a deep breath and straightened her shoulders before turning to see Kai. "You're actually about five steps behind."

Kai's lips twitched into an almost-smile and it made her belly flip. Maybe buried beneath that tough exterior was a sense of humor. Probably not, but a small part of her was determined to find out.

Not that she would act on that curiosity, of course. She'd work with him for her story and then forget him. A dragon-shifter would damage her career and without it, a small piece of her heart would be torn out.

He closed the distance between them and Jane forgot everything else as she looked up to meet his eyes. They were blue with a ring of green in the center. She hadn't noticed that before.

Kai spoke again. "Do you have a list ready for me?"

Clearing her throat, Jane held up her notebook. "Right here, but I want some tea before I share it with you."

He raised an eyebrow. "You do realize I could snatch it from your hand in the blink of an eye, don't you?"

Whatever spell his eyes had held, broke. "Don't even think about it. That's not how equals act around each other."

Nikki jumped in. "Well, not exactly true. If you had ever met Bram and Evie, you'd see what I mean. I imagine they snatch things from each other all the time."

Kai growled. "Enough, Nikki. Wait for us downstairs."

Whistling, Nikki left Jane alone with Kai in the hall.

# REAWAKENING THE DRAGON

~~~

Standing so close to Jane Hartley was dangerous. She smelled of strawberries and female, and that combination called to both man and beast.

His dragon spoke up. *Strawberries are one of your favorites. She is meant for us.*

*No. The one meant for us chose another.*

*Not her. The human. Pull her close and kiss her. She will taste good. Better than strawberries.*

Jane's voice interrupted his beast. "Why are your pupils flashing to slits and back? I think it means you're talking to your dragon, and if so, I'm curious about what he's saying."

Kai's dragon was smug. *Tell her I want to strip her naked and fuck her until she can't walk.*

Kai cleared his throat. "He's impatient to find the hunters. Show me the list."

Jane stared at him a second before pointing her forefinger at him. "You're lying."

*Tell her the truth. I know from last night she wants us, too.*

*Shut it, dragon.*

*You'll thank me later for pushing. Just wait.*

Kai forced his face into a bored expression. "Do you really want to waste time arguing about what my dragon did or didn't say? Each second we waste gives the Carlisle hunters another second to move their new headquarters. If that happens, you'll lose your story."

Jane paused and then raised her brows. "Fine."

The human turned and walked down the stairs. His dragon itched to grab her and haul her back so that her soft arse cushioned their cock, but Kai resisted the impulse and issued a warning. *We need to work. The clan depends on us.*

His beast paused a second and then replied, *There will be plenty of time after we help the clan. I can be patient.*

Kai nearly choked. Jane paused and looked at him, but he motioned for her to continue.

Shrugging, the female descended the stairs and Kai followed. *You've never been patient in the entire time I've known you.*

*Untrue. I didn't push when the other one wanted to wait to kiss.*

*That's because I warned Maggie about the mate-claim frenzy. It scared her.*

His dragon huffed. *She wasn't and isn't worth our time.*

Since Kai and his beast had argued about their true mate dozens of times over the years, he let it drop. His dragon's memory was faulty at best. At one time, all his dragon had wanted to do was to please Maggie Jones.

Banishing thoughts of Maggie and his past, Kai picked up his pace. Before long, they reached the same room from the night before.

Nikki wasn't there, which was unusual. Ever since the dragonwoman's capture by hunters, she'd mostly followed his rules and orders without complaint. The defiance was a sign of her old self.

He wasn't sure if that was a good or bad thing. No doubt, it was the human's influence.

Jane turned when reaching the table with the giant map of greater Newcastle and held up her notebook. "Tell me what you know and I'll do the same."

His dragon chuckled. *Someone is brave enough to give you orders.*

Ignoring his beast, Kai cut straight to the point. "Most dragon hunter gangs live in abandoned farms or houses. The

Carlisle branch is different. We found them last time in an abandoned warehouse."

Jane nodded. "Right, which makes sense considering just how many of them there are."

"How do you know their numbers?"

"Is that really important right now? How about just the facts relevant to our current task?"

His dragon chimed in. *It's a fact that I like her more and more. She has more spirit than the other one.*

Kai looked down at the map on the table, refusing to waste more time thinking about Maggie. "Let's lay out the facts. The hunters would avoid the posh areas which rules out these locations." Kai pointed to each one. "What I can't determine is if they'd choose to hide out in one of the forests or in a dodgy neighborhood. Simon Bourne is too clever to set up shop again in an abandoned warehouse. He doesn't like establishing patterns."

"Considering no one has ever seen Bourne, how do you know what he thinks?"

Kai hesitated. Then he realized if he held back, then Jane might hold back. So, he answered, "I've been collecting information on him for nearly a year. Before you ask, no, I don't have a picture. But that doesn't mean he doesn't exist. It just means he's intelligent."

Jane's voice was dry. "An intelligent bad guy. Lucky for us."

"A stupid one never would've been able to kidnap my clan leader's mate, let alone capture and kill one of my people." Something he swore was sympathy flashed in Jane's eyes, but he ignored it. "I've shared some information, now it's your turn."

"Would it kill you to ask nicely?"

"Stop wasting time."

At his order, Jane narrowed her eyes before looking down at the map. "What you didn't factor in to your choices is the ease of transportation and lack of CCTV coverage."

Kai shrugged. "I usually fly and don't have to worry about those things."

Jane met his eye. "Yes, well, humans can't. And while no one in Stonefire will tell me about your security cameras, let alone what they cover, humans in the UK use them everywhere. The hunters would want somewhere with several escape routes as well as the least amount of camera coverage." Jane tapped the map. "That rules out these three, which have too few escape routes. Give me some time on the internet and I can rule out a couple more that have large retail centers, which means lots of cameras."

"Good. That means we can start investigating this afternoon."

Jane motioned toward her body and Kai didn't pass up the chance to stare at the tall human female. Her top was extra snug over her lush breasts. Judging by the size, they would fit nicely into the palms of his hands.

His dragon spoke up. *There's only one way to find out.*

Before his dragon could start banging on again about sex, Jane stated, "I can't do my job looking like this."

He met her eye again. "I don't understand. You have clothes. That's all humans seem to care about."

"While I'm happy not to be running naked through the streets, I look suspicious. No doubt, the hunters have lookouts posted everywhere. A strange looking woman wearing too-small jeans and a slightly too small top chatting up strangers will send up a red flag."

Noticing how tightly the jeans hugged her thighs, Kai decided he didn't want any other male staring at her.

His dragon chimed in. *She's ours.*

46

Ignoring his beast, Kai nodded at Jane. "I can see how a woman putting herself on display in the middle of the day would attract notice."

"I'd hardly call this putting myself on display. You may not pay attention to human fashion, but these jeans are too long to be capris and too short to be regular trousers."

"The males won't be looking at your ankles."

Jane looked toward the ceiling and muttered, "Dragonmen."

He shrugged. "From my time in the army, I learned there is little difference between human males and dragonmen on this topic. We'll find some clothes that hide your body," Kai stated.

Jane met his eyes again. "Hiding my body would be suspicious, too. I'm a grown woman who knows how to blend in when needed. I'll be choosing my own clothes, thank you very much."

Kai crossed his arms over his chest. "You weren't blending in last night. Every male was staring at you."

"I'm not about to defend myself to the likes of you. But why do you care, anyway? Not that long ago, you were threatening to toss me aside somewhere."

"We're working together now and if you fuck up, it puts my clan at risk."

Before Jane could answer, Nikki entered the room carrying a tea tray. The dragonwoman winked at Jane and a thread of jealousy shot through his body. Kai wanted to be in on the secret.

Nikki set the tray down and poured tea. "Humans need tea or coffee to function properly. I figured giving some to Jane will make her more alert for our investigation."

"I'm sure that's the reason," Kai murmured. The human was definitely being a bad influence on Nikki.

Raising his voice to normal levels, he added, "Jane needs clothes. You have until noon to take her out and find some." Kai switched his gaze to Jane. "You'll be paying for them."

Jane crossed her arms over her chest in almost the exact same pose as him. "I'm not buying new clothes. I have perfectly suitable ones in my hotel room. We'll go there."

"Did you tell any of the blokes at the pub where you were staying?" Kai demanded.

"I'm going to pretend you didn't just insult my intelligence," Jane replied. "I used a fake name and even pretended to be American. You're the one who nearly broke my cover by calling me 'Janey.'" Kai remained silent, not wanting to admit she was right. Sighing, Jane continued, "Besides, they have no idea where I'd be staying. Especially since I have messy hair and no make-up on today. I look like a completely different person."

He grunted. "You look better when natural."

Nikki blinked at him, but Kai didn't care. He merely spoke the truth.

Jane cleared her throat. "Right, then Nikki can take me to my hotel after I drink my tea. I'll check out too, since I assume I'll be staying here. Correct?"

Jane staying in the same house as him was a bad idea. His dragon would keep pushing for him to kiss the blasted human. And if Kai let his guard down for even a second, he didn't trust his beast.

His dragon growled. *You want to kiss her, too. You dream about it all the time.*

Maybe, but he wasn't going to admit to it. He didn't have time to woo, let alone kiss, a human. Especially a human who would drive his dragon crazy.

Yet Jane staying with him was the logical choice. He'd just have to exercise his steely self-control for a few days. After that, he'd steer clear of her and never have to see the human again.

His beast added, *Except on TV. Or, when she's interviewing people in our clan.*

Kai looked Jane straight in the eye. "Yes. It'll be easier for us to share information if you stay here."

The corner of Jane's mouth ticked up. "And for you to keep tabs on me."

Careful not to show his surprise, he replied, "That too." He glanced at the clock on the wall. "You'd better hurry. I expect for you to narrow the list further as well as retrieve your clothes in the next four hours." He looked to Nikki. "Make sure she's back on time."

Nikki nodded slowly. "Of course."

Kai looked to Jane. "You have one chance. If you try to escape or withhold information from me, I will find you and lock you away until I finish my investigation. Understood?"

Jane rolled her eyes. "I'm not a child, nor am I your soldier to order around. You keep forgetting that, Kai Sutherland."

Kai grunted. "No, you're not, but you are a pain in my arse." She opened her mouth to reply, but Kai cut her off. "I have some business to take care of. I'll see you in four hours."

As he turned and walked out of the room, he heard Nikki whisper, "He's never that chatty. What did you do to him?"

Not wanting to hear the answer, Kai hurried down the hall toward his room. Exercise would help clear his mind of the human. She knew how to get under his skin. Next time, he'd be better prepared. The second he let his emotions take control, especially when it came to jealously and arousal, he might start compromising his mission.

His dragon chimed in. *If you want to concentrate, then fuck her and get it over with.*

*Is that all you can think about?*

*You starve me of sex. A dragon needs it as much as breathing.*

*Stop the exaggerations.*

His beast huffed. *You'll regret saying that to me. Consider it a warning.*

With a sigh, Kai entered his room and began stretching. If he worked out hard enough, his dragon might stop being so bloody dramatic. If not, Kai would have to find another way to calm his dragon down. It wouldn't be long before his damn beast would blare his lust through Kai's mind and give him a hard-on at all the wrong times.

And if there was one thing he was determined to do, apart from protect his clan, it was ensure Jane Hartley never knew how much Kai yearned to strip her naked and kiss every inch of her soft skin.

# CHAPTER FOUR

Thirty minutes later, Jane was in the car with Nikki, drumming her fingers on her thigh.

Not because Jane was impatient to get to the hotel, but rather she was impatient to return to Kai so she could finally put his bullshit in its place. Despite their earlier agreement, he was still treating her as a subordinate.

She needed to corner the dragonman and give him a dressing down. She may not have his muscles, but Jane had noticed him staring at her breasts before. There was more than one way to catch a man's attention and she wasn't above using her boobs to do it.

Jane smiled. If Kai thought she was a pain in his arse before, he would think she was a bloody nightmare before much longer, if she had anything to say about it.

Yet the chance to corner Kai was still hours away. What Jane needed was a distraction. Glancing at Nikki, she decided the dragonwoman would be it. With the right coaxing, Jane could find out some more information on the dragon-shifters.

While Nikki was quiet, Jane sensed the woman wanted to talk. Jane nudged, "You can ask me what you like, Nikki. Kai isn't here to growl or frown." She glanced around the car. "Unless he records the conversations from the car."

Nikki smiled. "Not for want of trying. Bram put his foot down on that one. My guess is because Bram likes to whisk his mate away and have sex with her in the car."

Jane eyed the dragonwoman and pounced on the opening. "For all that I've been working with your clan, few people really ever talk to me. Provided you don't endanger your clan, will you answer some questions?"

Glancing at her and back on the road, Nikki asked, "Is this to do with Kai?"

"Does it matter?"

Nikki shook her head. "Not really, but I hope you stick around. Few people stand up to him, but you act unafraid." Nikki looked at her. "Why is that?"

"Honestly? I've worked with worse. Besides, my older brother is in the Special Forces and is just as bad as Kai. I have lots of practice dealing with alpha male bullshit."

Something that looked like recognition flashed across Nikki's face, but then it was gone. Jane was about to question the emotion, but Nikki beat her to it. "What is it you wish to know? I hope it's nothing to do with Bram and Evie having sex in cars."

Jane chuckled. "No, although I've always wondered what would happen if a dragon-shifter shifted inside of a car. Would it just peel like a tin can?"

Nikki shrugged. "More like it pops open."

While it had nothing to do with finding out information on Clan Stonefire, Jane couldn't help but ask, "You know this from experience?"

"Let's just say I never turned down a dare growing up."

Jane connected the dots. "I've seen how some of the older clan members treat you differently. It's because you were the first child born to a human sacrifice on Stonefire, right? I think you're still trying to move past that label. Taking daft dares would create an entirely different one."

Frowning, Nikki looked at her. "I hope you're not writing a story on me."

"No, although it would be fascinating. While information is slowly seeping out on the dragon-shifters now, pretty much nothing was known in the 1980s apart from the rumors. If you ever want to tell your story, let me know."

Nikki readjusted her hands on the steering wheel. "Let's not talk about me. We'll be at your hotel in five minutes, so if you have questions, now is the time to ask them."

After nearly a decade of being a reporter, Jane could tell from Nikki's tone that she wouldn't talk more on the subject. Although, if things went well and Jane helped Stonefire take down the dragon hunters, Jane might have the chance to tell a lot more dragon-shifters' stories in the future, including Nikki's.

For the moment, however, Jane focused on something she'd been dying to ask for months. "How do the dragon and human halves co-exist? I know that when a dragon-shifter's pupils flash to slits, they're talking to their dragon, but not much else. Can the dragon half force you to do what it wishes?"

The corner of Nikki's mouth ticked up. "They always try, especially when it comes to sex, the randy bastards, but a well-trained dragon-shifter can maintain control."

"What happens to those who lose control?"

"The clan takes care of them unless they reach a major human city, then the DDA takes care of them."

"As in kill them?"

"Sometimes, if they can't be contained." Nikki tapped her fingers on the steering wheel. "Other times, they go through rehabilitation. The ones who usually crack are the ones who want to become Protectors. Because of the agreement with the British government, all prospective Protectors must serve in the army for two years before training with their respective clans. It's not always easy to take orders and sometimes serve in active war zones, all whilst keeping your dragon in check. It really is the ultimate test of a dragon-shifter over their dragon."

Jane knew the dragon-shifters helped fight overseas, but she'd never really thought about their role inside the army before. "Did you ever come close to cracking?"

Nikki glanced at her. "All Protectors have, even Kai."

"Somehow, I find it hard to believe that Mr. Self-control could ever lose it."

Nikki shrugged. "It happens."

"Then there's hope for me."

"Hope for what?" Nikki asked cautiously.

Jane grinned. "That I can get him to drop his commander persona and figure out the man beneath."

"And why, exactly, would you do that?"

"I like to know who I'm working with."

The dragonwoman straightened her shoulders. "I do, too. So I have a question for you."

"Ask away."

"Do you have a brother who serves in the army named Rafe Hartley?"

Jane tilted her head. "I was wondering when you were going to comment on my brother."

"What?"

She waved a hand. "I noticed your expression earlier." Nikki opened her mouth, but Jane continued, "Reading people is essential to my job. But to answer your question, yes, I do. He's older and in the UK Special Forces." Jane frowned. "He didn't do something daft, did he? I love my brother, but he tends to think with his dick instead of his brain."

54

Nikki blinked. "You sound like a dragon-shifter. Most humans would blush and say something such as 'man parts.'"

Jane waved a hand. "My mother is Australian and grew up on a cattle ranch with five brothers. Being delicate is not in her nature, and she passed that on to me." Jane turned a little toward Nikki. "But back to my brother. Tell me if he was a dick and I'll handle it."

Smiling, Nikki shook her head. "As much as I'd like to see that, I was just curious if you were related."

"And?"

Nikki raised an eyebrow. "You're quite demanding, aren't you?"

Jane shrugged. "I don't like dancing around and not getting answers. The truth usually speeds things up."

"I'll try to keep that in mind." When Jane remained silent, Nikki added, "While Kai would cut off his own arm before asking humans for help, humans like your brother could help us with the dragon hunters. I've tried to convince Kai to ask our colleagues from the army for help, but he refuses." Nikki met her eye. "Maybe you can convince him."

"Why ask me this? You barely know me."

"You've helped our clan more than Kai will admit. Plus, I know your brother's reputation. Those two combined tell my gut to trust you."

Her brother Rafe had two reputations—one with women and the other as a soldier. "Please tell me you didn't sleep with Rafe."

Nikki blinked, looked at Jane, and then away. "Um, no."

But judging by Nikki's response, the dragonwoman had wanted to.

That meant Nikki was basing part of her trust on Rafe's role as a soldier. By all accounts, her brother was a damn good one. "Well, asking Rafe and other soldiers unofficially for their help is an interesting idea. But I think we need to locate the hunters first and see what we're up against. Then I'll decide if it's worth the hassle of convincing your stubborn-headed boss to ask for outside help."

As Nikki nodded and turned into the hotel car park, the dragonwoman added, "If anyone can change Kai's mind apart from Bram, I think it might be you."

"All I do is ignore his growly orders and demand equal footing."

Turning off the engine, Nikki turned toward Jane. "He needs that more than you know."

Before Jane could ask for clarification, Nikki exited the car and Jane followed.

~~~

Kai ended the call to Aaron, his second-in-command back on Stonefire. Everything was in order and no new threats were detected.

While that was a good thing, it also meant Kai needed to find something else to occupy his mind until Jane and Nikki returned.

His dragon spoke up. *Thinking about the human now will avoid distractions later.*

*She's not a distraction.*

*Liar. You want her naked as much as me. I still say fuck her and clear your mind.*

*No fucking the human.*

His beast paused a beat before adding, *It's okay to want someone else. The other one chose a different male.*

56

Kai had spent the last eleven years not thinking about Maggie. But if his dragon was going to bring her up, Kai would, too. *And what if Maggie shows up tomorrow, newly widowed? She didn't want us then and I don't want her now, but will your instincts allow me to have someone else? Or, will they be a slave to the true mate pull?*

*I've waited a long time for you to talk to me about this.*

*Then talk, dragon.*

His beast huffed. *Don't order me around. I deserve better.*

Kai rubbed his hand over his face. If he didn't stop his dragon's near-tantrum, he would definitely have a headache in five minutes. *Fine, then please answer my question. Otherwise, I'll never fuck a female again.*

*Liar.*

*Care to dare me, dragon? My record is pretty solid when it comes to winning over you.*

After what seemed like an eternity, his beast replied, *Dragons can find another mate.*

*In theory. But you don't let things go.*

*I can and I will. Kiss the human and we can forget about the other one.*

*And what happens when the kiss is just a kiss? How long will your interest hold?* Kai asked.

His dragon's voice turned steely. *With Jane, it could be forever.*

*How do you know?*

*No more talking. Kiss her and then ask me again.*

Before Kai could press his beast for answers, the front door opened and two female voices drifted down the hall.

Jane and Nikki were back.

Shoving his beast into a mental prison, Kai exited the room and moved down the hall. He opened his mouth to bark an order when he saw Jane and forgot what he was going to say.

The female wore jeans that hugged her long legs, leaving no detail to the imagination. Her black top dipped to a V, revealing a creamy expanse of cleavage. A small mole lay on the top of her right breast. He wondered how many more moles and freckles she had on her body.

Not that he'd ever find out.

With herculean effort, Kai looked to Jane's face. Her long, black hair tumbled around her shoulders. He couldn't help thinking her hair was the perfect length to wind around his fist and tug her head back for a kiss.

Then amusement danced in Jane's eyes and her voice broke the spell. "Did you get a good enough look or would you like me to give a little twirl so you can see the rest?"

He longed to see how her jeans hugged her arse, but he dared not ask for it. "Don't be daft. That outfit is a bit revealing, but better than the dress from last night. You also look different enough from yesterday that few should recognize you, in the event you run into a hunter. Are you ready to go investigate now?"

Jane crossed her arms over her chest and Kai made every effort not to look at her plumped up breasts. "I'm surprised you aren't asking for a play-by-play on how the trip to the hotel went."

Kai looked to Nikki. "Any problems?" Nikki shook her head and Kai looked back to Jane. "Done. Now, answer the question."

Sighing, Jane shrugged off her short, faux leather coat. "Before we go anywhere, I want a word with you."

Kai frowned. "Then speak."

"In private," Jane stated.

"Whatever you want to say to me you can say to Nikki."

Jane raised her brows. "Oh, really? So if I wanted to rip your shirt off and asked you to flex, you'd be okay with Nikki watching, too?"

He shrugged. "Nudity is a human concern. Nikki has seen me naked before and will again."

"It's called teasing, Kai Sutherland. You should try it sometime," Jane replied.

His beast finally broke free. *I want to do a different type of teasing. Get her alone and we can try it.*

*No.*

Kai gave Jane his best stare. "You're wasting time. Speak."

Jane took a step toward him. "In private."

As they stared at one another, Kai almost admired the female's stubbornness. Most humans would back down from a dragon-shifter, especially if they were a Protector.

Yet Jane looked about ready to fight him if necessary.

The image of the human attempting to tackle him almost made Kai smile.

His dragon growled. *I think we should tackle her into bed.*

Ignoring his beast, Kai studied Jane's face. Judging by the firmness of her jaw, she wasn't going to back down.

Rather than waste time, Kai motioned down the hall with a hand. "Fine. Go to the map room from last night."

With a triumphant look on her face, Jane walked down the hall. As he watched her arse move in the tight jeans, Nikki cleared her throat.

*Fuck.* He didn't need Nikki teasing him later.

Kai met her brown eyes. "Zain arrived while you were out and took the two hunters to a secure location. Contact him and see if he's found out anything."

Before Nikki could do more than bob her head, Kai moved down the hall. Part of him was disappointed Jane's arse was nowhere to be seen, while the other part of him was glad the temptation was out of sight.

His dragon spoke up again. *Remember what I said before. Kiss the human and forget about the other one.*

He entered the room and lost the ability to speak. Jane was bent over the table with the map and he had a clear view of her breasts encased in a black bra.

Looking up, Jane smiled. "Do I have your attention now, dragonman?"

~~~

Jane bit her lip to keep from laughing. Kai blinking with his mouth open wasn't a sight she'd soon forget.

Since she needed him to think with the head on his shoulders, Jane stood up and placed a hand on her hip. "Can you speak now?"

Clearing his throat, Kai clenched and unclenched his fingers. "Tempting an unattached dragonman is a dangerous thing to do."

"Maybe with a regular dragonman, but not you. You're Mr. Self-control, after all."

Kai's expression turned neutral. "You put up a tantrum to get me in private to talk, so talk. You're wasting time we could be using to investigate the area for the hunters' hideout."

"I hardly think it's wasting time to get to know someone you're working with."

Kai grunted. "You appear clever. I'm sure you already researched me before this."

Jane sighed. "Just because I looked you up doesn't mean I fully know you."

"Get to the point."

Jane walked around the table until she was a foot away from Kai. "The point is you're still ordering me around. You need to fix that, or else."

He raised his brows. "Or else what?"

She smiled. "Oh, I have ways of making you agree to almost anything I say."

"I doubt that."

Taking another step closer, Jane stood about six inches from Kai. The heat of his body, mixed with the male scent that was uniquely his, made her heart rate kick up. She was overly aware of just how male Kai Sutherland was in that second.

But he wasn't just any male; he was a powerful dragon-shifter who was single and attracted to her.

Before she could relive the dream she had last night, when they'd both been naked, Jane took a deep breath. Focusing on her task, she whispered, "Last warning before I start using my box of tools."

"You will fail."

Jane lifted a hand but stopped an inch from Kai's chest. She studied his eyes, but they were unreadable. "Let me try. If I win and get you to admit to something you probably wouldn't admit to, then you stop giving orders. If you hold out and I lose, I'll do whatever you say."

His pupils flashed to slits and she wondered what Kai's dragon was saying to him.

Then Kai leaned his face closer to hers and she could feel his breath on her lips as he murmured, "Try your hardest, human. I will win."

For a second, Jane lost herself in the depths of Kai's blue-green eyes. The confidence staring back at her was only part of Kai's story.

She would bet her career that the dragonman was hiding something.

Not that she had time to think about that. Pushing aside her ever-present curiosity, Jane whispered, "It's a deal," before placing her hand on Kai's chest.

Even through his shirt, Kai's heat branded her palm. The hardness of his chest reminded her of the muscles underneath.

Lightly scraping her nails against Kai's torso, she focused on her task. There was no bloody way she was going to allow a little thing such as attraction get in the way of winning.

Running her other hand up and down his shoulder, Kai tensed under her ministrations. With a little more prodding, she could finally put the dragonman in his place.

She moved one hand to the back of his neck. The instant her fingers made contact with his skin a little jolt shot through her body.

Kai's eyes flashed again and Jane asked, "Are you ready to admit you want to kiss me yet?"

He grunted. "No. If this is all you have, then you're going to lose."

She raised an eyebrow. "Oh, baby, I'm just getting started."

Kai opened his mouth, but Jane moved her head to the side of his neck and nuzzled his warm skin. His scent was stronger there, and Jane couldn't resist licking his neck. The saltiness made her stomach flip. Kai tasted good.

Since the dragonman was still unmoving, Jane bit his neck where it met his shoulder at the same time as she leaned her body against his. The feel of his hard cock against her stomach made her wetter than she'd ever been in her life.

Kai growled and grabbed her arse. Pulling her flush against his body, Jane let out a squeak.

Kai's breath was hot against her ear. "Didn't I tell you it was dangerous to tease an unattached dragonman?"

Daring to lean back, Jane stopped breathing at the hunger in Kai's eyes.

Then she regained her wits. She had a bet to win. "Are you sure you don't want to kiss me?" She lowered her voice. "Don't you want to feel my soft, warm lips as you devour my mouth with your tongue?" His eyes flashed again and Jane knew he was close to losing control. Rubbing her body against his cock, Kai hissed. "Stop fighting it. You've been eyeing me since I first met you. Just admit you want one little kiss and you can finally stop wondering."

Kai's voice was husky as he asked, "Wondering about what?"

"What I taste like."

With a growl, Kai moved until his lips were a hairsbreadth from hers. "You play a dangerous game, human."

She blew across his lips and Kai's grip tightened. The dragonman was closer to giving in. "Stop stalling. Either claim a kiss and let me win, or walk away." She rubbed against his body again. "Although, your dick tells me you don't want to walk away."

Slapping her arse cheek, Kai murmured, "If I'm going to lose, then I'm going to lose properly."

And he kissed her.

# CHAPTER FIVE

As Kai Sutherland's lips touched Jane's, a possessive surge coursed through his body at the same time his dragon roared. Pulling the human even tighter against him, Kai pinched Jane's arse. When her mouth opened in surprise, he took advantage and invaded her hot, sweet mouth with his tongue.

For a second, Jane didn't respond and he wondered if she'd had second thoughts. However, once she stroked her tongue against his as she leaned into the kiss, it took everything he had to remain in control. His human definitely made him work for it.

His dragon growled. *Her taste…I want more. Much more.*

Before Kai could reply, Jane's nails dug into his chest as she took the kiss deeper. He growled and stroked harder. She may have won the first round by wearing down his self-control, but he wasn't about to let her win this one, too.

He moved a hand to her head and fisted her hair. Gently tugging for better access, he stroked, nibbled, and sucked her bottom lip. Releasing her warm, plump lip, he went in for another taste. It'd been too long since he'd had a female and he had forgotten what it was like to hold a soft body against his. And since she was human, Jane's body was softer than any dragon-shifter, and he loved the difference.

Jane leaned into him, her nipples pressing hard against his chest. He was torn between ripping off her shirt and sucking one of them deep, or turning her around to bend her over, tear off her clothes, and fuck her from behind.

His dragon chimed in. *Yes, do it now. I don't want to wait.*

*No. Fucking her would complicate things.*

*Then lick between her legs. Her mouth tastes good, but I want to taste her honey.*

An image of Kai spreading Jane's legs wide as he devoured her pussy flashed into his mind and his cock let out a drop of pre-cum.

*Stop it, dragon. That would also complicate things.*

His beast huffed. *Who cares? We want her and she wants us. The clan is safe, so seize the chance.*

Kai stilled and broke the kiss. What the hell was he doing? He was wasting time with a female while his clan could still be in danger.

Jane blinked and then frowned, her breathing still fast from their kissing. "I thought you were going to lose properly. That seemed like a half-arse job to me."

His beast scratched to take control. *I will make her forget how to speak. Let me have a go.*

After tossing his dragon into a mental prison, Kai forced himself to take three steps back. "Says the female who rubbed against me, begging me for more."

While Jane couldn't erase her kiss-bruised lips, her expression turned hard. Part of Kai regretted the change, but the rational part of his brain was grateful to get back to business. His clan was counting on him to keep them safe.

The human crossed her arms over her chest. "Hide behind your badass expression and attitude all you like, but your actions and body didn't lie. You were enjoying yourself."

He shrugged. "Of course. Who wouldn't enjoy kissing a pretty female?"

Kai was so used to being honest that it took him a beat to realize he'd just admitted he found Jane Hartley attractive.

Triumph flashed in Jane's eyes before she spoke up. "Sometimes your honesty is annoying, but other times, it reveals some of your secrets."

It was on the tip of his tongue to press for details, but glancing at the clock on the wall, it was almost one o'clock. He couldn't afford to waste any more time, so he changed the subject. "Since I'm not supposed to order you around, are you ready to get to work?"

Jane raised an eyebrow. "Asking me a question must've been difficult for you." Kai grunted and Jane smiled. "Okay, I'll stop teasing, for now." She lowered her voice. "But this is far from over, dragonman."

"I assure you, it won't happen again. Once I make a mistake, I learn from it."

"I'm a mistake now?"

His dragon huffed. *Don't be an arsehole. She is not a mistake. The other one was a mistake.*

Ignoring his beast, Kai answered, "Kissing any human is a mistake."

She studied him a second and then shook her head. "I'm not sure if I'm offended or intrigued." Jane moved to the door and stopped to look over her shoulder. "Are you coming?"

Good. The female was getting back to business. Kai could handle that. "Where are we going?"

"South Gateshead."

Jane exited the door and Kai could do nothing but follow.

# REAWAKENING THE DRAGON

~~~

The second she was out of Kai's sight, Jane couldn't resist touching her lips with her fingertips. Not even his comments dismissing their kiss as a mistake could clear the dragonman from her mind.

Kissing Kai had been a strategy to prove to the unshakeable dragon-shifter that he could lose control like anyone else. Yet she hadn't expected his lips and tongue to set her skin on fire. She'd never felt such a primal need to kiss a man back before, either. Because of her stubbornness, all Jane wanted to do was kiss the man again and have him beg for more.

Yes, he'd been an arsehole, but Kai's dismissal was part of the armor he used. Jane was beginning to see how Kai used work as an excuse for everything. However, she sensed there was something else holding him back from his attraction to her. It was plain from his erection and the stroking of his tongue that he wanted her. Yet he fought against it at every turn.

Jane wanted to find out the reason for it.

Still, the best thing would be to forget about the dragonman and his secrets so she could focus on her story. As much as she wanted to strip Kai bare and tease him until he lost complete control, she wasn't about to tarnish her reputation or ruin her career. If she slept with him, no matter how careful she was, someone would find out and then no one would take her reports on the dragon-shifters seriously. She would be labeled a dragon's whore, or worse.

Once she had exposed the dragon hunters and helped raise the esteem of Stonefire with the public, she could chance sleeping with a dragonman. Maybe even the one she'd been dreaming about for months.

*Get a grip, Jane.* Kai was more work than she could handle. There were others who would sleep with her after nothing more than a glance.

Yet looking over her shoulder, she knew none of them would compare to Kai.

*Ruining your reputation isn't worth it, Hartley. There will always be other men but there won't always be another career-making story.*

Straightening her shoulders, Jane picked up her pace and entered the living room before Kai could catch up with her.

Nikki was standing at the far window, talking in a language Jane couldn't understand. But she recognized the rise and fall of the syllables enough to know it was Mersae, the old dragon language.

Kai's heat came up behind her and Jane just prevented herself from shivering. She wouldn't let the bloody dragonman know how he affected her. The next however many days were going to be the ultimate test of her own self-control. Yet with her story as the prize, she would find a way to resist.

Kai's low voice filled her ears. "Despite what I said, I still expect for us to work together. Is that clear?"

*Don't answer, don't answer.* Telling him to fuck off wasn't the best idea.

As the silence ticked by, Kai grunted in what she would almost call amusement. The bloody dragonman must've read her mind.

The urge to tell him off was strong, but Jane merely straightened her shoulders even more and waited for Nikki to be done. Arguing would only delay exchanging information with Kai.

A minute later, Nikki lowered the phone from her ear and turned around. Kai moved to Jane's side and Nikki looked back and forth between Jane and Kai. "I didn't hear you two come in."

Kai spoke up. "What did Zain say?"

# REAWAKENING THE DRAGON

Nikki tucked her mobile phone into her pocket. "The hunters are secure, but he hasn't had a chance to interrogate them yet. He'll call when there's news."

"Good." Kai then turned to Jane. His eyes were unreadable again and she didn't like it. "Tell me why you picked South Gateshead."

If he was going to pretend they hadn't just shared a passionate kiss a few minutes ago and treat her like an information source, then she would do the same. "The more I researched the Tyneside area, the more Gateshead made sense as my top choice for several reasons. Not only would they want to be on the edge of the city, but they would want access to new recruits."

"Go on," Kai stated.

"Well, there are a lot of economically disadvantaged areas in mid-to-south Gateshead. Since most of the dragon hunter recruits join for the money, it would be easy to persuade men and women living there to join—pick out the most financially vulnerable with the desired skills sets, dangle money in front of them, and voila, you have new recruits."

Kai nodded. "And their street smarts could help, provided Simon Bourne has them trained well enough not to fuck up."

"Correct," Jane answered. "But while they will recruit from those areas, they won't base themselves there since they'd stick out quite easily. I believe they're either on the edge of Gateshead or in the farms not too far from the city limits."

Nikki frowned. "The former Carlisle-based gang has never used farms as their headquarters before."

Jane smiled. "Exactly, so the DDA won't think to check there for a while. By the time they do, the hunters will be long gone."

Grunting, Kai looked between Jane and Nikki. "It's logical and makes sense. Let's hurry up and check out the area. The longer the two hunters we captured are missing, the greater the chance Bourne will move his people."

Holding up a hand, Jane added, "Please tell me you have a different car we can use. The big SUV from before will stick out like a sore thumb in some sections of Gateshead."

Kai shook his head. "That's the only car we have. Remember, we're dragons. We prefer flying."

Jane sighed. "Flying into Gateshead would be even worse." Kai opened his mouth, but she cut him off. "My brother's friend lives nearby and I can call him about borrowing a car, but it's best if I talk to him alone whilst you two wait in the SUV."

"Do you trust him?" Kai asked.

"It's a friend of my brother, Rafe, and if Rafe recommends him, he's golden. Older brothers don't recommend other men lightly to their single sisters."

Nikki bit her lip, but Kai grunted. "I know. I have a half-sister."

Jane blinked. "You have a sister?"

Kai took out his phone and held it out. "That's not important right now. Call the human."

Jane raised an eyebrow. "I have my own phone, you know."

"Yes, but this way, I have his number in case I need to track him down."

Jane wanted to rub her temples. "Do I want to know why you'd need to track him down?"

"If he betrays us, he will learn to never do it again," Kai answered.

Jane raised her brows. "Get in line, dragonman. He'll have to deal with me and my older brother first. No one messes with the Hartleys and gets away with it."

She swore approval flashed in Kai's eyes, but it was gone before she was certain.

Nikki spoke up. "Forget the Hartleys, love. He'll have to deal with Clan Stonefire."

Despite Nikki's almost delicate appearance for a dragon-shifter, thanks to her half-Chinese ancestry, the woman's voice was like steel. As much as Nikki had been joking and talking earlier, Jane needed to remember Nikki was a Protector. And not just any Protector—one who was out to prove herself.

Taking Kai's phone, Jane nodded at Nikki. "Just this once, we can call our threats a draw."

Nikki laughed, but it was Kai who spoke up. "I hardly think you and your brother are a match for an entire dragon-shifter clan."

"You haven't met my brother."

Nikki added, "Maybe you should call your brother up here. I'd love to see him and Kai circle each other."

"As tempting as that is, let's focus on our current task. If we don't get moving, Kai may have a stroke." The dragonman merely grunted and Jane grinned. "Okay, okay. Let me call Jeff."

Jane pulled out her own phone to get the number for her brother's friend and inputted the number into Kai's. As she waited for him to pick up, the image of Rafe and Kai growling and grunting at each other popped into her mind. Someday, she would like to see that.

Jeff answered his phone and prevented Jane from wondering why she wanted her brother to meet Kai.

~~~

Jane moved a hand to the door handle and Kai growled, "I still say I should talk with him first to ensure he's trustworthy."

The human raised an eyebrow. "And as I've said twenty times, you can't read minds. Maybe if you shifted your fingers into talons Jeff would spill all of his secrets, but he can't know you're a dragon-shifter."

Kai glared. "I can be persuasive without revealing I'm a dragon-shifter."

Jane shook her head. "I'm going. Now, stay here."

Before he could reach out a hand to stop her, Jane exited the SUV and headed toward Jeff's flat.

Nikki's amused voice filled the car. "She's not one of your soldiers, Kai. You should try a different approach with her."

A human male opened his door and smiled at Jane. Even from his position in the SUV, Kai could see the male giving Jane a once-over.

As if the human was worthy of someone like Jane Hartley.

Kai leaned closer to the car window. "We know nothing about Jeff. If not me, then at least you should have accompanied her."

Nikki sighed. "Jane's survived thirty-plus years on her own. I think she can handle ten more minutes."

As Kai watched Jeff and Jane walk from his apartment to the footpath, Kai uncrossed and re-crossed his arms. The human male named Jeff had just touched Jane's shoulder.

After snarling, his beast spoke up, *She shouldn't be alone with the human male. We know nothing about him.*

*She wouldn't let me vet him first. I tried.*

*But not hard enough.*

*She is stubborn.*

His beast huffed. *We are more so.*

*I'm not so sure about that. She's as bad as any dragon-shifter. She'd take on the hunters by herself if she had to.*

His dragon growled. *We will help her.*

72

# REAWAKENING THE DRAGON

*And if she sneaks away?*
*We will track her down.*

His beast's words worried him a little. Kai knew Jane wasn't a true mate since he'd kissed her and hadn't gone into a mate-claim frenzy, but his dragon was acting as if she were theirs to claim. His beast hadn't acted that way around anyone since Maggie.

Nikki's voice interrupted his thoughts. "Worrying won't help anything, boss. Trust Jane. She knows how to take care of herself."

He glanced at Nikki. "She's human and fragile with no formal training."

Nikki raised an eyebrow. "Considering how you've taken every precaution to avoid Jane Hartley since her first interview on Stonefire, I'm curious why the sudden interest now."

"If she screws up, the clan could suffer."

Nikki studied him a second before replying, "What happened between you two whilst I was on the phone? It's as if you won't look at each other longer than absolutely necessary. I would say it's because you're afraid to let your desire show."

Kai grunted. "Ridiculous."

"You two also smelled of each other."

Kai's dragon chimed in, *Why won't you declare the human ours? We should be kissing her again, right now.*

Ignoring his beast, Kai watched Jane laugh at the human male's words. When the male touched her arm again, Kai dug his fingers into his thigh. He was close to exiting the car and tugging Jane out of reach. The time she spent flirting with the human took time away from them chasing down the dragon hunters. This operation was time sensitive and Jane knew it.

Yes, saving time and finding the hunters was the only reason he wanted to rip her away from the male's arm now

73

around Jane's waist. It had nothing to do with Kai's dragon wanting to stake a claim on her.

*Liar*, his dragon stated.

Thankfully, Nikki's voice prevented his dragon from saying anything else. "It's okay to want her, Kai. Because of Melanie's persistence, the rules have temporarily changed for Stonefire, for a trial period. Dragon males are allowed to take human mates of their own choosing, provided they apply with the DDA. Besides, considering all that Jane's done for our clan, Bram would welcome her if she accepted you."

Glancing at Nikki, he asked, "Why are you saying this?"

"Because I once watched a human male just like you're watching Jane. If it wasn't against the law, I would've gone after him. You don't have that worry and you deserve someone. You're one of the best males I know."

Studying the younger dragonwoman, Kai saw more than a soldier or a kidnapping victim. Nikki had been denied a love, just like Kai had. On top of that, she had wanted a human.

Since female dragon-shifters were much rarer than males, they still weren't allowed to mate outside the dragon clans, not even on Stonefire, who had the public's good graces.

Or, at least, that was how things stood so far.

Clearing his throat, Kai answered, "Mention your predicament to Melanie and Evie. Given how stubborn they are, they'll find a way to change things for you."

Nikki shook her head. "I'm over the male now. But maybe you could mention it for the future and then that way, I wouldn't have to put up with Mel and Evie's scrutiny."

Kai nodded. "Once the hunters are no longer a threat, I'll talk with the females."

The car fell into a comfortable silence. Well, for about thirty seconds and then Nikki smiled. "This is nice."

He raised an eyebrow. "What is?"

"You actually talking about something other than work."

With a grunt, Kai looked back out of the car window. The talking had helped him forget about Jane, but as the human male named Jeff moved his hand to Jane's lower back and guided her down the footpath, Kai couldn't prevent growling.

Before Nikki could stop him, he exited the car and walked toward the humans.

~~~

Jane was going to kill her brother, Rafe.

Even if Jeff was as trustworthy as Rafe had declared, the man was a huge flirt and kept touching her. It was taking twice as long as it should to simply walk to the man's car.

Still, Jane kept a smile on her face. If she offended Jeff and he walked away before she secured the car, then they would lose precious time trying to find another nondescript vehicle. While the bus or Metro would take them to some parts of Gateshead, they needed the car to reach the farms.

And Jane had learned the hard way that hiring a car was too easy to trace back to the person who signed for it. Since she didn't condone stealing vehicles, Jeff was her best bet.

The man in question rubbed her lower back in slow circles as they walked. Jane forced her voice to remain light. "Which one is yours?"

Jeff waved toward a blue economy car that looked a few years old. "She's gotten me out of a scrape or two." Since Jane was about six inches taller, Jeff looked up at her. "I don't care if I owe Rafe a favor or not. If you don't bring her back in one piece, you'll owe me."

Jane knew where this was going. "I'll bring her back safe, don't worry."

Jeff leaned close. "If you don't, then you'll owe me a date."

Jane opened her mouth to reply when Kai appeared in front of her and Jeff, blocking their path. Kai crossed his arms and met her gaze. "Is this man bothering you?"

*Well, at least he didn't say human.* The jumper hid Kai's tattoos, but dragon-shifters had some unique phrasings that often gave them away. "You were supposed to wait in the car."

Kai shrugged. "You're taking too long."

Jeff looked between Kai and Jane. "Is he your boyfriend?"

Jane had an idea of how to speed things along. Moving away from Jeff, she leaned against Kai's side. "Yes. He's a former colleague of Rafe's."

Jeff eyed the snug material around Kai's bulging biceps and his face went neutral. "Then maybe your boyfriend can find you a car."

"You owe Rafe your life."

As Jeff stared at them, Kai wrapped an arm around Jane's waist and encased her in his marvelous heat. She would never go cold with a dragonman at her side.

Not that she would ever have a dragonman of her own.

Jeff finally held up his keys. "Take them. But if you damage her, then you're paying to repair it."

"Fair enough." Jane swiped the keys. "We'll even bring it back with a full tank of petrol."

Before Jeff could reply, Kai turned them around and moved toward the car. She half expected Kai to let go of her waist and move around to the driver's side. Instead, Kai squeezed her tighter against him.

She really should protest. But the feel of his hard body next to her made her belly clench. She could only imagine what would happen if Kai brushed his fingers against her bare skin.

Kai growled. "Stop doing that."

Frowning, she looked over at his profile. "Doing what?"

"Wanting me so much I can smell it."

Jane's cheeks flushed, but she quickly recovered. "Sorry if my scent offends you."

He glanced at her. "It doesn't."

She blinked. "Then why bring it up? It's not like I can control how attractive you are."

They stopped in front of the car and Kai turned her to face him. There was approval in his eyes. Maybe she should've lied about him being hot, but if she lied, then it provided an excuse for Kai to do it, too. The easiest way to write her story was to keep the dragonman honest.

Kai lowered his head and her mind went blank as his firm lips moved closer to hers. Stopping just short of kissing her, he murmured, "Because your scent drives me crazy and tempts me to do something I shouldn't."

He moved a hand to her back and pressed her close. Between his heat and the desire in his eyes, Jane's heart rate kicked up. Even to her own ears her voice was strangled. "What do you want to do?"

Kai nuzzled her cheek, the roughness of his almost-whiskers sending a thrill through her body that ended between her legs.

*Shit.* The dragonman would take her arousal as encouragement.

Kai's husky voice caressed her as he answered, "I want to kiss you again." He pulled back to meet her eye. "Although, if I'm

77

playing the role of your boyfriend, I probably *should* kiss you. It will make the ruse more convincing."

Her heart thumped harder. "Not all couples kiss in public."

Kai's voice was husky as he replied, "Maybe for humans."

As Kai's pupils turned to slits and stayed that way, Jane stopped breathing. Did the change mean his dragon was in charge? And if so, what would he do?

In that second, she forgot all about the dragon hunters or her quest for a good story. She wanted to find out more about the dragon-half of the man in front of her.

And foolish as it was, she then wanted him to kiss her. To keep up their ruse, of course. Nothing more.

Maybe if she said the lie enough, she'd actually believe it.

Determined not to lose her nerve, Jane leaned into Kai's touch and asked, "What is your dragon saying to you right now?"

~~~

Kai's dragon growled. *Tell her I want to lick every inch of her body. Then bend her over a table and brand her pussy with our dick.*

*That will scare her away.*

His dragon paused a beat. *Are you finally admitting that you want her?*

Rather than admit his dragon had been right earlier, he merely replied, *Any straight male would want her.*

*Then tell her we want her.*

*I won't equate attraction with more. She may get the wrong idea.*

Jane's voice interrupted his conversation with his dragon. "Answer me, Kai, or I'll walk away and leave you panting after me."

He frowned. "I don't pant."

A playful twinkle filled Jane's eyes. "Does that mean sex is as efficient as everything else you do?"

His dragon hissed. *Definitely not.*

Kai pressed Jane's body closer. When the human drew in a breath, Kai murmured, "With a dragon in charge, you will tire long before I do."

Jane's heart rate kicked up and he nearly smiled.

The female cleared her throat before replying, "You still haven't told me what your dragon has been saying. I have a feeling it's about me." She raised her chin. "I have a right to know."

Moving a hand to Jane's face, Kai traced her cheek bone. The human's skin was so soft. "As equals, I should tell you."

"I sense a 'but.'"

"But you didn't win against my dragon. He wants another form of payment."

Jane tilted her head. "Let me guess, he wants sex in a car?"

Kai's dragon grunted. *Cars are too small. I want her in a field. There are several nearby.*

Blinking, Kai forced his voice to work. "Is it a secret fantasy of yours to have sex in a car?"

Jane grinned. "Not necessarily. I just like confusing you. I need to do it more often."

Kai growled. "Enough teasing. My dragon wants a kiss."

She raised an eyebrow. "Does he, now?"

He moved a hand to her right arse cheek and squeezed. "Yes."

Jane's scent grew stronger and he wished he could strip off her jeans and taste the honey that kept tempting his nose.

The human stared at him for a few seconds. Uncertainty filled her eyes, but she finally nodded. "Okay, but not in view of Jeff."

"I don't like his name on your lips."

She slapped his chest lightly. "Don't get any ideas about telling me what I can or cannot say. I'm not a thing to be controlled."

His dragon chimed in. *Stop wasting time.* She agreed. *Find a place to kiss her properly.*

Reluctantly, Kai released his grip on Jane. Taking her hand, he tugged her toward a nearby alley. "No more talking."

For once, Jane didn't fight him. Judging by her strides, she was as anxious as he to kiss again.

He liked the fact Jane wasn't hiding or blushing. It was the opposite of what he'd had with Maggie.

His beast spoke up. *Don't bring up the other one. I want to only think of Jane.*

Kai wished he could turn off his memories as easily as his dragon. But the image of him trying to coax a kiss from Maggie and her turning her head and asking him to chase her flooded into his mind. For all that Kai's dragon had wanted Maggie, Kai had never had the chance to kiss her. She'd been afraid of the mate-claim frenzy, and at the first sign of hardship, Maggie had run to another.

He glanced at Jane. Nikki's words from earlier had made him believe he could at least have a chance with the female. He wondered if kissing the human was a mistake; it would only make both man and beast want her more.

Given his track record, Jane might even abandon him at the first sign of trouble.

His dragon sighed. *It's just a kiss. Enjoy it and worry about the future later.*

*That's what you said before.*

*This time is different. Jane is no blushing virgin flirt. Enjoy this kiss.*

If it will make you shut it, then fine. I'll do it just this once.

80

After all, once he could stop thinking with his cock, he and Jane had work to do.

As soon as Kai guided them into the alley and around a corner, he stopped and tugged Jane against his body. As he leaned down for a kiss, he forgot about the future. For the first time in over a decade, Kai was going to steal a few minutes for himself.

# CHAPTER SIX

There were a million reasons why Jane shouldn't waste time kissing Kai Sutherland in a private alley. But as his lips moved toward hers, she forgot about all of them. Her whole body was on fire and Kai Sutherland was the only one who could feed the flames.

His warm, firm lips touched hers gently at first before he took her bottom lip between his teeth and nibbled. Then he tugged and released. She leaned forward for more, but Kai retreated an inch and moved a hand to her breast. Even through her bra and top, his touch sent a tingle through her body.

As he traced her hard nipple, he whispered, "Later, I'm going to touch you properly."

"I never agreed to any such thing."

His eyes turned predatory, reminding her he was half dragon. "You will."

Never one to back down, Jane leaned into his hand and traced her fingers down Kai's chest to the waist of his trousers. Moving her hand under his jumper, she touched the warm, hard planes of his stomach and Kai sucked in a breath. As she rubbed against the trail of hair above his waist, she wanted to touch what lay at the end of it.

Kai's voice was rough when he added, "I don't have time to fuck you, Jane Hartley. But just know that my kiss is a preview of what's to come."

"I didn't—"

The dragonman shut her up with a kiss.

As his tongue found hers, Jane moaned. She would never get enough of the heady male taste that was Kai Sutherland.

Then the dragonman ran his hand up under her top and she gasped as his large, rough hands brushed against her skin. The pulse between her legs increased as she waited to see what else he would do.

But damn the man, he removed his hand and fisted her ponytail. She should be offended at the caveman-like action, but each gentle tug only made her wetter. Craving any kind of relief, Jane hooked her leg around his and rubbed against Kai. The friction brought her closer to the edge.

Kai broke the kiss, spun around, and pushed her behind him. Jane blinked a few times before she realized what happened. "What's wrong?"

The dragonman put up a hand. Anxious to know what was happening, Jane peeked around the solid mass of dragon-shifter in front of her, but the alley was empty.

After Kai scanned the sky, he took Jane's hand and tugged. "Let's go."

Keeping her voice low, Jane asked, "Are you going to tell me what happened?"

Kai remained silent until they were almost out of the alley. Glancing at Jane, he raised an eyebrow. "As much as I wanted you to come against my leg, someone was climbing on the roofs."

"I didn't hear anything."

"My hearing is better."

When Kai didn't elaborate, part of Jane wanted to kick him in the shin. She knew he was remaining quiet for their safety, but she hated being in the dark. She whispered, "Is it safe to move?"

"I don't know." Kai glanced around until his eyes landed on a metal skip bin behind them. "When I give the word, hide behind that skip and send a text to Nikki. Ask her to come to the alley."

"Fine, but don't do anything daft."

Kai briefly met her gaze. "I ask the same of you." Before Jane could reply, Kai ordered, "Go, now."

Knowing Kai would better handle the situation than she, Jane ran toward the skip. The second she reached it, the sound of someone jumping onto the cobblestones echoed through the alley. The urge to check on Kai was strong, but he was trusting her to have his back. Jane wasn't a soldier, so she followed Kai's orders and sent a text to Nikki, asking for the dragonwoman's help.

She trusted Kai's abilities, but who knew how many men and women could be waiting on the roofs of the surrounding buildings.

The wait to find out what was happening was going to kill her.

~~~

Kai tensed, waiting for the threat to appear.

What he hadn't told Jane was that the footsteps were still audible; someone kept shifting their feet against the roof tiles.

At least the female had listened to his orders and would hopefully remain safe. The possible threat had taught him a lesson, though. Females were distractions. If he hadn't been kissing Jane, Kai would've picked up the sounds straightaway.

He wouldn't be so reckless again.

A male jumped down in front of him and remained crouched low. From the height and build, there was no way the male was a dragon-shifter.

Kai flex his hands. Taking out one human wouldn't even wind him.

Kai watched the male, waiting for him to make the first move. Eventually, the human stood up and drew a knife.

Normally, Kai would extend a talon or two and easily finish off his opponent. But he couldn't risk exposing he was a dragon-shifter to the human before him, especially since he still needed to track the hunters and find a way to take them down.

As they stared at one another, a car pulled into the end of the alley. From the corner of his eye, Kai could see it wasn't Nikki.

Right, he needed to take this male down before he had a group attacking him. If that happened, he couldn't guarantee Jane's safety.

His dragon growled. *Take care of them. We must protect her.*

Kai faked a lunge and the knife-wielding male moved to the side. Drawing on his speed, Kai rushed the male, hitting him in the stomach before he could swing his knife.

The weapon clattered to the ground. Kai adjusted his grip and slammed the male's head against the wall. Tossing the unconscious human aside, Kai turned toward the car.

Five men stood in front of it.

The odds might actually be even now.

Drawing them further down the alley was his best chance at picking them off one or two at a time, so Kai moved a few feet backward.

Then the five bastards pulled out guns.

*Fuck.* It was time for a new plan.

Running, Kai jumped and gripped the edge of the gutter and pulled himself up onto the roof. Aware that he needed to draw the guns away from Jane, he ran in the direction of the men on the ground below. If he could just make it to the edge of the roof and jump off, the men should follow.

He half expected the men to shoot at him, but they didn't. If they didn't want to draw attention to themselves, then Kai was dealing with something much more than a random gang. He wondered if they were Carlisle hunters. They were the only dragon hunter group to possess such restraint.

Kai paused at the edge, waiting to see what the men would do. However, they moved further down the alley. Could it be they were after Jane?

His dragon roared. *We must protect her.*

Giving a sweep of his surroundings, he spotted Nikki running toward his location. But then the human named Jeff darted out from a hedge and grabbed her. Since Kai trusted Nikki to handle herself against one mere human, Kai ran back toward the alley. He'd deal with the male later.

Running as fast as he could, Kai quickly arrived at the location he'd use to make his attack. He jumped onto the ground in front of the five men. "What do you want?"

The tallest one spoke up. "Move out of the way, mate. This is your only warning."

Kai growled. "No."

Raising his gun, the same man replied, "We're going to take the reporter, one way or another."

Kai lunged low. A gun went off and hit the skip bin behind him.

After throwing the nearest human against the wall, he turned toward the leader. But the leader was already heading toward the skip.

# Reawakening the Dragon

Drawing on his dragon's strength, Kai ran for the male. He couldn't let him reach Jane.

Just as Kai landed a punch to the man's kidney, gun shots rang out behind him.

~~~

Jane clutched her can of pepper spray and waited. For whatever reason, a group of weapon-wielding men were after her.

She had no idea why anyone would want her. The Dragon Knights had harassed her the most over the last few months, but ever since the DDA helped to capture a large group of them on Lochguard the previous month, things had turned quiet. And since she'd yet to report anything on the hunters, she didn't think they would target her. After her story, yes. But not before.

As the sound of running feet and then a thud filled her ears, Jane pushed all other thoughts away. She only hoped Nikki came to help soon. Kai might be good, but from the quick peek she'd had a minute ago, he was vastly outnumbered.

Another thud sounded at the same time as gunshots rang out. The urge to check on Kai was strong, but Jane resisted. She couldn't afford to distract the dragonman from his task.

Then things fell silent except for the sound of footsteps coming toward her.

Her heart pounded. Maybe it was Kai.

A brown-haired man with a hard face appeared in front of her. Seizing on her split second advantage, Jane turned her head away as she sprayed her pepper spray into the man's face.

Once he screamed, "You bitch," Jane ran around him and saw one other man. It wasn't Kai.

Kai was unconscious on the ground next to some of the others. But he was also covered in blood.

*Shit.*

That was all she could think of before the man waved his gun at her. "Drop the pepper spray, love."

*What to do, what to do?* There was no way she could reach the man before he fired. She guessed he wanted her alive or she'd be dead already, but there was a lot a person could do without killing you.

A whoosh swept through the alley right before a purple dragon flew over them. Taking advantage of the distraction, Jane kicked the gun out of the man's hand and smacked his nose with the heel of her hand. She was about to kick him again when the dragon flew past again, but this time, the beast knocked the remaining attackers against the wall.

Everyone was on the ground unconscious, except for Jane.

Jane looked up. While she had never seen Nikki in dragon form, she had a feeling that was who the purple dragon was.

Hovering over them, the dragon motioned her front talons toward Kai's arm.

Jane forced her gaze away from the purple beast and rushed to Kai's side. She wasn't a doctor, but Jane knew she needed to stop the bleeding.

Ripping a section from her shirt, Jane tied the material tightly around Kai's injury. While not the most sanitary of methods, it was the best she could do.

The dragon gave a low growl above her. Looking up, Jane saw the dragon motion her to the side. While Jane wanted to stay with Kai, the dragon knew what was best for him.

The second Jane was out of the way, the purple beast gently lowered her form until she could maneuver her back talons around Kai's body. She lifted her talons and then the dragon looked at Jane and nodded.

# REAWAKENING THE DRAGON

Jane didn't speak dragon, but she assumed Nikki was saying everything would be all right.

What Jane didn't expect was the dragon to then wrap her other set of back talons around her middle. As the dragon beat her wings and carried them into the air, Jane's stomach flipped. Unstable heights weren't really her thing.

Yet glancing over at Kai's unconscious body, she swallowed and willed her stomach to behave. Kai had been hurt protecting her. She could survive a short dragon flight to help him.

Still, she avoided looking down as the dragon carried them away from Gateshead and toward the west. It looked like Jane was going back to Stonefire.

She only hoped they made it in time to save Kai.

~~~

Nikki beat her wings as if her life depended on it.

Well, truth be told, Kai's life depended on it, and given all that he'd done for her over the years, she would make bloody well sure he lived. All she needed to do was reach Stonefire, and Dr. Sid could patch him up.

Not caring that she'd feel sore the next day, Nikki beat her wings faster. There was still a good thirty minutes to Stonefire.

She could spend the journey fretting over something she couldn't control, such as Kai's life, or she could use the time to sort through the facts she'd learned from the human named Jeff. Once she'd had a grip on his bollocks, he'd told her anything she'd wanted; sometimes it was useful to have the ability to extend a talon or two.

Jeff had sold out Jane to the Dragon Knights. Nikki, like much of the dragon-shifter community, had taken their previous month of silence as a sign they were fading back into history.

89

While Jeff hadn't known anything about the inner workings of the Dragon Knights or what plans they had in store, the knights had put out a £5,000 reward for Jane Hartley. Jeff had found out about the bounty through his less-than-legal contacts and had merely wanted the money.

Nikki stole a glance at the human female. The news about the reward was going to complicate things, especially since Nikki didn't know how many people knew about it. If the bounty became public knowledge, every wannabe lowlife would be after Jane.

She only hoped Bram was ready for this headache.

Putting aside all of the problems they would encounter once they landed, Nikki studied Jane. She was pale, but conscious and looking intently at Kai. There wasn't any guilt, just concern. The human wasn't screaming or fainting as most did on their first dragon flights.

Jane was tough, which was exactly what Kai needed.

Nikki would just need to convince Bram to keep the human on their land. Knowing Kai as well as Nikki did, he would push the human away after what had happened in the alley. But Nikki knew Jane was Kai's best chance at even a smidgen of happiness; no female in her recent memory had stirred the head Protector so much. Sure, she knew the story of his true mate denying him, but Nikki had been young at the time, not even a teenager, and hadn't paid attention.

But she understood the pain of not having someone you truly wanted.

Her dragon spoke up. *You never bloody tried. We are a catch. He would've wanted us.*

*And then what? Female dragon-shifters aren't allowed to have human mates. You know that.*

# REAWAKENING THE DRAGON

*There are always ways. Humans and dragons have hidden their relationships for years.*

*Times are different now. There are cameras everywhere.*

Her dragon huffed. *You are the one who wouldn't act. Either go after the male again or find someone else. I'm starving for sex.*

*Kai could be dying. Have a little compassion.*

*He is stubborn and will most certainly live. I'm more concerned about us.*

Tired of her dragon, Nikki locked her into a mental prison and pushed aside all thoughts of the male who had caught both her and her dragon's eye a few years earlier. He wasn't worth her time.

Her dragon broke free and spoke up again. *Any male will do. The one awkward encounter last year wasn't enough. We are young and I want sex. Lots of sex.*

Nikki gritted her teeth. *Now is not the time. Your complaining isn't going to instantly change my mind.*

*It has in the past.*

*Yeah, well, I'm much stronger now.*

Her dragon chuckled and Nikki ignored her. She knew that a male's inner dragon thought about sex even more than a female one, but Nikki's beast was slowly making her crazy.

Sleeping with random males would take away time from proving herself to the clan as a dedicated Protector. Only then would the older members of the clan see her as more than a blessing because of her birth.

Double-checking that her dragon was locked up tight, Nikki surveyed her surroundings again to pinpoint their location. She spotted the peaks in the distance that marked Stonefire's territory. Good. She could feel Kai's heart still beating, but the sooner Dr. Sid fixed him up, the better.

Ten minutes later, she made the final approach. Delicately beating her wings, Nikki lowered herself to the landing area used for injured dragons, but hovered before touching the ground. She laid Kai down gently before doing the same with Jane. Moving to the side, she plopped down and imagined her wings shrinking into her back, her talons becoming fingernails, and her snout turning into a nose. The second she was human again, she raced to Kai's side.

Jane was already there, but Nikki ignored her to check on her leader. Thank fuck, he was still breathing.

Sid raced out of the building about twenty feet away, her ponytail swaying in time with her strides. Jane moved out of the way to allow Sid to take her place. As the doctor checked his pulse, she asked, "What happened?"

Nikki grimaced. "He was shot about forty minutes ago."

Sid glanced up with irritation in her brown eyes. "Why did you wait so long to bring him here?"

"We were in Tyneside. I came as soon as I could."

"Bloody hell," Sid whispered. She ripped off Kai's shirt and bandage before checking the gunshot wound in his arm. "Given the location, he should be okay as long as I get him into surgery and stop the bleeding." She motioned to two young dragon-shifters behind her with a stretcher. "Get him inside."

Nikki stepped back as the two dragon-shifters maneuvered Kai onto a stretcher. Sid added, "My job is to ensure Kai lives. You can take the reporter to Bram and sort out the rest."

Before Nikki could do more than nod, Sid was moving with her team back to her surgery. Once Kai was no longer in sight, Nikki met Jane's gaze. "We need to talk with Bram. Are you well enough to do that?"

Jane bobbed her head. "Yes, but will Kai be okay? It's my fault that he's hurt."

92

Nikki waved a hand. "There's more to this story than you know. Come, let's go to Bram's cottage and I'll explain it to you there." She watched as Jane looked back toward the surgery, so Nikki added, "Kai's a tough bastard. He'll make it through, if only to hunt down those who hurt him." Nikki smiled. "If you truly want to help him, then we need to talk with Bram."

"Why me?"

"You have information we need."

Without another word, Nikki turned and headed in the direction of Bram's cottage. Two seconds later, she heard Jane following.

# CHAPTER SEVEN

Rationally, Jane knew there was nothing she could do as long as Kai was in surgery, but she couldn't help but glance one last time at the building Kai had been carried into.

The doctor had seemed confident, which she took as a good sign. Despite the fact Jane had never interviewed Dr. Sid, the dragon doctor had a good reputation. Jane only hoped it was true.

Looking back to Nikki, who was ahead of her, Jane increased her pace, taking deep breaths to calm her heart. What Bram would want with her, Jane had no idea. But since it was Jane's fault Kai was hurt, she fully expected Bram to revoke her interview privileges with his clan. He might even banish her from stepping foot on Stonefire ever again.

A few days before, the news would've devastated her. Even though a small part of her would always wonder about Kai and the spark between them, in that moment, she could accept being banished because of her actions. It was no one's fault but her own.

Just like with the 'incident' she'd caused a decade before yet again someone had been hurt while she'd been pursuing a story. Even if she hadn't planned to use someone for her own personal gain, someone had still been hurt in the process, just like before. All she could do was try to find a way to make it right.

In other words, no matter what happened with Bram, Jane would find a way to gather information on the former Carlisle-based hunters and pass it on to Stonefire.

They approached the two-story cottage located in the middle of the main living area that belonged to Bram and Jane focused on the upcoming meeting.

Nikki knocked on the door, but it was Bram's heavily pregnant mate who opened it.

Evie Marshall eyed Nikki and then glanced to Jane and back. "You're supposed to be in Newcastle. What happened?"

Nikki answered, "We need to talk with Bram."

Evie stepped back and motioned them inside. "You can talk to the both of us."

Once they entered, Evie shut the door and guided them into the living area. She motioned toward the couch. "Sit down. I'll fetch Bram. He's upstairs putting Murray to bed for his afternoon nap."

Evie looked at Jane with curiosity again before ascending the stairs. While Jane had met Evie Marshall once or twice, Jane had never stepped foot inside Bram's cottage before. All of her meetings had been conducted inside the Protectors' central command building. No doubt, the former DDA employee was wondering why she was there.

Nikki plopped onto the couch and patted the spot next to her. "You may as well sit down. I'm surprised you're still standing after that flight."

Jane started pacing. "How are you so calm? Kai's in surgery because of a gunshot wound. He lost a lot of blood. He could die."

Nikki shrugged. "He was hit in the arm, but he's had far worse in the past. It comes with the job. His injury history is pretty impressive."

95

Nikki's attitude made her frown. "Even putting aside Kai's injury, there's the little fact those men were after me. Don't you think we should investigate why?"

"I already know why."

When the dragonwoman remained silent, Jane sighed. "Fine, I get it. We need to wait for Bram."

Bram's accent, a mixture of Northern English and Scottish, drifted into the room. "I'm here." He walked into the room with Evie at his side. The tall leader looked at the blood on Jane's shirt from when she'd knelt next to Kai earlier. "Now, tell me why Jane Hartley is standing in my living room and covered in blood."

Nikki replied, "I wouldn't say covered in blood. It's just a splash."

Bram growled. "Tell me what happened, Nikola Gray, or I'll assign you to the teenagers' watch duty for a month."

Jane had no idea what that entailed, but Nikki immediately stood up. "We had an incident while looking for the dragon hunters." Bram cocked an eyebrow and Nikki continued, "The Dragon Knights have a reward out for Jane. Someone reported her location and the knights had come to collect."

Jane interjected, "What? How did they know where I was?"

Nikki met her eye. "Jeff."

Shaking her head, Jane put up her hands. "That's impossible. He served with my brother. Rafe trusted him."

Bram's voice interrupted, "Aye, well, it looks like that trust is now gone."

Evie jumped in. "Stop dangling information piece by piece, Nikola. Just bloody tell us what you know."

Nikki glanced to Jane and back to Evie. "I wasn't sure how much I was allowed to share."

Bram crossed his arms and stared down at Jane with his ice blue eyes. "This is off the record, lass, are we clear?" Jane could do nothing but nod at the dominance in his voice. Bram looked to Nikki. "Tell us, and quickly. Starting with where's Kai."

Jane should keep her mouth shut, but she blurted out, "He's been shot."

"With a regular or electric blast gun?" Bram asked.

Nikki answered, "Regular one. But Sid has it under control and thinks he'll be fine."

Evie leaned against Bram. "Sid doesn't give platitudes, so it must be true."

Jane placed her hands on her hips. "Something could go wrong and Kai could still die. Why are you all so calm?"

Bram paused and then asked, "I think the bigger question is why are you so concerned?

Jane huffed. "He was protecting me, so of course I care. If you start accusing me of being only here for a story and not giving a damn about the good of the dragon-shifters, I swear I will kick you in the balls. A reporter can have ethics and real feelings, you know."

Amusement flashed in Bram's eyes, but then vanished. "I never said they couldn't, Ms. Hartley. I believe you have a heart. Reporting on my kind isn't easy and can lead to dangers such as what happened today. The fact you've stuck around tells me volumes about your character." Bram paused a second and added, "I also know about the moving flats and the death threats."

"How—"

Bram cut Jane off. "I may not be a reporter, but I have my sources." He looked to Nikki. "Fill us in on the rest, Nikki."

Nikki bobbed her head. "The knights have been wanting Jane for some time. Her reports helped drown out their social media campaigns, which curtailed a lot of their momentum."

Evie looked to Jane. "Were the knights the ones sending you the death threats?"

97

Jane shrugged. "For a while, but then things died down after the Lochguard attack. I figured they were no longer a threat."

Bram grunted. "Well, they are. Until all of this is sorted, you're staying here." Jane opened her mouth, but Bram cut her off, again. "I'm sure your boss will understand when you mention the danger. I can mostly control the outside threats while you're on my lands, barring a surprise attack. If you leave before things are taken care of, then you'll be on your own. And trust me, lass, not even your reports can help stave off the bloody Dragon Knights. You support us, therefore, you're the enemy, end of story."

"I know," Jane stated. "But why help me? Keeping me on Stonefire will only endanger your clan."

Bram smiled. "Stonefire has had enemies as long as we've been based here in the Lake District. It's nothing new."

She should let it drop, but Jane's curiosity never quit. "That still doesn't answer my question. Why?"

Bram shrugged one shoulder. "I have my reasons. Stick around long enough to earn my trust and you might learn what they are."

Judging by Bram's tone that was all the answer she was going to get.

That didn't mean she couldn't start earning Bram's trust. No doubt, Bram already knew Kai's reasons for being in Newcastle, but not hers. She needed to fix that.

Rather than think about why she wanted Bram's trust, Jane straightened her shoulders and added, "The only issue I have with remaining here is that Kai and I had a lead on the former Carlisle-based hunters. We were close to pinpointing their new base's location when we were attacked."

Bram shook his head. "As much as I want the bastards out of the way, I won't risk you or any other members of my clan. Since I saw Nikki flying in, I assume she was near Newcastle in dragon form. The DDA will probably soon be on my case, not to mention the hunters will be on high alert now. It's best to wait and pounce later, once things calm down."

Jane strummed her fingers on her thigh and her eyes went to Nikki. An idea hit her. "I agree, but I may have a solution of how we can still try to take the hunters down whilst remaining under the radar."

Bram raised his brows. "Oh, aye? How?"

Jane kept her gaze on Nikki. "Tell them your suggestion."

Nikki blinked. "I thought we talked about this. You were supposed to discuss it with Kai first."

Evie threw up her hands. "Kai isn't here, is he? Now, I don't bloody well care who tells me, but someone had better speak up because I really need to pee. And you don't want to upset a pregnant woman. Trust me. Bram's learned that lesson the hard way."

Bram's voice was dry. "Aye, you'd best do what she says, Nikki."

Nikki widened her stance and clasped her hands behind her back. "Well, I thought it might be a good idea to unofficially invite our trusted comrades from the British armed forces to help us hunt the dragon hunters. They're human, but skilled. They have ways of monitoring the knights whilst remaining under the radar. I don't think even Simon Bourne would see their help coming."

Jane jumped in. "I thought we could ask my brother to help, along with suggestions from your Protectors. They could gather intelligence on the hunters whilst your clan and I stay here.

Once they have the information we need, you and Lochguard could make a surprise attack."

Bram replied, "After your brother's recommendation of the human named Jeff, I'm a little leery of trusting him."

Jane raised her chin. "My brother is a decorated soldier who has always put friends and family first. We all screw up once in a while, and I'm sure there's a reason his judgment was wrong about Jeff. Talk to my brother yourself and then make a decision. That's what you keep asking humans to do, isn't it? To talk with a dragon-shifter before deeming them monsters."

Bram studied Jane and she willed herself not to fidget.

Stonefire's leader finally smiled. "Your backbone will come in handy. Never lose that core of steel."

Jane blinked. "Pardon?"

Bram waved a hand in dismissal. "I want to interview your brother, and only your brother, first. Then I can make my decision, as you suggested. Is it possible for him to come up here in the next few days?"

Jane nodded. "Probably tomorrow, as it's one of his usual days off. If I use some of my little sister tricks, he won't be able to say no."

The corner of Bram's mouth ticked up. "I have a feeling not many people say no to you."

Jane grinned. "I can be quite persuasive."

Laughing, Bram hugged his mate closer. "I'm sure you can be, but I think it's more because you're stubborn." He looked to Nikki. "Take her to the command center to ring her brother. After that, find Jane a place to settle in and report back to me." Bram looked to Jane. "You and I will chat some more later. For now, the adrenaline will wear off soon and you'll probably crash. Take a little time to rest and recover."

Jane crossed her arms over her chest. "I'll shower and change, but I want to see Kai as soon as he's out of surgery."

She didn't like the twinkle in Bram's eyes. "Aye, I bet you do. I'll tell Sid's people to put you on the visitors' list." He waved toward the door. "Now, go. Evie's trying not to dance at my side and my dragon isn't happy with her discomfort."

Nikki stepped next to Jane and put a hand on her back. "I'll report back as soon as I can."

Nikki pushed against Jane's back and they started walking just as Bram's voice rang out. "Well done today, Nikki. You probably saved Kai's life."

Jane looked over her shoulder and watched a faint blush rise on Nikki's cheeks. The dragonwoman murmured, "I was just doing my job," before pushing Jane quickly out the door.

As soon as they were about ten feet from Bram's cottage, Nikki stopped and growled before saying, "You were supposed to suggest the idea to Kai, not Bram."

Jane looked her dead in the eye. "If you want to move past who you are because of your birth, you need to start speaking up. How else are people supposed to know how brilliant you are?"

"I'm still young and inexperienced. Kai always helps me improve. I needed to talk with him about things first."

Jane placed a hand on her hip and pointed a finger. "Embrace your self-confidence. Do you really think Bram would endorse a plan that could easily go wrong?"

Nikki mumbled, "No."

"Right, then what are you worried about?"

Nikki's gaze turned fierce. "The hunter bastards killed one of my comrades and played mind games with me. I need to make sure any plan I have to help take them down is as flawless as can be. Kai's experience would've helped with that."

"We can still talk with him later, once he wakes up."

"And how long will that be? Each day we waste is a day the hunters could run."

"Exactly, which is why I suggested your idea in the first place."

Nikki's voice was dry as she replied, "Don't take this the wrong way, but you're not exactly a military strategist."

Jane waved a hand. "Of course not, but Rafe is. Until Kai wakes up—and believe me, I'm going to get him to wake up as soon as I can without endangering his health—you can hash out details with Rafe. He's good at the soldier strategy stuff."

"If Bram approves of him."

"Oh, I suspect he will. A decorated soldier who has worked with dragon-shifters in the past is quite the asset. You approve of him, after all."

Nikki sighed. "Fine, whatever. Let's get you to the command center so you can ring your brother and set things in motion." Nikki dropped her voice to a murmur and added, "And let's hope Kai wakes up soon so you can pester him instead."

"I heard that."

Nikki started walking. "It's true. You're like a chatty female version of Kai."

Jane jogged to catch up with Nikki. "I somehow doubt that. I have yet to see Kai's sense of humor."

"From what I've heard, he had one once."

"Then what happened?"

"Maggie Jones."

Jane frowned. "Who's that?"

Nikki turned to meet her eye. "That's something only he should tell you."

With that, Nikki upped her pace and Jane struggled to catch up. Maybe she could use her time on Stonefire to exercise a bit more.

As they walked in silence, Jane wondered how one woman could change Kai so dramatically. To imagine him with a sense of humor was quite a stretch.

Not that she could find out anything about Maggie Jones until Kai woke up. Until then, she needed to concentrate on convincing Rafe to come to Stonefire. Because of lifelong practice, Jane was fairly certain she could sway Rafe, as long as he wasn't grumpy.

Too bad her brother had been grumpier as of late.

Pushing the doubt aside, Jane walked with purpose. She had a job to do. Even if she had to call in every favor her brother owed her, she would get Rafe Hartley's arse to Stonefire as soon as possible. She needed to make things right with the clan who had been willing to work with her over the last few months, even if it ended up costing Jane her reputation. Living with Stonefire for any period of time would render her opinion biased.

Her heart ached at not proving herself as a journalist. Yet if she could help the Stonefire dragons and change opinions about them on her own terms, that might not be the worst thing. If she was fired from the BBC, Jane could still try things on her own.

To be honest, she rather liked the idea of being in charge of her own stories and what she shared with the public.

Ideas raced around her mind, but before she could work on fine-tuning any of them, she needed to convince Rafe to come to Stonefire.

Increasing her pace, Jane thought of everything she could use to blackmail her brother, if need be, to get him to the Lake District within the next twenty-four hours.

~~~

Kai was vaguely aware of something poking him in the arm, but he couldn't really form a thought about it. All he knew was that each touch sent a low pulse of pain through his body and it bloody hurt.

His beast's voice was sleepy as it said, *That's because we were shot.*

At the mention of being shot, Kai remembered the searing pain followed by a blow to the head. After that, he remembered nothing. *If you're talking to me, then I'm still alive.*

His beast paced inside his head. *Open your eyes and find out where we are. Then we can find out what happened to Jane.*

Jane. Had the humans taken her?

There was only one way to find out.

Kai had been shot before, but no amount of preparation steeled him enough for the light hitting his eyes or the thousand pinpricks of pain stabbing his brain. Unable to stop it, he groaned.

"You're awake."

*Jane.* Anxious to ensure the female was safe, Kai forced his eyes open. After blinking a few times, Jane's face came into focus. He murmured, "Where are we?"

His dragon growled. *Make sure she's okay.*

Ignoring his beast, Kai stared at Jane and she motioned around the room. "If you look around, you can tell you're in a hospital room. Are you really Stonefire's head Protector?"

Kai growled, but then moaned as the vibration sent a shot of pain through his shoulder and arm. Jane stood up and placed a hand on his forehead. "Are you okay? Dr. Sid said the wound wasn't serious, but if you're in pain, cut the alpha crap and tell me straight."

"Did anyone ever tell you that you're bossy?"

Removing her hand, Jane raised an eyebrow. "That's the pot calling the kettle black."

Too tired to argue with the bloody human, Kai returned to his original question. "A hospital could be anywhere. Just bloody tell me where I am."

"Stonefire. Nikki brought us here. Even though the wound wasn't serious, you lost a lot of blood. She saved your life, Kai. Make sure to thank her."

Taking a deep breath, Kai managed not to growl again. The less pain, the better. "You don't need to tell me, human. I can manage it by myself."

Jane answered, "You don't have to do everything by yourself. The sooner you get used to that idea, the better."

He frowned. "What are you talking about?"

"Bram made me promise not to tell you, so you'll have to ask him."

"I don't like secrets, Jane."

She shrugged. "Take it up with Bram. He should be along shortly. I already pushed the alert button. One of the nurses should be contacting him as we speak."

His dragon jumped in. *Make sure she is okay before Bram comes. She is clearly fine if she can argue.*

His beast grunted. *Ask her.*

To shut up his bloody beast, Kai studied Jane's face. But it was the same pale, yet healthy skin she always had. There were a few smudges under her eyes from lack of sleep, but he'd just have to make sure she slept after this.

He nearly blinked at that thought. Jane wasn't his concern, especially not if they were back on Stonefire. After all, the distracting female had gotten him shot in the first place. Not only that, he would have to wait who the hell knew how long before he could track down the hunters again.

For both his health and the sake of his clan, Kai would put distance between him and Jane Hartley as soon as possible.

His dragon roared. *Don't send her away. She is ours. We must convince her to stay.*

*No. What she does after today is not my concern.*

*Liar. You think having her near is a distraction, but wait until you push her away. I will think of her often, to the point you will beg her to return.*

*Shut it, dragon. If I survived you after Maggie, I can do the same with Jane.* Using what strength he had, Kai tossed his beast into a mental prison and added, *We'll recover faster if you remain calm. If you don't, then I'll mention it to Sid. I'm sure she has something to block you out for a while to allow me to heal.*

Even locked away, his beast paced. Good. With the threat of drugs, maybe his dragon would actually listen. They'd been drugged once before, in the army, and his dragon had been silent for days. As much as his bloody dragon irritated him, days without him were too long.

But he kept that thought tightly locked away. If his dragon ever found out, he'd never hear the end of it.

Jane's voice interrupted his thoughts. "Since your pupils are round again, are you quite finished with your dragon?"

"I'm not sure how I should answer that."

Jane crossed her arms over her chest. "I wanted to thank you for saving my life, but if it's too much of a nuisance, then I won't mention it."

Kai really missed grunting. "I wouldn't be a Protector if I let them take you while you were under my care."

"I didn't realize I was under your care."

106

"Of course you were." He paused a second and added, "And you still are until I can find a suitable replacement."

"Do I get any say in the matter?"

"No."

Jane rolled her eyes. "When you start threading dominance into your voice, it becomes harder to be nice to you." She winked at him. "And I was really trying."

"This is trying? Remind me not to piss you off."

Jane grinned. "Oh, believe me, you don't want to do that."

The sight of Jane's face when she smiled stole his breath away. He'd always found the human attractive, but her winks and grins were dangerous. They made him want to kiss her again.

And he definitely couldn't do that. He was home. He didn't have time for a female. Not even one with eyes the color of a deep blue lake in summer.

*Bloody hell.* He'd never had such a poetic thought in his life.

Even in his cage, Kai sensed his dragon's laughter.

Clearing his throat, Kai finally answered, "They didn't hurt you, did they?"

"No. Although I'm not sure I want to fly gripped in a dragon's talons ever again."

"Nikki."

She nodded. "Yes. I only hope the DDA doesn't punish her for shifting inside a city."

Kai started to shrug, but then grimaced as his bicep and shoulder throbbed at the movement. After a few deep breaths, he found his voice again. "Leave it to Evie. She'll sort it out somehow." Kai moved his legs and tested out the pain. Luckily, moving his lower body didn't hurt as long as he was careful. He hated sitting still. "What happened to the men in the alley?"

"We left them behind. But while I've been here waiting for you to wake up, Bram might've done something else to find them. You'll have to ask him when he arrives."

"I don't like the fact that the threat to your life is still out there."

Jane studied him a second and Kai resisted moving his legs again. Given enough time, the human could wrestle out all of his secrets.

He wasn't sure if that was supposed to be a good or bad thing.

Jane opened her mouth, no doubt with another bloody question, when Sid entered the room carrying a clipboard. The dragonwoman's face was stern as she assessed him with her brown eyes. "You look well. How do you feel?" He tried to answer, but Sid cut him off. "Give me the truth, Kai Sutherland. I'm not about to dance around to get it, either. I have ways of making you talk. You bloody well know that."

Sid had once withheld his pain medication for five hours until he'd told her the truth. Kai could handle pain if need be, but those had been some of the longest hours of his life. "My arm is sore and if I move it, it bloody hurts. But with a sling and some pain medication, I can probably go home."

Tossing her clipboard onto the side table, Sid moved to Kai's injured shoulder. "Let me be the judge of that."

As Sid poked and prodded his shoulder, arm, and chest, Kai set his jaw and kept his face stoic. He wasn't about to show weakness in front of Jane.

Though why the hell that mattered, he had no idea.

# Reawakening the Dragon

~~~

Jane watched Dr. Sid exam Kai. Despite the fact the doctor was doing her job, Jane didn't like the other woman touching Kai's bare skin.

Tapping her fingers, Jane studied Kai's expression, the one she was coming to call "badass Protector face." She wondered what the true Kai Sutherland was like beneath the mask. More importantly, she wondered if there was still humor buried deep inside of him.

Thanks to Bram, she might actually have a chance to find out the answers to her questions, as well as satisfy her curiosity about the mysterious Maggie Jones.

But Jane was getting ahead of herself. She continued tapping her fingers until Sid stepped back and nodded. "Provided you follow my instructions to the letter, you can probably go home in the next hour or so." Sid looked to her. "I was told you are going to look after him."

"What?" Kai demanded.

Ignoring him, Jane nodded. "Bram said it was part of my duties whilst I stayed here."

Sid eyed her for a second before reaching into the pocket of her white coat and taking out a folded piece of paper. Offering it to her, Jane took it as the doctor said, "Dragon-shifters are a little different than humans. Since we heal faster, the first twenty-four hours are the most important when it comes to treating infection or other complications. If we don't catch them early, it could have a devastating effect on a dragon-shifter's ability to shift properly." Nodding toward the paper, Sid added, "Keep an eye out for everything on that list. I wrote my own personal mobile number at the bottom. Call me if you spot anything."

Kai chimed in, "Do I get a say in this at all, Sid? I'm more than capable of looking after myself. I've done it before."

Sid moved her brown-eyed gaze back to Kai. "Yes, but never when the dragon hunters were within your grasp. If you want out of this surgery, then you'll allow Jane to look after you. Otherwise, I'll have Ginny do it."

At Kai's sigh, Jane had a feeling this Ginny wasn't someone you wanted looking after you.

Kai finally answered, "Fine. Anyone is better than Ginny."

"Gee, thanks," Jane murmured.

Sid looked at her and the corner of her mouth ticked up. "Don't take it personally. All dragon-shifter males turn into big babies when they're injured. Ginny is one of the few who won't turn sympathetic and disregard my orders. She handles all of my most alpha patients."

Jane waved the folded piece of paper. "I'll make sure to follow the instructions. Even if Kai bats his eyelashes and gives me puppy dog eyes, I won't deviate."

Sid stuck her hands inside the pockets of her lab coat. "Good. If you do that and need another task whilst you're on Stonefire, you can help me here in the surgery. I need all the alpha females I can get."

Kai muttered, "More alpha females in the surgery are the last thing we need."

Sid looked down her nose at Kai, and Jane wanted to fidget from the doctor's intense look. "Say that again, Kai. Ginny is on duty and can care for you straight away."

Jane blinked as Kai sulked, actually sulked, but before Jane could reply, there was a knock on the door.

Bram walked inside the room and moved to the foot of Kai's bed. "You're alive, I see." Bram looked to Sid. "How long will he be out of commission?"

Sid answered, "If he follows my instructions, he should be able to shift again in five or six days. If he doesn't, then I have no bloody idea how long he'll be out."

The corner of Bram's mouth ticked up as he glanced to Jane. "With Jane looking after him, it should be fine. You won't let him boss you around, will you, lass?"

Jane noticed the change of Stonefire's leader calling her 'Ms. Hartley' to 'Jane,' but she tried not to read too much into it. "He hasn't been able to do it so far."

Kai jumped in. "I may not be able to shift, but I can still work intelligence and give orders. The Carlisle bastards are within our reach, Bram. We shouldn't pass up this chance."

"Aye, I know. But you'll hear the rest tomorrow, provided you've rested and done as Sid instructed, and don't kill Jane in the process."

Kai frowned. "A day is a long time when your enemy might know you're on to them."

Bram crossed his arms over his chest. "I have plans in motion. I'll know the full details tomorrow. Until then, rest, Kai. We need you in full health as soon as possible. Even if the hunters and the people of Newcastle saw a dragon today, there's still time to take them down. After all, it takes a while to move a group as large as the Carlisle hunters, especially with all the kit they have."

When Kai gave a slight nod, Jane bit her lip to keep from smiling. Her dragonman really didn't like being out of commission. She almost pitied any nurse who had cared for him after a more serious injury.

Once Rafe arrived, Kai might return to his own growly self. She had a feeling her dragonman didn't act this way in front of strangers.

She blinked and tried not to read too much into it. She and Kai may have technically known each other for months, but she'd only had a real conversation with him the day before. By definition, she should be deemed a stranger.

Pushing the thought aside, Jane turned to Bram. "Is there anything else you want to tell him? Otherwise, I'd like Sid and her staff to prep him for discharge. It's been a long day and I'm sure Kai needs his rest."

Amusement danced in Bram's eyes. "Playing the role already, I see. I may soon lose a bet to Evie."

"A bet?" Jane echoed.

Bram waved a hand. "Forget I mentioned it." He turned toward Kai. "I know you hate being kept in the dark, but there are a lot of uncertainties at the moment and you don't need the stress. Concentrate on healing properly. I need my head Protector at my side as soon as possible."

"I'll be well in two days, if I can manage it."

Sid rolled her eyes. "I'll be the judge of that." She made a shooing motion with her hands. "Everyone leave so I can have my people bring in the necessary medication and supplies. The sooner Kai is out of my hair and in Jane's hands, the better."

For some reason, it seemed like everyone was in on a secret that Jane had no idea about.

Given she was still the outsider, she decided to wait for the right time to ask for an explanation.

Bram motioned toward the door and Jane followed. She half expected Bram to interrogate her about her brother, but all he did was smile and say, "Take care of Kai. I'm not sure what the clan would do without him."

"Of course." Bram's smile gave her the encouragement she needed to ask, "What's the bet you keep talking about?"

112

Bram grinned. "I'm sure you'll figure it out by yourself soon enough."

With a wave, Bram left.

Jane stood in the empty hall and released a long breath. Dealing with dragon-shifters was exhausting. She wasn't sure how the other human women managed it twenty-four-seven.

Depending on how long it took to take care of the Dragon Knights and ensure her safety, Jane might seek out their advice sooner rather than later.

To distract her from thinking about her future, Jane opened Sid's list of instructions and went to work memorizing them. Knowing Kai as she did, he might try to swipe the instructions, burn them, and then dictate his own. Jane wanted to be prepared.

# Chapter Eight

While Kai had talked his way out of being pushed out of the surgery in a wheelchair, he'd been forced to wear the sling. The strap itched against his skin, but as he moved to scratch it, Ginny cleared her throat. "Stop it. You're the one who wanted to go bare-chested."

"Can I go now?"

The brown-and-grey haired nurse scrutinized him for three long seconds before moving to the door. "Let's find Jane."

His dragon was free inside his mind and spoke up. *Good. It will be nice to have Jane take care of us.*

*Don't get any ideas, dragon. I'm only doing this so I can leave the bloody surgery.*

He followed Ginny into the hallway and spotted Jane sitting on a bench with her eyes closed. The strange part was the human was moving her lips without making any sound.

At their approach, her eyes opened and she stood. "Is he ready to go?"

"The 'he' in question is standing right here."

Jane raised her brows. "You're not the one who has to sign off on you leaving."

Ginny patted Jane on the shoulder. "You'll do, Ms. Hartley. Kai is a sneaky one. I should know since I've been taking care of his scrapes and bruises since he was a boy."

Kai was about to grunt, but remembered it irritated his arm. "I'm supposed to go home and rest. You'll have to save your embarrassing stories for later."

Ginny stared at him with her dark brown eyes and Kai tried not to fidget like he'd done as a teenager. "I never said they would be embarrassing, but now that you mention it, I do have plenty of those." She winked at Jane. "I can share them later."

Kai gritted his teeth. "I've done what you asked, Ginny. Just let me go."

Ginny signed the clipboard in her hand with a flourish. "Go, you troublemaker, and try not to scare Jane away. I like her."

"You only just met her." Ginny gave her trademark stare, filled with disapproval and exasperation, and Kai did grunt. The pain was worth it. He looked to Jane. "Let's go, Jane. You look tired and I don't like it."

Jane's eyes moved to his bare torso and Kai's dragon took notice. *It's too bad we're injured. Now we can't fuck our human for a few days.*

*I'm surprised you actually acknowledge that.*

His beast growled. *If we aren't careful, we might never shift into a dragon again. If that happens, we both might go insane.*

It was true. If a dragon-shifter lost the ability to shift forever, sometimes the dragonman or woman would lose their mind. Others, like Sid, had learned to adapt through sheer stubbornness.

Cassidy "Sid" Jackson may not be a Protector or clan leader, but she was one of the strongest dragon-shifters he knew.

Jane's voice interrupted his thoughts. "Your compliance worries me, but I'm going to take advantage of it. If you're sure you won't freeze to death in the cool October air, then let's go."

"I've been naked in freezing temperatures. I think I can survive a ten-minute walk."

"Fine, then lead the way."

"I never expected to hear you say that."

Jane rolled her eyes. "I've never been to your place, or I would take the lead."

He nearly smiled. "That sounds more like you."

When all Jane did was glare at him, the corner of Kai's mouth ticked up. For some reason, irritating Jane was fun.

His dragon chuckled. *Yes, and we have a few days to enjoy it. By the end of it, you won't want to push her away.*

His beast's words were like cold water tossed over his head. *Thanks for reminding me I need to keep my distance.*

As his dragon growled, Kai walked out the front of the surgery without a backward glance.

~~~

If Kai wasn't injured, Jane would've punched the bloody dragonman.

His half-smile had stunned her for a second, but then he'd gone back to his arsehole self, ruining the moment. It didn't help that she could do nothing but follow his lead.

Another item to add to her list was to learn Stonefire's layout. Then she wouldn't be so dependent on everyone else to get around.

She tossed on her cardigan as she tried to catch up to Kai's back. Maybe dragon-shifters gave off extra body heat. That was the only way Kai wasn't freezing to death. Autumn in Northern England was rainy, cold, and often windy.

As the breeze blew, Jane fisted her fingers and tried not to shiver in the light cardigan she'd borrowed. Picking up her pace, she hoped the exercise would keep her warm. Sure, she'd rather lean against Kai's side and absorb his heat, but she wasn't about to ask him to do that.

Kissing her whilst away from his clan was one thing, but kissing Kai or leaning against his bare chest in full-sight of anyone on Stonefire was quite another.

Not that she was going to think about their shared kiss. That would distract her from what was more important for both the clan and her future career.

For one, Jane needed to prove herself to Bram. Especially since she had ideas she wanted to propose to the clan leader once the dragon hunters were taken care of.

To distract herself, Jane ran through story ideas and in less than ten minutes, they reached a two-story cottage. It was similar to the rest in that it was made of stone and looked to be a few hundred years old, but there was one major difference—the cottage had bars over the windows and an extra-solid-looking door. Before she could stop herself, Jane asked, "Just how many enemies do you have? No one else has bars on their windows."

As Kai unlocked the front door, he glanced down at her. "The bars were installed a little over ten years ago to keep me inside."

She frowned. "What the bloody hell are you talking about?"

She half-expected for him to grunt and remain silent, but he murmured, "Not out here."

Kai disappeared into his cottage and Jane followed. Shutting the door behind her, Jane turned toward Kai. "Well?"

"There's not much to tell. I was having a difficult time controlling my dragon. I've since moved past it."

"Then why keep the bars on?"

"Just in case."

Jane sighed. "It's as if you give me just enough to answer the question and pique my curiosity, but no more. If you don't give me more information, I'm going to keep coming up with theories until it drives me crazy."

Kai studied her a second before his pupils flashed to slits. A few seconds later, they were round again. She opened her mouth to ask about his dragon, but Kai beat her to it. "I'll explain a bit more provided you promise not to ask any more questions."

"Are we back to you dictating orders again? If you remember, I'm the one in charge of you."

"Only Bram is in charge of me."

"Well, he put me in charge of you, so you need to listen to me."

Kai looked unimpressed. "You can try."

Jane growled in frustration. "What happened to you? Right before the men in the alley and you being shot, you were telling me you wanted me. I thought we'd made some progress."

Kai clenched his jaw and then said, "I wasn't thinking properly. I would've kissed any attractive female who threw herself at me."

His words were like a slap in the face. "You're a real charmer, you know that."

"I never said I was charming. I never should've kissed you, let alone propose anything more. We should both forget about it."

Jane kept her mouth shut. She wanted answers from the dragonman, but she could bide her time. After all, Kai was stuck with her for the next few days, at least.

If Kai was going to be brusque and dismissive, then she'd just have to steer the situation back toward her favor.

Jane turned and walked into the living room and then the kitchen. As expected, Kai followed her and demanded, "This is my bloody house. If you want a tour, you should ask first."

"Oh, and if I had asked, you would've given one with a smile? I'm too tired to argue. I figured it was easier to show myself around."

His eyes flashed again and then Kai placed the hand of his good arm on her lower back. Despite his recent arseholery, heat flared at his touch.

Damn the dragonman.

Kai pressed gently on her back. "You need to sleep. I'll show you around afterwards."

She looked up at him. The concern in his eyes confused her. "Why do you care if I sleep? I would expect you want me to fall asleep on the job so you can slip away."

Kai frowned. "It's not me, but my dragon. He doesn't like you looking tired."

"What is that supposed to mean?"

He applied more pressure to her lower back. "I thought you were a journalist. You should know how our dragons work."

"Yes, because you lot are so chatty about your inner dragons."

The corner of Kai's mouth ticked up. "Believe me, not hearing my dragon's voice is for the best."

"I somehow doubt that."

Kai leaned closer to her. "If it takes telling you a bit about my dragon to get you to go to sleep, then I'll do it. But only after you've taken a nap."

She searched his eyes for any sort of deceit, but there was none. "Is there some sort of dragon-shifter vow you can make so I know you'll keep your word?"

Kai's voice was low when he replied, "I promise to talk a little about my dragon." He leaned another inch closer. "And when I promise, I always see it through."

There was truth in his tone, but she needed something else from him. "I will take a nap if you also promise to stay put. I don't want to worry about you sneaking off. Bram gave me a job and I plan to do it properly."

"I promise I won't sneak off whilst you're asleep."

She scrutinized his face. "You just don't want to face Ginny."

Kai grinned and she sucked in a breath. His smile lit up his whole face. "You've got me there."

She battled a smile and lost. "Thanks for that. I now have something I can use to keep you in line."

Kai opened his mouth and promptly shut it. She wondered what he had wanted to say.

Still, as much fun as it was to tease Kai Sutherland, it was getting difficult to stand and concentrate. The sooner she rested, the better.

Jane nodded toward the kitchen door. "Take me to my room." Looking back to his face, she added, "And wake me up in two hours. I need to check your dressing and inspect your wound for infection."

Pressing against her back, Kai guided her out of the kitchen. "I can do better than promises. There's an alarm clock in the spare bedroom."

Jane studied Kai. "You're going to take a nap, too, aren't you?"

"I'm not daft. The more I sleep, the quicker I'll heal."

"Then just be prepared for when I wake you up to check your wound. Even if I have to dump a pitcher of ice water over you, I'll do it."

"Duly noted. Now, follow me."

Kai ascended the stairs and it took everything she had to make her legs climb them. For once in her life, she was tempted to ask a man to carry her.

Somehow she resisted and reached the top landing. Kai turned right and stopped at the second door. Turning the knob, he motioned inside.

Jane walked past him and entered a sparsely furnished room. There was a bed, a nightstand, a clock, and a closet. The paint was white and the walls lacked any decorations. She would hazard a guess that Kai didn't have many visitors or overnight guests.

She turned back around to face him. Pointing a finger, she narrowed her eyes. "No escaping whilst I'm asleep."

He placed a hand over his heart. "I wouldn't dream of it."

At the sight of Kai trying to placate her, Jane smiled. "I like how much more relaxed you are inside your own cottage."

Kai's face shuttered and he pointed to the bed. "Just go to sleep."

So much for drawing out Kai's sense of humor. She liked to believe it was inside him somewhere.

With a sigh, Jane motioned for him to leave. "I'll see you in a bit."

Surprisingly, Kai nodded, turned, and closed the door behind him. The fact he hadn't issued an order or a demand told her he was tired too, even if he was trying not to show it.

As she fiddled with the alarm clock, Jane pushed aside thoughts of why Kai would be almost teasing in one instant and cold the next. It was almost as if the dragonman didn't like to express extreme emotions.

There had to be a reason for it.

Yet her mind was fuzzy and Jane knew thinking about the possibilities for Kai's behavior would have to wait.

With the alarm set, Jane crashed onto the bed. About five seconds after her head hit the pillow, she was asleep.

~~~

Kai lay on his bed, staring at the ceiling, and willed his mind to calm down enough so he could fall asleep.

Yet after nearly two hours, he was still wide awake. His dragon chimed in. *That's because you're counting down the minutes until Jane's soft hands touch our skin.*

*No. After she changes my dressing, it means I get more pills to help with the pain and to counter infection.*

*Right. You keep telling yourself that.*

The constant throbbing in his arm almost made him admit the truth. While it might be the best thing for his clan and career to push Jane away and forget about her, both man and beast were having a difficult time doing so.

Her asking about the bars on the windows reminded him of the last time he'd tried to stay away from a female.

His dragon huffed. *That was different. This one wants us.*

*You seem pretty sure about it.*

*You saw how upset she was when you started acting like an arse again. You should tell her the truth about the bars. It's time to break with the past.*

*Well, someone's quite the psychologist today.*

His beast growled. *I am only trying to help.*

*Right, only so our chances of fucking Jane become reality.*

*Fuck you.* Snarling, his dragon retreated to the back of his mind without another word. Only through years of practice did Kai know not to call his dragon's actions a tantrum.

# REAWAKENING THE DRAGON

Glancing to the clock, Kai noted Jane should be up in a few minutes. Since falling asleep would be a waste of time, he decided to get up and do something he'd secretly longed to do for years—watch a pretty female wake up in his cottage.

At one time, all Kai had wanted was to wake up next to his true mate and maybe a child, but Maggie's choice had changed all of that. He'd long ago accepted he'd be alone for the rest of his life; few female dragon-shifters wanted a male who'd found his true mate but couldn't have her. If the male wasn't strong enough, he might leave if a true mate showed up wanting him.

Yet even if he'd accepted his future, watching Jane's sleeping face wake up might be the only chance he had to glimpse what his life could've been.

Standing up, Kai moved silently out of his room and down the hall. He wanted to make a memory he could draw on for the rest of his life.

Once he reached Jane's door, he turned the doorknob bit by bit until it clicked. He pushed it open.

When the door was wide enough, he locked his gaze onto Jane's sleeping form.

His human slept on her side with her mouth slightly open. Her expression was calm and relaxed, as if she didn't have a care in the world. While he much preferred her fire and sass, Jane's gentle expression reminded him of the fact that she was a vulnerable human.

Back in the alley in Newcastle, he'd been terrified something would happen to her. When the human enemy had made a go for the skip, terror had gripped Kai's heart. One stray bullet could take Jane's life away forever; she'd never tease him or call him out on his shit.

And she'd never be able to tell the stories she wanted to tell.

Although why that mattered to him, he didn't know. He'd kissed her twice. It wasn't as if he owed her a bloody thing.

His beast returned to the forefront of his mind and growled. *You know why it matters. Stop being so bloody stubborn.*

*I can't let down the clan.*

*Stop using that excuse. Even Bram senses something between us and the human. If he disapproved, he never would've put Jane in charge of us.*

His dragon had a point. If Bram wanted Jane gone, she wouldn't be sleeping inside Kai's cottage. *Allowing her to stay so we can protect her is one thing. Us fucking her, or more, is another.*

*Bram only wants you to be happy. Don't be afraid to seize it.*

Kai gave a bitter laugh inside his head. *I don't have the best track record with females.*

*Stop whining. You go after everything else you want, why not this?*

He stared at Jane's pink lips and then her dark eyelashes against her skin. She was beautiful, it was true, but he wanted her for much more than her beauty.

His dragon's tone was smug when he said, *You just admitted to wanting her.*

Jane snuggled into her pillow and Kai's heart warmed at the sight. A part of him wanted to keep her here so he could protect her always. The Dragon Knights were unpredictable. If Jane left Stonefire, she'd be looking over her shoulder for as long as the knights existed.

His dragon spoke up again. *Stop being a wishy-washy arsehole and she might stay.*

*And give up her career? I doubt it.*

*She is clever. I bet she will find a compromise. She is our second chance. Don't push her away. At least try to win her over.*

Kai paused for a moment and then replied, *She might say no.*

*We won't know until we try*, his dragon stated.

# REAWAKENING THE DRAGON

Kai wasn't sure if it was the constant throbbing pain in his arm, the drugs, or the weakness of the moment, but he was tired of fighting his beast.

Maybe he should try with Jane and see what happened. After all, the worst she could do was run away. If that were the case, he could go back to focusing solely on his work.

Roaring in excitement, his beast replied, *I won't let you forget what you just thought.*

As Kai tried to think of what to say to his dragon, the alarm clock beeped on the far side of the room. Jane rolled over with a groan and flicked it off.

In that moment, Kai wanted to drop kick the clock out the front door for waking up his human. She needed her rest.

Ignoring his dragon's chuckle, Kai stated, "I'm awake, so you don't need to dump water on me."

Jane slowly turned over and rubbed her eyes. "Why are you standing in the doorway? Watching someone sleep when they're a guest in your house is a bit creepy."

He really wished he could shrug. "I saw it more as me watching over you to keep you safe."

Jane blinked and then narrowed her eyes. "If you're trying to butter me up to avoid me checking on your wound, it's not going to work."

Kai decided honesty was the best policy. "You were right before, about me changing into an arsehole. I wanted to kiss you in the alley and I still do. I'll never have the chance if something happens to you."

Jane sat up and rubbed her eyes with her arms. "Am I still dreaming?"

The corner of his mouth ticked up. "No."

"What happened in the two hours whilst I was asleep then?"

"My dragon."

"Again with the minimum. Do you ever elaborate? You know, just for fun?"

Kai did smile then. "Maybe."

Shaking her head, Jane moved until she was sitting cross-legged on the bed. "Let's go back to the bit about you still wanting to kiss me. Say you're telling the truth, how do I know you won't go back into 'arsehole mode' five minutes later? I understand you're used to giving orders, but I will only put up with so much crap from you."

His dragon hummed. *She is fantastic.*

Kai took a step toward the bed. "Give me time, and I will show you."

Crossing her arms over her chest, Jane shook her head. "I need more."

He took another step. "I'm afraid to ask, but what would convince you that I'm serious?"

Jane studied him a second. "I want you to answer something honestly and completely without changing the subject."

"Always the reporter."

She sat up a little taller. "Of course. Now, stop stalling. Will you do it?"

Giving Jane free rein to ask him anything was dangerous. His dragon chimed in. *It might be our only chance. Giving Jane information is akin to giving flowers to another female.*

His dragon had a point. "Right, so what do you wish to know?"

Jane searched his eyes. "Tell me who Maggie Jones is and what the hell she did to you?"

# CHAPTER NINE

Jane's heart thudded inside her chest as she held her breath and waited for Kai to answer her question about Maggie Jones. Until he did, she wasn't going to get her hopes up. Hearing the dragonman wanted to kiss her had sent a little thrill through her body, but she wasn't about to live a life of him being nice one minute and an arsehole the next. As hard as it would be to walk away, she would do it if Kai didn't pass this test.

Kai remained silent as his pupils flashed to slits and back again. She really wished she could hear what Kai's dragon was saying to him.

After a full minute had passed, Kai's low voice filled the room. "Maggie Jones was my true mate."

Jane let out the breath she'd been holding. "Was, as in past tense?"

His jaw clenched a second before he replied, "She's still alive. However, she chose another."

"Wait, how is that possible? I thought once a dragon-shifter found their true mate, they went into a frenzy?"

Kai moved to the edge of her bed and sat down. The action reminded her that her dragonman had been shot only a few hours ago and wasn't at full-strength.

Still, if Kai was in pain or tired, she couldn't tell. He really was a master of self-control in all areas.

Well, except when it came to her.

Kai's deep voice filled the room again. "While a male dragon-shifter will often know their true mate when they see him or her, it's usually their first kiss that brings on the frenzy." Kai's piercing blue gaze never moved from hers. "Maggie never let me kiss her."

Jane fisted the sheets on the bed. "So what did she do, then? Tease you and string you along? Is that why you needed the bars on the windows? So you wouldn't go after her?"

"How do you know I wasn't the one to run away?"

She raised her eyebrows. "That goes against everything I know about you."

"This all happened eleven years ago, when I was twenty-one. Young dragon-shifter males spend their early twenties battling their dragon's need for sex. In a small way, Maggie was right to be cautious."

"Even with hormones raging through your body, I can't see you forcing anyone. Stop stalling and tell me the rest of your story."

Kai stared at her, but Jane didn't look away. He stated, "I will if you stay quiet." Jane motioned with her hands and Kai continued, "The bars came later, so let's back up a bit." Kai turned a little more toward her. "I met Maggie when I visited my mother, who lives with the Welsh dragon clan, Snowridge."

Jane frowned, but her expression must've conveyed her question because Kai answered, "I was raised on Stonefire, but my mother moved there after my father's death, after meeting her second—and true—mate and later had my half-sister. Since I was sixteen when she met her new mate, I decided to stay here with my uncle. However, I would visit her every once in a while."

When Kai paused, Jane tucked away the information about Kai's mother for later and waited patiently. In her experience, when you interrupted a story at an emotional point, you sometimes broke the spell and a person wouldn't divulge their whole story.

Her silence paid off as Kai spoke again. "A few years after my sister was born, I was visiting and spotted Maggie for the first time. With her short black hair and brown eyes, my dragon knew instantly that she was meant for us.

"I was still learning to control my dragon. At the time, my beast often swayed me to his decisions. So when he demanded we pursue her, I didn't fight him.

"I was twenty-one then, but Maggie was a few years younger than me and inexperienced with males. While dragon-shifters are a lot less prudish about sex than humans, there is still an awkward period like with adolescent humans." Kai looked away and stared out the window. "I decided to be honest with her and told her she was my true mate. At first, she ran and avoided me. But after a few days, she started to seek me out. We would take long walks and go for flights over the mountains. It soon became a game for me and my dragon to try to make her laugh.

"I thought I was lucky at finding my true mate so early." He looked back at Jane. "If we find our true mate at all, it's usually a bit later."

Jane reached out to touch Kai's uninjured shoulder, but then pulled back, lest she break the spell. "Then what happened?"

He gave a bittersweet smile. "I'd only gone to visit my mother on Clan Snowridge because I was about to join the British Army for two years. I had always wanted to be a Protector, like my uncle. But I needed the military training and experience before I could even apply.

"I had thought about giving it up for Maggie, but she encouraged me to go. She needed time to digest what the mate-claim frenzy would be like and the two years would give us both time to grow up a little more. While I didn't want to leave her, I figured having her two years later was better than never having her at all.

"So, I went. The army suited me. I always had a place to be, a schedule, and a task. I excelled at all of my training and eventually learned to control my dragon so I could fight in the harshest environments, such as combat zones. While it was hard to be away from Maggie, I knew I had made the right choice. At least, I thought so until I finished my service and returned to Clan Snowridge to visit her, my mother, and my baby sister."

Kai paused and Jane waited with bated breath. She had a feeling that whatever happened next had changed him from the young dragonman who had liked long walks and making a young woman laugh to the stoic workaholic sitting next to her.

With a sigh, Kai's voice filled the room again. "The instant I landed, my mother was there to greet me with a look that told me something was wrong. When I finally wheedled the information out of my mum, I found out that Maggie had recently mated one of the clan's accountants, a shy male who worshiped the ground she walked on. To say I was upset would be putting it mildly."

Jane frowned. Something was missing from his story. "Wait a second. If you kept in touch with Maggie, how did you not know something was wrong?"

Kai shrugged his good shoulder and grimaced. "I later found out she was afraid I'd come racing back, force a kiss, and then she'd be under the spell of the mate-claim frenzy. Instead, she thought pretending everything was fine was a better idea. Especially since if I had challenged her mate or had attempted to kill him to claim Maggie, it could've started a war between Stonefire and Snowridge. And she knew I wouldn't want that, or I'd never see my mum or sister again."

"Rubbish. I can't imagine you ever forcing a female, not even in your youth."

Kai shook his head. "I never would. But some mate-claim frenzies go wrong and Maggie's cousin had suffered one. Instead of talking about her fears, Maggie ran away from them.

"To be honest, I did the same with my anger. I came back to Stonefire and ranted at the previous clan leader, Victor Holmes. While Victor was different than Bram, he had been a good leader. He gave me two options—stay on Stonefire and get a grip on my dragon, or leave the clan until I could do so."

"Judging by the bars, I'm guessing you stayed."

"Yes." Kai met her eyes and she wished she could read his expression. "Although I sometimes think it would've been easier if I had left."

~~~

As soon as Kai started talking about his past and problems with Maggie, he hadn't been able to stop.

Not even Bram had been able to get so much out of him. The old clan leader before Bram had known, of course, but Kai had wanted a fresh start with Bram. While Bram had known the basics and had seen him a few times during the worst three weeks of Kai's life, Stonefire's current leader had never really pushed on the subject. He sometimes wondered why Bram trusted him; there was always a small chance Kai could regress and go after Maggie if he saw her again.

Pushing thoughts of Bram aside, Kai studied Jane's face. Telling even a small part of his past to Jane made him feel lighter. Especially since his human was looking at him with curiosity instead of pity.

His dragon spoke up. *Jane just wants the story. Yet another reason she is perfect for us.*

*You're really cheering for her now, aren't you, mate?*

*Of course. I will never see her naked if I don't. You're too stubborn and never go after what you want.*

Jane's voice cut into his thoughts. "You can't just stop there. Something must've happened between then and now or you never would've admitted to wanting to kiss me."

His eyes darted to Jane's mouth and he lingered on her full bottom lip. Despite the pain and his exhaustion, he burned to kiss her again.

Jane cleared her throat and he met her blue gaze. He couldn't help but smile at the faint blush on her cheeks.

"Finish the story so I can check on your wound," Jane ordered.

The image of Jane's hands on his skin made Kai shift his position. His dragon chimed in. *I want to feel her soft fingers. Hurry up.*

Too tired to argue with his beast, Kai raised an eyebrow on Jane. "Yes, ma'am."

Her smile warmed his heart. "Glad to see you finally acknowledge that I'm in charge of you until you're better."

"I wouldn't say in charge, but if saying yes means I can have you touching me, then it's a small price to pay." Jane merely shook her head and he smiled as he continued, "Fine. Although if you're looking for a happy ending, it's not going to happen."

Jane tilted her head. "I just want the facts."

His dragon crooned. *She is perfect.*

Kai replied, "Well, I was young and my dragon didn't take it well. He roared and clawed his way out of any mental prison I constructed. All he wanted was Maggie.

"I spent three weeks locked inside this cottage. A guard was posted near my place at all times and the old clan leader checked on me every day. Bram checked on me too since he had been one of my schoolmates and had been concerned. Bram has always cared about the clan, even before he was leader.

"Anyway, after three weeks, once I was able to keep control of my dragon for several hours at a time, Victor sat me down and told me about his brother, who had gone through the same experience with his true mate denying him. That time, it had been one of the human sacrifices who had run away and left her child behind. You actually know that child, by the way. It was Nikki. Being the first child of a human sacrifice has been much tougher than people realize."

Jane nodded and waited for him to go on. He liked that she could remain quiet if a situation needed it. Not that he didn't love matching wits with his human, but it showed her in a new light— one where he could imagine her helping him with his Protector duties.

He paused at that. He'd barely kissed the human. It was a bit early to be thinking of a future with her.

Pushing aside that thought, he carried on with his story. "Victor's brother eventually found someone to love within the clan and is mated to her to this day. Knowing it was possible to survive a true mate's denial was the missing piece I needed to get my life together. After that, I focused all of my energy on my work. I became head Protector shortly after Bram took over the clan, and the rest is history."

Jane remained quiet for a minute. Then she moved closer to him and placed a hand on his cheek. "You are much more than a muscled fighting machine. You're strong inside and out."

His dragon chimed in. *I've been patient, but I want her to fix our wound and touch us. Ask her.*

*We need rest, so if you're hinting at her touching our cock, it's not going to happen.*

His dragon growled. *I'm not stupid. If you don't get well, I may never be able to shift into my true form.*

*Well, with you, I'm never sure.*

With a huff, his beast faded into the back of his mind. Good. Kai could focus on Jane without his dragon banging on about a kiss or more.

For a split second, he wondered what the hell he was doing. Jane had grand plans for her future, as did Kai for his clan. He should ask her about them first and ensure she knew what getting involved with him would entail. But as she stroked her thumb over his cheek, Kai trusted she knew what she was doing. Jane was clever. She would never do anything without understanding the consequences.

Well, almost everything. She'd been daft about going into that pub in Newcastle alone, armed with nothing but a can of illegal pepper spray.

He didn't even want to know where she'd managed to purchase that. The female was too stubborn and determined for her own good.

Too bad that was why he liked her.

Making his decision, Kai raised the hand of his good arm and placed it over Jane's. She met his gaze and he nearly growled at the desire in her eyes. "You're teasing me with what I can't have on purpose, aren't you?"

She leaned closer and her breath tickled his cheek. "No, I'm trying to encourage you to heal faster so you can have me."

He blinked. "Just like that?"

Jane smiled. "You told me about your past, despite it being painful. If you can do that, then I think you can stop being an arsehole to me. I have a feeling you do it to push people away so they won't ask questions." She searched his gaze. "But let's get one thing straight right now—I'm not Maggie Jones. I'm not going to tease you and then run into the arms of another man, provided you don't drive me away. And, most importantly, I'm not afraid of you or your dragon. I can take whatever you throw at me."

Kai growled, barely noticing the pain in his shoulder as Jane's scent surrounded him. "You better be telling the truth, Jane Hartley, because once I'm well again, nothing is going to stop me from kissing the living shit out of you before I rip off all of your clothes."

Jane's shiver sent a surge of pride through Kai's body. Even his bloody dragon was smug. *She is different than the other one. She is ours.*

~~~

Jane loved the feel of Kai's late-day stubble under her palm. Combined with his growl and look of hunger, she nearly proposed for him to lie on the bed while she rode him.

*Stop it, Hartley.* According to Dr. Sid's list, Kai wasn't to do any sort of mildly intense physical activity for at least the first twenty-four hours. The doctor had also underlined "NO SEX" with three lines.

Still, it didn't mean Jane couldn't tease Kai a little. She'd made up her mind to give Kai a chance and once Jane made up her mind, she gave up all doubt and embraced the decision.

Sometimes, it didn't work out. But if she always played it safe and never took a chance, she never would've volunteered to cover the dragon-shifters.

And she wouldn't be here with a hot, stubborn dragonman whose gaze alone could make her shiver.

Moving behind him, she traced the edge of his sling. "Take this off so I can check your wound."

"I don't have any of the medical supplies in here."

Brushing his skin along the edge of his shoulder, she answered, "I was given a stash too, if you remember."

Kai remained silent a second before his deep voice caressed her ears. "I need your help taking off the sling."

Jane bit her lip and then said, "Asking for so much help in a day must be hard for you."

Kai turned his head to meet her eye. "Aren't you supposed to be nice to me?"

She tapped her chin. "That wasn't on Sid's list of instructions, so no."

"It will help me heal faster."

"Oh? How, exactly? Does your dragon-shifter super-healing abilities go into overdrive when someone says or does something nice?"

Kai grunted. "Don't be daft."

Grinning, she figured Kai had suffered enough, so she helped to ease the sling off and tossed it to the side of the bed. Then she moved to stand in front of him, in between Kai's legs. She went to work removing the bandages when she felt Kai's gaze on her breasts. Glancing over, his eye level was in line with her nipples.

At the intensity of his gaze, her nipples turned into hard points.

When he smirked, Jane's voice was dry when she asked, "Enjoying yourself?"

He grinned. The twinkle in his blue eyes made her heart skip a beat. "Immensely. Maybe being an invalid won't be so bad this time around."

"So does that make me better than Ginny?"

"It's too early to tell."

Rolling her eyes, Jane went back to removing the gauze and exposed his wound. Kai's skin had already started to knit back together. "Dragon-shifters really do heal fast."

"Yes. You're welcome."

"For what?"

"I can tell you want me. If I were human, you'd have to wait a week or longer. With me, it's a day or two."

"Don't get cocky just yet. I need to check for infection and give you a shot."

"Then hurry up. My pain medication is wearing off."

She shook her head before studying his wound. "If you hadn't stared at my nipples, I'd be done by now." Gently, she checked the stitches and tested the temperature of his skin. "The good news is your skin isn't overly hot or swollen. I also don't see any pus or ooze." She glanced to Kai, only to find him staring at her breasts again. "Kai Sutherland, can you stop that for now?"

"Hmm?"

She murmured, "Men," before stepping back and turning toward the dresser.

Jane tried not to think about how she missed Kai's heat or being surrounded by his masculine scent as she grabbed her supply kit. Not really touching the marvelous man for one or two days was going to be bloody difficult now that she knew she could have him.

Pushing aside her lusty thoughts of stripping the dragonman and seeing his control break, she cleaned Kai's wound with antiseptic, replaced his bandage, and took out the pre-filled syringe. Removing the stopper on the needle, she tapped the side and pressed the plunger a fraction to ensure there wasn't any air in the needle before looking at Kai again. "I need you to stand up and pull down your boxers so I can give you a shot in the bum."

After she took three steps back, Kai stood up. "I only have one good arm." His look turned heated. "Will you help me?"

"I think you're doing this on purpose. You clearly took off your trousers earlier by yourself."

"And I nearly ripped my stitches." He placed the hand of his good arm over his heart. "I'm just trying to be a good patient."

Jane snorted and held out the syringe. "Take this." He did, and she moved closer. "And just know that you brought this on yourself."

~~~

Kai watched Jane as she ran her hand down his side and dipped a finger into the hem of his boxers. The light touch branded his skin and he wondered what it would feel like to have her long fingers gripping his dick.

His dragon growled. *You're teasing me. Stop it.*

*You're the one who wanted to feel the softness of her skin.*

*Yes, but now she's close to our cock and it's painful to not touch her.*

In that, Kai agreed. His dick was hot and heavy, pressing against his boxers. He was fairly sure that Jane knew he was aroused, too.

Not that he was embarrassed. Humans tried to hide their desires and sexuality. Kai was a dragon-shifter. He may not have much experience pursuing females, but he wanted Jane and would do whatever it took to have her.

Sure, his injury prevented him from tossing his female onto the bed and making her scream his name as she came, but he would rectify that as soon as possible.

Jane tugged down the hem of his shorts. Her soft skin brushing against his hip made his dick harder.

His dragon grunted. *Heal as fast as possible.*

138

Jane put out a hand and met his eye. She knew full well the effect her touch had on him and she was enjoying it. "Syringe."

He waited a beat to commit Jane's scent of vanilla and female to memory before handing her the syringe. "Do it quick."

She raised an eyebrow. "Is someone afraid of needles?"

"Don't be ridiculous."

Grinning, she looked back toward the exposed top of his arse. "Good." She stuck him, pushed the medicine into his body, and removed the needle. She gave his bum a pat. "Good boy."

He frowned. "I'm not a boy."

Jane looked from his eye, to his cock pressing against his boxers and back again. "I agree."

His dragon spoke up. *We must think of the best way to tease her when we're well. We have some time to think about it.*

*Yes, and they're going to be the longest hours of our life.*

*Good to see you're not denying you want her.*

*She knows about Maggie and didn't blink an eye. I want time to know her secrets, too. I know she bloody well has them.*

*Then just make sure to not scare her away. She is ours.*

Jane reached around him to her bag of supplies. "Here are your special dragon-shifter strength pain pills. Take them and then go to sleep."

He took the pills and swallowed. "I'm also hungry."

"Then I hope you have something easy because I'm not a very good cook."

The image of Jane in his kitchen, burning her latest attempt to cook breakfast, made him smile. "I know how to cook, but I'm too tired to do it. Sid probably knew that. Look in the medical bag. She usually packs me protein bars."

Jane rummaged around until she pulled out two carefully wrapped protein bars. She sniffed them and shook her head. "They're not poisoned, if that's what you're worried about."

"Don't be silly. I'm trying to figure out if they're human-friendly. The last thing I need is to eat something that is the equivalent of a billion calories."

"A billion, huh? You clearly don't know anything about dragon-shifter metabolism."

Jane glared. "I never said I did." She shook her hand with the bars. "If you want one, then tell me if I can eat one too. I'm starving."

His dragon growled. *Our female should never be hungry. Feed her.*
*I like teasing her first.*
*Not this time. The sooner we sleep, the sooner we heal.*
*Right, and then you can have Jane naked.*
*Exactly.*

Mentally shaking his head at his beast, Kai focused back on Jane. "They're the equivalent of one human meal. Now, may I have one?"

His question eased the frown from Jane's face. "You being polite makes me uneasy."

He growled out, "You didn't want me to be an arsehole, so I'm trying. Make up your mind, Janey."

No one had called her Janey since she was a child. But for whatever reason, she liked it when Kai said it.

With a smile, Jane handed him one of the protein bars. "Good. Just checking."

He murmured, "Bloody female," before tearing off the wrapper and taking a bite.

Jane did the same and she made a face. "What flavor is this?"

"Roast beef."

He waited until Jane took another bite before doing the same. As they ate in silence, Kai was relaxed in a way he hadn't felt in over a decade. For so long, he'd never expected to share a quiet, mundane moment with a female.

He didn't want it to end.

Kai was afraid that if he let Jane leave his sight, the ease and playfulness would disappear. He knew it was fucked up, but after what had happened the last time he'd set his sights on a female, he was afraid Jane would run away, too

After finishing his protein bar, Kai tossed the wrapper aside and cupped Jane's cheek. When she leaned into his touch, both man and beast hummed in contentment. He murmured, "You're fed, but you still look exhausted. How about you sleep with me?"

"I'm not so sure that's a good idea."

Kai wasn't one to tiptoe around the truth. "Because you don't want to?"

"No, because it might be too much of a temptation."

"For whom? You or me?"

She didn't miss a beat. "Both of us."

Her answer stroked his ego. "Just for sleep. The sound of your voice has helped me relax for months. Your warmth and scent should be even better."

She searched his eyes. "What do you mean my voice has helped you relax? We've barely spoken before yesterday."

His dragon growled. *Tell her the truth.*

Kai rubbed his thumb against her cheek and decided what the hell. She already knew his biggest secret. "I've listened to all of your news reports. And most of them more than once."

Her brows came together. "But why? You always acted like you hated me before."

"It wasn't hate. I was trying to keep my distance. You caught my eye the first day I saw you, when you did your interviews. You're the first female I've wanted in a very long time."

141

"How long exactly?" she asked.

"Years. But even the females I've slept with in the past were nothing compared to how much I want you right now."

"And how much is that?"

Kai lowered his voice. "So much that I'm tempted to take you right now, even if it means I can't ever shift into a dragon again."

Jane's expression softened. "There's so much more to you than meets the eye."

Before he could think about it, Kai winked. "And you've barely scratched the surface."

Jane laughed and replied, "I'm sure I'll be doing plenty of scratching before long."

He moved his hand and patted her arse. "Tease." Squeezing her arse cheek in a possessive grip, he asked, "So, will you sleep with me?"

She held his gaze for a few seconds and then shook a finger at him. "No funny business. You try to cop a feel or worse, and I'm kicking you out of my bed."

"Your bed, huh? Mine's bigger."

"Bigger isn't necessarily better."

The corner of his mouth ticked up. "You will sing a different tune soon."

When her breath hitched, warmth rushed through his body. After all these years, he might actually have a female he wanted who also wanted him for more than a quick fuck.

Turning them toward the bed, Kai reluctantly released his grip on Jane's soft arse and pulled down the duvet. "After you."

"No, I sleep on this side, so you go first."

He stared at her. "This is my side of the bed."

She raised an eyebrow. "If you want in my bed, then you sleep on the other side."

With an exaggerated sigh, he moved to the other side of the bed and carefully laid down. "You win this time, but the war has just begun."

Jane snuggled next to him and laid her head on his good shoulder. Kai wondered if she'd chosen that side of the bed on purpose, so she could lay next to him.

Her voice was muffled against his skin. "I'm being easy on you because you're injured. Once you're well, the kid gloves are coming off."

Smiling, Kai turned his head and breathed in Jane's scent. "We'll just see if a mere human can win against a man and his dragon."

"Wrong thing to say, dragonman, wrong thing," Jane murmured.

At the exhaustion in his female's voice, Kai leaned against Jane and waited until her breathing was even. Satisfied his female was asleep, Kai drifted off into a relaxed sleep. One he couldn't remember having in years.

# CHAPTER TEN

As Jane slowly came out of oblivion, she snuggled into the solid warmth at her side. After a few seconds, a large, warm hand rubbed up and down her back and Jane opened her eyes to see Kai's broad chest in front of her.

Blinking, she half-expected to wake up from a dream, but as she looked up to meet Kai's eyes, he smiled and the rumbling of his voice under her palms told her she was awake. "Good morning, Janey."

She frowned. "Morning?" Jumping up, she gently slapped his chest. "I was supposed to check your wound and give you more pain medication hours ago. Why didn't you wake me up?"

"I'm fine and you needed your sleep." Rolling her eyes, Jane tried to move from the bed, but Kai kept his grip on her waist. "You worry too much."

Jane sighed. "Gee, why would I worry? If your wound becomes infected and Stonefire loses its head Protector, it will all be because of me. I'm sure that's nothing to worry about."

The bloody dragonman smiled and Jane wanted to slap him. The twinkle in his eye, however, melted her heart a little when he replied, "You're a little feisty and sarcastic in the morning. I rather like it."

"Only because I can't punch you right now since you're injured. Trust me, without my morning cuppa, you don't want to deal with me."

Kai's gaze dropped to her breasts and heat spread through her body. "I'm sure I can think of ways to make you forget about your cup of tea."

"Kai, stop it."

Grinning, he looked back to her face. Despite the trouble he was giving her, the sight of the stony Protector smiling at her warmed Jane's heart. Kai had suffered for years, all whilst doing his best to protect his clan.

Kai deserved a slice of happiness.

Maybe, if he didn't drive her crazy first, she could try to give it to him.

For the present, however, Jane needed to make sure Kai was okay. Especially since Rafe would be arriving soon and her dragonman would need his strength to deal with her older brother.

Putting her alpha brother and her alpha dragonman in the same room was going to be interesting, to say the least.

But she was getting ahead of herself. Making her face as stern as she could, Jane waggled a finger. "Let me up. The sooner I finish my exam of your injury and go through the checklist, the sooner we can get ready and go see Bram."

"Does getting ready entail me helping you in the shower?"

The image of Kai slowly caressing her body with a wet washcloth flashed into her mind. He'd probably linger on her breasts, her abdomen, and then finally reach between her thighs.

Jane shifted her position, hoping her dragonman couldn't smell her arousal.

As his pupils flashed to slits and back, she knew that hope was smashed.

Kai's voice was husky when he said, "I can behave, if that's what you're worried about."

"Even putting aside the fact you're not supposed to take a shower until twenty-four hours after your surgery, there's no time for a long shower." She looked pointedly at his hand. "Let me up."

She swore she saw disappointment in Kai's eyes as he released his grip on her waist. Before he completely pulled away, Jane took his hand in hers and looked Kai straight in the eyes. "I'm not going to string you along forever, Kai Sutherland, but I'm not about to let Sid or Bram down by making your condition worse. You know sex would do that."

"Then how about if I just lie here and you give me a kiss?"

She raised an eyebrow. "You're not going to give up, are you?"

He tightened his hand around hers. "You already know I'm stubborn and when I make up my mind about something, I don't pull punches. I may have done that as a young dragonman, but no more. I want you, Jane. Kiss me."

The sincerity and hunger in his voice shot straight to her heart. "Just a quick one and no funny business, or I may just nudge your sore arm by mistake."

"Then hurry up, Janey. Your kiss will help me heal faster."

Rolling her eyes, she leaned down. "Sid mentioned nothing about kisses helping you heal."

"It can't be just any kiss, human. Only yours."

Melting at his words, Jane moved until she was a whisper away from Kai's lips. "You can be charming when you try."

He opened his mouth to reply, but Jane shut him up with a kiss.

# Reawakening the Dragon

~~~

Kai's dragon hummed as Jane's face lowered to theirs. *Let her know we want her.*

*Give me a bloody chance.*

Once Jane's lips touched his, Kai raised his good hand and threaded it into her hair. Jane didn't waste time and pushed her tongue past his lips and into his mouth.

He met hers stroke for stroke and he threaded his fingers through her hair. When she groaned, the sound shot straight to his cock.

Kai had survived flying for eight hours without a break as well as not eating for two days during a training exercise. But not taking his human right then and there was by far the hardest thing he'd ever done.

Except for maybe not killing Maggie's mate when he'd first heard the news.

*No.* He didn't want to think of anyone else but the human in front of him. Kai focused on Jane's taste, the heat of her tongue, and the scent of hers that made him crave more, much more.

All too soon Jane pulled away. She smiled and the mischief in her eyes made his stomach flip. Life would never be boring with Jane Hartley.

He'd just have to ensure she stayed around.

Jane murmured, "I kissed you, so I expect you to get your arse up and not put up any sort of fuss."

"I don't put up fusses."

She chuckled. "Sid was right about alpha dragonmen turning into big babies when sick or injured."

147

Kai gently tugged Jane's hair. "Just remember that when Sid clears me, you have a lot of payback coming your way."

"Oh, is that so?" Jane sat up and he let go of her hair. "I should probably say something clever, but I'm looking forward to it too much."

Kai's dragon spoke up. *We'd better be cleared later today.*

*And if we're not?*

*Then we'll find creative ways to skirt Sid's rules.*

*For once, dragon, I like your way of thinking.*

Jane snapped her fingers and motioned up. "Stop dawdling. There's lots to do today." He opened his mouth to ask what when Jane beat him to it. "The sooner you cooperate, the sooner we can talk to Bram."

She moved off the bed and retrieved her medical kit as Kai sat up. Each movement caused a thread of pain to shoot down his arm and across his shoulder, but he didn't regret letting Jane rest. Having his human curled up at his side had given Kai the best sleep he'd had in years. If he could have that every night, with Jane next to him, he'd be a happy dragonman.

His beast spoke up. *Just make sure she stays.*

*I'm going to try, but I'm not sure I can make Jane do anything.*

*Once she's naked, that will change.*

Jane handed him his pain medication. After he swallowed the pills, she stood in front of him and removed his bandage. As her soft fingers brushed his skin, he stared at her breasts. The temptation to lean forward and suck one of her hard nipples through her shirt was strong. He bet when he nibbled, Jane would moan and thread her fingers through his hair.

Since sucking her nipples might be too much too soon, Kai raised a finger and lightly brushed the taut peak. Jane sucked in a breath and he did it again. When she murmured, "Kai," he looked up into her eyes.

148

# Reawakening the Dragon

Never ceasing the strumming of her nipples, he watched Jane's pupils dilate. He half-expected her to scold him, but she placed a hand on his good shoulder and leaned into his touch.

Taking her actions as encouragement, he moved his hand down her stomach to the waist of her trousers. He traced her skin under the waistband and whispered, "Unbutton them."

The scent of Jane's arousal grew stronger and his dragon roared. *Rip them off. She wants us. We'll make her come with our fingers.*

Kai waited to see what his human would do. After a few seconds, she answered, "We shouldn't."

He raised an eyebrow. "Does it say anywhere in your list of instructions that I can't touch you?" He rubbed his hand under her top and back down again. "We'll both focus better afterward."

"For me, yes. But I can't see how you going into a meeting with a hard-on will help things."

Kai grinned. "Oh, tasting your sweet honey from my fingers will do for now. Not even I will risk Sid's wrath by disobeying her orders." He ran his hand higher and cupped her breast through her bra. He squeezed gently and a small moan escaped Jane's mouth. "Let me make you come, Janey. It'll make my dragon happy."

The corner of her mouth ticked up. "And let me guess? A happy dragon means you'll heal faster?"

"But of course."

Jane laughed and the sound warmed both man and beast. His dragon growled, *Rip off her trousers. I want to feel how hot and wet she is for us.*

*Not until she says yes.*

His beast paced, but didn't fight him. Deep down, even his dragon knew how important this moment was. Neither one of them would force it.

Jane traced his jagged flame tattoo on his left arm and the whispers of her touch made his dick pulse. When his human spoke, her voice was husky. "If you can think of a believable excuse to tell Bram why we're so late meeting with him, then do it quickly."

"Do what, my little human?"

"I'm over six feet tall. I'm not exactly little."

He massaged her breast and Jane bit her lip. "Okay, my rather tall human, tell me what you want."

Her eyes grew even more heated. "I want you to fuck me with your fingers."

His dragon roared. *Do it. Now.*

Kai removed his hand. "Take off your trousers and underwear."

Never taking her blue eyes from his, she unbuttoned her trousers and slowly slid them down her legs. Kicking them aside, she placed her thumbs in the waist of her underwear and Kai watched as she slowly slid them down to reveal a patch of dark hair between her long, shapely legs.

*Mine.*

Kai didn't know if it was him or his dragon who'd said it, but he didn't care.

Meeting Jane's eyes, he ordered, "Come here."

~~~

Jane's heart thudded in her chest. Part of her knew she shouldn't be doing this, but Kai had been right. Nothing in Sid's list had said he couldn't touch her. Moving his fingers and hand most definitely wouldn't count as mildly intense physical activity.

And to be honest, she could do with some release. She needed a clear head to face Bram and Rafe.

150

# REAWAKENING THE DRAGON

Kai's deep voice ordered, "Come here," and for once, she didn't feel like challenging him.

Each step she took toward her dragonman only made her wetter with his flashing pupils and heated looks. She'd never thought she'd be with a dragon-shifter because of her career. But since her reputation was already damaged and Jane had plans of her own, she wanted her dragonman more than anything she'd wanted in a while.

And not just because they worked well together as a team, which would be useful for her plans to succeed. Kai was the only man who could make her heart race and breasts tingle with little more than a glance. With a little more time, she might even be able to draw out the rest of his humor. She loved it when he laughed.

Reaching Kai, she placed a hand on his cheek and stroked his skin. "Make it count, dragonman. If you can't make me come, then I may have to rethink this whole staying with you thing."

Kai growled and placed a possessive hand on her arse. "You're staying with me."

She lowered her eyelids to half-mast and whispered, "Then convince me why I should."

Instead of words, Kai moved his hand from her arse to her hip and finally to her lower abdomen. As he strummed his thumb an inch above her clit, Jane moved her hand from his face to his good shoulder. Digging in her nails, she ordered, "Stop teasing me."

He stilled his thumb. "I told you payback was coming."

She opened her mouth, but he ran a finger between her folds and his touch sent a rush of heat through her body. Her pussy pulsed with each stroke of his finger. Without thinking, she widened her stance to allow him better access.

Kai chuckled. "Impatient, aren't you?"

She growled. "We have an appointment—"

He plunged his finger into her and she forgot what she was going to say.

Kai retreated and thrust again. As he continued in a steady pace, it became harder for her to stand. If not for her grip on his shoulder, she would fall over.

Her dragonman suddenly ceased his movements and she dug in her nails. "Don't stop."

His gaze was on her breasts, which were in front of his face. "I want to taste your pretty nipples first. Give me one."

As he licked his lips, her breasts grew heavier. In any other situation, she would tell him not to order her around. But in the moment, she wanted nothing more than to feel his wet mouth around her sensitive flesh.

Using her free hand, Jane bunched her shirt under her chin and held it while she tugged her bra over her breasts. In the next breath, Kai sucked one deep into his mouth and twirled her bud with his tongue. She moaned and Kai moved his fingers inside her pussy again. Between him nibbling her nipple and fucking her with his finger, her body wanted more, so Jane started to move in time with Kai.

The vibrations of Kai's growl around her nipple shot straight between her legs. In the next second, Kai released her nipple with a pop. His pupils were slits as he barked, "Kiss me. Now."

Jane kissed him without hesitation and threaded her fingers through his hair. His taste made her want to do much more than stand and let him fuck her with his fingers. She wanted to feel his long, hard cock moving inside of her.

But as her dragonman moved inside her again, adding a second finger, Jane moaned. The man had found her G-spot.

Slowing his movements, Kai strummed her clit and her knees nearly buckled. She loved the friction of his rough skin against her bundle of nerves. Yet each pass turned her bones a fraction more into jelly.

When he started rubbing her nub in slow circles, she whispered, "Please, Kai. I'm close."

He stilled his thumb and Jane cried out. "What are you doing?"

Rather than respond with words, Kai spread her legs wider and Jane had no choice but to sit on his thighs with her legs open.

Kai broke the kiss and stared into her eyes. "Don't look away. I want to see you come."

As the pulse between her legs increased, Jane merely nodded.

Kai's eyes flashed again and he growled before saying, "Good."

He stopped finger-fucking her pussy and concentrated on her clit with his thumb.

Jane dug her nails into his good shoulder and Kai's circular motions grew faster and rougher.

Somehow, the man already knew how she liked it.

Then he pinched her clit and Jane closed her eyes as she lost all coherent thought. If he would just pinch her one more time, she'd finally have her release.

Kai stilled. "Look at me."

Close to whimpering, Jane did as he said. The second her eyes met his, he lightly squeezed and twisted her hard nub.

Jane cried out as spots dotted her eyes and pleasure coursed through her body. Each spasm made it harder to keep her eyes open, but she didn't want Kai to stop rubbing her clit. The combination of her orgasm and his touch was pleasure to the point of almost pain.

Once the last spasm wracked her body, Kai smiled, removed his fingers, and licked them slowly.

Despite her recent orgasm, the sight made Jane's pussy pulse again in anticipation.

After a good twenty seconds and never breaking eye contact, Kai removed his fingers and licked his lips. Combined with the genuine hunger in his eyes, Jane desperately wanted to feel his tongue and mouth between her legs.

Leaning over, Kai kissed her. He took his time exploring her mouth and nibbling her lips. Each slow stroke made her hunger for more than his tongue.

When he finally pulled away, he whispered, "You're staying with me."

She tilted her head and tapped her chin. "I don't know. I might need another orgasm or two to convince me."

Moving his good hand to her back, he pressed her close against him until she could feel his hard cock between her legs. "If Sid clears me today, then I'll be fucking you until you can't walk straight. You're mine."

She laced her hands behind his neck. Dancing her fingers against the edge of his short hair, she moved her hips and rubbed against her dragonman's dick.

Kai hissed. "You're killing me, Janey."

Jane smiled. "If you're cleared today, then I have a few tricks of my own. I might wear you out before you can fuck me hard enough to mete out your threat."

"Bring it on, human. In this, I will win."

"We'll see, dragonman, we'll see." As much as she wanted to stay on Kai's lap all day, reason was returning to her brain. Bram was probably wondering where they were.

Jane tried to stand up, but Kai tightened his hold on her. She frowned. "We're already late. We can't keep Bram waiting forever."

"Bram will understand."

She raised an eyebrow. "The other visitor due today won't. Trust me on that."

Tracing circles on her back, he murmured, "I don't care if it's the bloody Prime Minister. They can wait."

His words were sweet and she nearly leaned down to kiss him. But then the thought of explaining to her older brother that she was late because she'd been fooling around with Kai gave her the strength to resist. She shook her head. "No. Let me up so I can freshen up and we can go. Your clan needs you, Kai. The meeting with Bram is important."

He searched her eyes for a second before he released his hand. "If you say it is, then I'll trust you."

She knew his words signaled an important shift in their relationship, but she pushed it aside. She would sort out everything later, after dealing with her brother.

Getting Rafe up to Stonefire had been hard enough; it'd taken nearly an hour to convince him to come. She couldn't imagine what it was going to take for him to agree to help the dragon-shifters.

There was only one way to find out. She needed to get Kai and herself to Bram's cottage.

Standing up, Jane took a second to find her balance. When she could finally stand, amusement danced in Kai's eyes as he smirked.

She placed a hand on her hip. "Don't look so happy with yourself. I'm only holding back because of your bloody shoulder."

"Go ahead and say that, Janey. I'll make you beg next time and you won't be able to use my injury as an excuse."

She glared, and Kai chuckled as he stood up.

Deciding that Kai needed a little payback, she zeroed in on his cock straining against his boxers. His laughter died instantly and Kai's voice interrupted her visions of taking his hard length into her hands. "Stop it, Jane. Now you're just torturing me."

She grinned and met his eyes. "Then try not to get shot again."

"Then try not to be daft and go after dragon hunters by yourself again."

"We'll see about that." Jane motioned toward her doorway. "Now, go get dressed. I'll meet you downstairs in five minutes."

Kai closed the space between them and placed a gentle kiss on her lips. "I'll be ready before you."

"Right, then it's on, dragonman."

Kai winked. "I think we should start keeping score. If I reach twenty points ahead, then I get to tie you to my bed and do whatever I want with you."

Heat spread across her body as she visualized Kai caressing her body and making her come over and over again with both his tongue and his cock.

Clearing her throat, she replied, "Until I decide what I get if I get twenty points ahead, the deal is off."

He nuzzled her cheek. "Then think of something quickly, Jane, because I want to earn my prize."

She pushed against his chest and motioned toward the door again. "Go get ready. We can talk about my prize later. Consider it an incentive."

"Right, so I can spend the whole meeting thinking of what you want to do with me."

She gave a light shove. "Go."

With a grin, Kai exited.

# Reawakening the Dragon

The room was empty without her dragonman. But as much as she wanted to spend all day with him, she needed to fix her screw up back in Tyneside. That meant garnering her brother's help. Without help from humans such as Rafe, Stonefire would have to spend who knew how many more months searching for the hunters again.

Jane righted her top and headed for the bathroom. Despite the uncertainty of the future and the upcoming meeting with her brother, Jane couldn't stop smiling as she cleaned up.

# CHAPTER ELEVEN

Nikki stood in the security room at one of Stonefire's side entrances and tried not to fidget. Bram had trusted her with meeting Rafe Hartley and bringing the human male to one of the remote, abandoned cottages on Stonefire's lands undetected.

She didn't have a choice, of course, but she'd said yes. After all, it'd been almost four years since she'd last talked with the human.

True, she'd kept abreast of his accomplishments and had glimpsed him a few times over the years whilst serving in Afghanistan. But it wasn't quite the same.

Her dragon chimed in. *It may have been four years, but I still think you should kiss him.*

*Why? He's attractive, yes, but female dragon-shifters can rarely tell a true mate until they kiss a male. I don't understand your persistence.*

Her beast huffed. *I'm curious, is all. None of the other human soldiers ever caught your eye.*

*We can't kiss any humans, dragon. You know that, or we could end up in prison. How will we protect our clan then?*

*Find a way. The males here only see us as the first child of a sacrifice or as a friend. A human male won't care about us being the child of a sacrifice, especially if we don't tell him.*

Nikki mentally sighed at her beast. *If only it were that easy.*

Her conversation was interrupted by Sebastian, the guard manning the side entrance gate for the morning. "Nikki, he's here."

Nikki glanced at the monitor, which broadcast the live feed of the sole incoming road to the rear entrance. A dark economy car drove toward them, the same color as what Rafe had reported the night before. Nikki kept her eyes glued to the screen as she ordered, "Wait until he steps out of the car before removing the camouflage barrier."

Seb's voice was dry as he replied, "You're senior to me by a few months, Nikola Gray. The formality seems a bit much."

She raised an eyebrow and met Seb's near-black eyes. "I'm still senior, Sebastian Randall. Do you really want to let a human point out our lack of control or order?"

"Fine. But if you order me to fly laps to impress the human male, I'll just tell you to sod off."

"What's that supposed to mean?" Nikki demanded.

"We served together in Afghanistan. Whenever Hartley was nearby, you hid. I think you fancied him."

Maybe Nikki hadn't been as smooth or secretive as she'd thought she'd been back then.

Still, she was several years older, with more experience. Schooling her face into the expressionless mask she'd learned from Kai, she shrugged. "Fancied, as in past tense. Right now, he's a stranger about to set foot on our land. Our job is to ensure he's not a threat."

Seb waved a hand. "Fine." He paused deliberately and then added, "Ms. Gray."

Nikki rolled her eyes and then watched as the car came to a stop. Rafe Hartley stepped out of the car and studied the trees in front of him.

The video was low quality, but the rugged features of his face, dark hair, and broad shoulders hadn't changed. Just looking at him made her dragon roar inside her head. *While he's here, kiss him. I don't want to wonder what if any more, especially since you won't kiss any males on our land.*

*We're young. We have time.*

*You use that as an excuse. Young dragons need sex and kisses. Find me some.*

*Shush. We need to protect the clan.*

Grumbling, her dragon retreated to the back of Nikki's mind. The clan's safety was one of the few things that would quiet her beast.

Rafe crossed his arms over his chest and looked up. After a few seconds, he stared directly into the camera and didn't blink.

Clever human.

After the attack on Lochguard's rear entrance last month, Kai had installed the tree and shrub dummy wall. But a trained soldier could still spot something was off. Nikki just hoped the Dragon Knights and dragon hunters weren't as clever.

She looked to Seb. "Let him in."

Seb thankfully kept his mouth shut and did what she asked.

Nikki went to the door, gripped the knob, and took a deep breath. She could face Rafe and be professional. She couldn't let Kai or Bram down.

Her dragon growled and Nikki quickly said, *I will find someone else once this mission is complete. Now, will you behave?*

Her beast retreated to the back of her mind and Nikki took that as a yes.

Turning the knob, she opened the door and walked up to the bars separating her and Rafe. Looking up to meet his green-eyed gaze, Nikki used every bit of training she had to keep her face neutral. She didn't have time to notice the sexy planes of his

160

face. Or, how his dark, wavy hair was a little longer than regulation length and fell across his brow, making his light green eyes stand out.

In the back of her mind, her dragon laughed. *Who are you lying to?*

Ignoring her beast, she nodded at Rafe. Even though she knew full well who he was, it was best to play it as this being the first time they'd met. She asked the secret question. "Who was Mr. Tiggles?"

"My sister's ridiculous cat." She arched an eyebrow and Rafe shrugged. "You have images of me already, I'm sure. I'm doing my sister a favor by being here. So either open up or I go take a real holiday."

Nikki wasn't about to let him take control of the situation. "Who was Mr. Tiggles?"

Rafe stared and she stared back. Finally, the human male growled and answered, "Jane's beloved tabby."

"Right. Now, was that so hard?"

Rafe glared. Good. She didn't think he recognized her. That would make working with him easier.

She punched in her code and the gate opened. She motioned with her head. "Follow me."

As she turned and started walking, she heard Rafe murmur, "Jane owes me for this," before he followed.

When he caught up to Nikki's strides, he asked, "Speaking of my sister, where is she? She still needs to tell me what's so bloody important that I had to come north in October."

She looked up at Rafe. "You'll find out soon enough."

Rafe studied her for a second and Nikki's heart rate kicked up. *Please don't let him recognize me or I'll never live it down.*

Then the human looked away from her face and picked up his pace. With a frown, Nikki caught up to him. "If you wanted us to hurry up, then you could ask."

"Why? This way is faster."

Rafe half-jogged and Nikki growled. She wasn't going to play games with him.

Nikki stopped in her tracks and waited. A few seconds later, Rafe turned around and jogged in place. He raised his brows and she raised hers back. Shaking his head, Rafe returned to where she was standing and bit out, "Why are we bloody standing still? I'm impatient to find out what the fuck is going on."

Her dragon spoke up. *He's different from before. He is confident and straightforward. I like it. He's like a dragon-shifter.*

*No, no, no. The last thing I want is some alpha male growling at me and barking orders.*

*If you say so.*

Her beast laughed and then fell quiet.

*Bloody fantastic.*

Nikki answered Rafe, "Only a handful of my clan know you're here. Go, run off, and see what happens when they find you. For all they know, you're a dragon hunter."

"I can handle them."

She raised an eyebrow. "Right, so when they shift into a dragon and dangle you from two talons, you'll pull out some special moves to defeat them?"

Rafe stopped moving and peered down at her. "I might."

She shook her head. "This isn't the army, Mr. Hartley. You're on dragon-shifter land."

He crossed his arms over his chest. "And what is that supposed to mean?"

"It means we do whatever it takes to protect our own. Mess with my clan, and you'll suffer the consequences."

Rafe's piercing green gaze reminded Nikki of one of her commanding officers, but she resisted squirming. Bram and Kai needed her strong. She could do it.

Eventually, Rafe nodded. "That I can respect. Now, Miss…?"

"Call me Nikki."

"Right, Ms. Nikki. How about we hurry? Whatever your clan leader wants with me is important. The longer you try to assert your control over me, the more time you take away from your clan."

He was right, the bloody human, but she wasn't about to admit it. "Then follow me and don't wander off."

As Nikki jogged away, she heard Rafe follow.

The exercise gave her time to digest what had happened. It seemed Rafe didn't recognize her. She should be elated, but a small part of her was disappointed.

Still, she needed to forget her adolescent fantasies about Rafe Hartley and focus on protecting her clan. She had yet to prove herself as a worthy Protector. Helping Kai had been a step in the right direction, but tracking down the dragon hunters and taking them down would most definitely earn respect from the other clan members.

Or, so she hoped. The elders would be the toughest to persuade she was more than just the start of repopulating their clan.

Nikki picked up her pace and pretended her past with Rafe had never happened. Once her mission was over, she'd maybe visit one of the other clans to ease her dragon's sexual appetites. Lochguard was friendly now.

Yes, she'd find a nice Scottish dragonman and sleep with him. Humans were too complicated and fragile. And she definitely didn't need that in her life.

~~~

Jane secured Kai's sling and gave his chest a little pat. "Even if it means I win this round, that wasn't so bad, was it?"

Kai scratched his chest. "Celebrate winning this time because it won't happen again."

She rolled her eyes. "You're such a sore loser."

She moved away from Kai and picked up the borrowed jacket from the bed. At some point, she would find a way to have her own clothes again.

Kai grunted and she smiled. "You must be feeling better if you can grunt."

He grunted again and Jane laughed. Her dragonman's voice filled the room. "I like your laugh. You should laugh more often."

"You're just trying to change the subject, Mr. Sutherland."

"No. I like how your eyes sparkle and your cheeks turn slightly pink."

She resisted covering her cheeks. "It's strange when you're nice to me."

"I thought you didn't want me to be nice one minute and an arsehole the next."

She decided to change the subject. "Instead of arguing the point, let's go."

"You just don't want to admit you're wrong."

"Says the stubborn head Protector."

Kai came up to her and placed a hand on her lower back. "This isn't over, but let's go. I want to hear what Bram has to say. Unless you've changed your mind and want to tell me everything?"

She raised an eyebrow and pointed to her face. "Does it look like I'm going to tell you? This is my stern face." She exaggerated her frown and slight glare.

Moving his hand to her backside, he squeezed her arse cheek and Jane squeaked. "I don't see any such thing."

"Wow, I've really coaxed out the incorrigible flirt, haven't I?"

"No comment, Ms. Journalist. Let's go."

Kai pressed gently against her bum and she started walking.

The dragonman never severed contact, though. She never thought she was the type of woman to want a possessive man, but she was starting to like it. No matter Kai's faults—and there were probably many she still didn't know about—he had no problem displaying his interest and intent.

Add in the mundaneness of them waking up together earlier, and Jane was honest enough with herself to admit she wanted more of it. The only question was whether she could have it. If Rafe refused to help Stonefire, the dragon-shifters might not welcome him back to their land. If she stayed, and she was starting to warm up to the idea, she would miss her brother.

Kai's voice interrupted her thoughts. "You're only quiet when you're thinking. Tell me what's on your mind."

Jane blinked as she realized they were outside already. She hadn't been paying attention.

Since she couldn't tell him the full truth, she stuck as close to it as possible. "My brother. I was wondering how he'd do here."

He frowned. "No one is allowed on Stonefire until I run a background check."

She fought a smile. "Is that so? And what happens when the badass Protector gets shot? Will everyone just line up at the gates and wait until you have a chance to screen them all?"

"Don't be daft. If Bram can't do it, then their visits are rescheduled." He paused and then added, "Your very first visit was nearly postponed, but I managed to find out just enough about you beforehand. Good thing, or Mel would've had my head."

"Oh? And what secrets did you uncover? I bet you didn't find anything about my secret life as a treasure hunter."

"Treasure hunter, huh? You must be a lousy one then because no one ever mentioned it. Not even on the internet, and you can find everything there."

She tried to look affronted, but then laughed. "Fine, I'm not a treasure hunter. But I'm sure you didn't find out everything about me."

"No, but you owe me a secret once we're done with Bram."

"And why, pray tell, do I owe you anything?"

He leaned down to her ear and whispered, "It'll help me stop visualizing you naked and at the mercy of my fingers, my tongue, and my cock."

Jane's heart skipped a beat. She whispered back, "Stop it. We're in public and dragon-shifters have sensitive hearing."

"Does it matter?" He patted her rear. "Any male who sees me with my hand on your plump arse knows I've made a claim."

She moved a hand to Kai's firm buttocks and squeezed. "There. Now it runs both ways." She dug in her nails a little. "Flirt with others at your own peril."

Amusement danced in Kai's eyes. "And how do you plan to take down a dragon, Janey?"

Straightening her shoulders, Jane lifted her chin. "I'm resourceful. After a few days here, I'll find a way."

Kai chuckled as they approached Bram's cottage. Despite his recent claim, Jane still half-expected Kai to step away from

166

her. Yet he pulled her tighter against his side as they approached the door and the action warmed her heart.

Just as he'd stated before, Kai truly didn't hold back once he'd made up his mind.

Kai raised his hand to knock, but the door opened before he could do so. Bram stood on the other side. After looking between Jane and Kai, the clan leader smiled and motioned inside. "Come. Evie's going to be happy to see you two. She just won a bet."

~~~

Kai squeezed Jane tighter against his side. "Explain what you mean, Bram."

Laughter danced in his clan leader's eyes. "Not right now. Evie can tell you."

"Hiding behind a pregnant female isn't very leader-like," Kai stated.

Bram shrugged. "It'll make her happy and I'll do whatever it takes to make my mate happy."

Kai sensed what was left unsaid—Kai would understand that fact himself if he ever took a mate.

Kai's dragon growled. *Hurry up. I want to spend time with Jane. What about the clan?*

*We can do both as long as you learn to delegate.*

Ignoring his beast, Kai glanced at Jane. She was being unusually quiet. "I see you're quiet for Bram."

Jane smiled up at him. "Oh, it's not for Bram."

Kai looked from Jane to Bram and back again. "Can one of you just bloody tell me what's going on already? I don't like secrets."

Bram motioned with his head. "Step inside first." Kai guided them in and Bram shut the door. His clan leader continued, "Jane is probably quiet because her brother was scheduled to arrive thirty minutes ago." Bram glanced to Jane. "And he came."

Jane let out a breath at his side. "Good."

Kai jumped in. "Wait, what does Jane's brother have to do with anything?"

Bram answered, "He's going to help us with the hunters." Kai raised his brows and Bram added, "I'll fill you in on the plan with Rafe in the room."

Jane spoke up. "So he passed your interview?"

Bram nodded. "I have a few things to look into, but I've cleared him for now. It was hard to get any answers out of the bastard until I mentioned the hunters are a threat to his sister. Then he became a lot more serious and cooperative."

Evie's voice drifted down the hall. "Bram."

They turned and Evie appeared, followed by Nikki and a tall male with dark hair and green eyes.

Those green eyes darted to Kai's grip, Kai's dragon-shifter tattoo, and then looked to Jane. "What the hell is going on, Jane? Since when are you cozy with a bloody dragon-shifter?"

Kai jumped in before Jane could. "Don't talk to her like that."

Rafe met Kai's eyes. They were neutral. Despite the human's tone, his emotions hadn't taken complete control of him. Rafe's voice was steely as he answered, "Be careful, dragonman. Until I know more about you, I'm going to be watching your every move."

Rafe stared and Kai stared back. Jane sighed and poked him with a finger. "Stop it." She looked to her brother. "And you, too. I'm standing right here. You could talk to me, you know, Rafe, instead of acting as protective as any dragon-shifter. Maybe even say hello to your favorite sibling."

"You're my only sibling. Besides, you're the one who asked for my help, little sister. How convenient of you to not mention you're sleeping with a dragonman," Rafe answered.

"If I am, it's none of your business. I don't go around lecturing you about your numerous women. You're a grown man and I trust you to know what you're doing. Do the same with me."

Rafe glared at Kai. "This is different."

Kai growled and took a step toward Rafe, but Bram's voice boomed out, full of dominance. "Enough. You two can circle each other later." Bram looked to Rafe. "If you want me to honor our deal, then go back inside with Evie and wait for me." Bram looked to Kai. "And you stay here. I want to talk with you."

"And me, too?" Jane asked.

Bram shook his head. "Go in with your brother and have your row. I want everything to run smoothly once we start discussing plans and tactics."

Jane nodded and Kai squeezed her hip. "Jane stays with me."

Bram gave him a piercing stare. "You and I need to chat alone."

Jane touched his cheek. "It'll be fine. Learn what you need to know from Bram and I'll sort out my brother."

Rafe mumbled something in the corner, but Kai ignored him. "If you feel the need to punch him, then give him an extra one from me."

Bram growled. "Kai."

Jane bit her lip. "I'll keep that in mind."

With one last look, Jane left his side and joined Rafe and Evie. Evie threw a look at Bram before the trio disappeared.

Kai focused all of his attention on Bram. "Tell me what the bloody hell is going on, Bram. And quickly."

His leader raised an eyebrow. "I should ask the same of you. You and the human smell of each other."

Kai wished he could shrug. "It wasn't planned, but she's mine. I would think you'd understand."

"While I'm glad you finally found a female you like, you have bloody awful timing."

"Some would say the same of when you mated Evie."

"Aye, well, as long as Jane is the one you want, I'll allow it. If it becomes serious, then you'd better hope the DDA grants you a special license to mate her. Evie and I only negotiated that deal for Stonefire a few weeks ago."

"I'll let you know." Kai studied Bram a second and added, "Now, tell me why Rafe Hartley is here."

"He's going to help us with tracking down the dragon hunters," Bram stated.

Kai frowned. "How is he going to do that? He's still active with the army."

"That's exactly why he's useful."

Kai's dragon spoke up. *I don't care if he's useful. If he tries to take Jane away, I will claw my way out and take care of him.*

*Let's try to avoid mauling humans, if at all possible.*

His beast huffed and fell silent. Sometimes, Kai wondered how he'd been paired with such a pouty dragon.

Kai focused back on Bram. "You're holding back information, Bram, and I don't like it. Just tell me what the bloody hell is going on."

Bram shook his head. "Rather than repeat myself, let's discuss this all together. I just need to make sure you won't kill the human male."

"I can't promise anything, but I'll try. If he betrays our clan, then he's fair game."

"Fair enough." Bram motioned toward the door. "Then let's join the others."

As they started toward the door, Bram lowered his voice and added, "I'm glad you've found someone, even if it's only for a little while."

"Jane is mine and she's staying."

Bram chuckled and Kai clenched the fingers of one hand.

Before Kai could say anything else, Bram exited the room and Kai followed.

As happy as he was that Bram approved of Jane, Kai still had to survive the meeting with Jane's brother. Not killing the bastard was going to be difficult.

His dragon spoke up. *As much as I'd like to kick the human male off our land, if he helps us and succeeds, then the clan and Jane will be safer. Maybe we should hold off on killing him.*

*Gee, thanks, dragon. I never would've thought of that.*

His beast huffed. *Maybe I won't try to help you, then. We'll see how far you get without me.*

Kai mentally sighed. *Everything is happening at once. I will need your help. Don't go.*

*Fine. But only to help Jane.*

Sensing dramatics, Kai remained silent. His dragon would only become moodier until he finally fucked Jane.

Pushing aside all distractions, Kai schooled his face into a neutral expression. It was time to deal with Jane's brother.

# CHAPTER TWELVE

Jane waited until Evie shut the door to Bram's office before turning toward her brother. Maybe she should care that the clan leader's mate was watching, but Jane had a feeling Evie understood being surrounded by alpha males, so Jane ignored her and pointed a finger at Rafe. "You need to calm the hell down, brother. I'm thirty-one years old. You need to trust that I know what I'm doing."

Rafe crossed his arms over his chest. "Oh, really? I heard you were nearly shot and had to be rescued by a dragon. Let's not even get into how daft it is to go into a pub full of dragon hunters by yourself."

*Fantastic.* Bram had told her brother everything. "I took precautions."

"Not enough, apparently," Rafe replied.

"I would've been fine if it hadn't been for your 'recommendation' turning me in to a bunch of Dragon Knights for a few quid."

Rafe narrowed his eyes. "I had no idea there was a bounty on your head. Five thousand pounds can change a person's intentions. If I'd known, then I never would've recommended Jeff."

"Right, so you only would've recommended him if there wasn't a bounty. I'm starting to question your judgment."

"Says the woman who volunteered to work with the dragon-shifters and have a crap ton of hate thrown your way. Did you ever think of Mum and Dad?"

She took a step toward her brother. "I talked with Mum and she encouraged me to try working with Stonefire. Unlike you, she supports my choice of career."

"Bloody hell, Jane, I support you. It's only your recklessness I have a problem with."

Jane pointed a finger at Rafe. "Your criticizing me isn't going to change what happened. Let's focus on the future."

"Right, the future. From what I've heard, you might not have one if I don't help."

"I'm sure we could manage without you. I'm quite resourceful, if you remember."

"Maybe," Rafe answered. "But my skills would speed up the process of finding and capturing the dragon hunters."

"We could find someone else," Jane spit out.

"Ah, but would they be as skilled or trustworthy as me? You know I won't fuck you over."

"I'm not so sure about that."

Rafe shrugged. "It doesn't really matter to me if I stay or go. I don't have time to argue it out with you. If you want my help, then stay away from the dragonman."

Jane raised her chin. "Don't be daft. As if I would bow down to your ultimatum. If you don't want to help, then leave. I'm not about to beg, Rafe Daniel Hartley. The door is over there. Use it if you wish."

The silence ticked by for a few seconds before Rafe smiled. "I see that age has only made you stubborner. You're not going to change your mind, are you?"

She answered dryly, "Right, I'm going to acquiesce to everything you say if you just scold me a bit more."

Rafe walked up to her and lightly punched her in the arm. "I'm never going to stop trying." His face turned serious. "One day your luck will run out and your recklessness will get you killed, Jane. If nothing else, think of Mum and Dad."

"Really? You're going to use our parents to make me feel guilty, again?" Rafe nodded and Jane sighed. "I forgot how irritating you are."

The corner of her brother's mouth ticked up. "But you know you love me anyway."

"If you loved me, then you'd trust me to make my own decisions without barking orders."

"As much as I've come to rely on a few dragon-shifters during certain operations, they're different, Jane. The public targets them, and by extension you. I know they've been threatening you ever since you did the first interviews here. If you stay here for an extended period, word will get out and you'll become a full-blown target," Rafe replied.

Evie cleared her throat from her position in a chair at the side of the room. "I'm not sure what all the fuss is about. If I'm not mistaken, Jane called when the threats became reality and she needed your help, Rafe Hartley. If a bossy, overprotective brother is all she gets when she calls, then I wouldn't expect her to call you again. If you're so concerned, then help her. She clearly isn't going to change her mind about staying just because you told her to."

Rafe studied Evie a second and then answered, "I don't know much about you and I'm not about to threaten a pregnant lady, but this is none of your business, miss."

Evie raised her eyebrows. "Isn't it?" Evie looked to Jane. "If something were to happen to Jane, then one of our clan members might become unstable. I say that bloody well is my business."

Jane moved between Evie and Rafe. "Rafe, you've worked with dragon-shifters firsthand. Give Stonefire a chance before you judge them. That's all they ask."

Rafe met Jane's eye. "I'm not judging them harshly, Jane. You've seen the attacks by both the Dragon Knights and the dragon hunters. Watching you report on them was bad enough, but to live with a clan of dragon-shifters is downright dangerous."

Kai's voice drifted into the room. "Not if I have anything to say about it."

Jane hadn't heard the door open, but Kai entered, with Bram right behind him.

Once Kai reached her side, he placed a gentle hand on her back and looked to Rafe. "I'm Kai Sutherland and I'm Stonefire's head Protector. If you're ready to make plans and strategize, then you're welcome to stay. But if you're only here to scold your sister, then you can leave. What will it be, Hartley?"

Jane held her breath as Kai and Rafe stared at one another. No doubt, they were sizing each other up. The question was whether Rafe could put aside his role as her big brother to help the dragon-shifters or not.

She waited and hoped her brother didn't do anything foolish.

~~~

Kai had to give the human male credit. He didn't so much as flinch, let alone look away from Kai's gaze.

Still, as Kai rubbed circles on Jane's lower back, he wouldn't hesitate to banish the human if Rafe tried to take Jane away from him.

Rafe finally answered, "If staying here and helping you lot is what Jane wants, then I'll help, provided it doesn't do anything that might get me tossed out of the army."

Bram's voice filled the room. "Between Kai's, Nikki's, and your experience, Rafe, I'm sure we can make sure your career is safe."

Rafe nodded. "Right, then let's get down to business. I only have so much leave and I'd like to get this assignment done and spend some of it on a beach with a pint in my hand."

Bram stood at Evie's side and massaged her shoulder. "As much as I admire your ambition, this isn't something that can be done in a matter of days."

Jane interjected, "But if we don't act, the former Carlisle-based dragon hunters will move again. It could take months to find them."

Bram answered, "Aye, it could if we let them escape and had to start from scratch. But thanks to Rafe, we can monitor their activity from afar and bide our time for an attack."

Kai frowned. "You want to let them move locations on purpose?"

Bram nodded. "Right now, between two of their members missing and Nikki's shifting into a dragon, I bet they're on high-alert. If they move, all whilst thinking they're safe, they will let their guard down."

Kai grunted. "That's risky, Bram."

Rafe chimed in. "Maybe, but it could result in a bloody big payoff."

Kai looked to Rafe. "Say you tap your friends in the military and intelligence. Can we trust you to help when the time comes?"

"I always finish a job I start. Ask Jane."

Jane murmured, "It's true." She patted Kai's side and he looked down at her. Jane continued, "Waiting would work best for you, too. Not only because you'll be healed, but you can hand-pick a team made up of both humans and dragon-shifters to plan the attack. Lochguard might even help, if Arabella asks Finn."

Bram added dryly, "Or if I ask him."

Kai grunted. "The longer we wait, the higher the risk the hunters or the Dragon Knights could come after you."

Jane tilted her head. "I may not be much help with the hunters, but I have an idea about how to handle the remaining knights. Well, at least those in the UK."

Bram spoke up. "This is the first I've heard of it, lass. What's this plan of yours?"

Kai added, "I haven't heard it either. Tell us."

From the corner of his eye, Kai saw Rafe smile. He hated that the bloody human knew more about Jane than Kai. Had she told Rafe about her plans?

His dragon growled. *One day soon we will know more than the brother. Just make sure not to scare her away.*

Not willing to dignify his beast's words with a response, Kai squeezed Jane's hip. "Tell us, Janey."

Jane tilted her head. "Well, I wasn't going to say anything just yet, but now that it's come up, I'll mention it." Jane looked to each person in turn as she continued, "Staying here means I will have to hand in my notice to the BBC." Kai tried to protest, but Jane beat him to it. "No, it's true. Interviewing members of Stonefire is one thing, but living with them is quite another."

Kai interjected, "But what about your dreams of becoming an investigative reporter?"

Jane smiled up at him. "Oh, I'm not giving up on that. I'm just going to accomplish it on my own terms."

Bram's voice filled the room. "Then tell us your plan, lass, and quickly."

177

Jane nodded. "Right, then. The knights like to post things on popular and obscure online hangouts. Sometimes with videos, sometimes with message boards. They always ask for information and tips about the dragon-shifters. If we have someone give them specific information, the knights would come to us." She looked to Kai. "I'm sure you can think of ways to handle them from there."

"The knights are clever with technology. They won't take information from just anyone," Kai stated.

"Of course not. But you forget, I've been working on stories about both the hunters and the knights for months now. I have someone monitoring and interacting with the online places of the Dragon Knights. Discreetly, of course."

Evie jumped in. "That's brilliant, Jane. Will that person be willing to help you, even if you're no longer with the BBC?"

Jane bobbed her head. "They should." She looked up at Kai and raised an eyebrow. "It means we'll have to work together again. Are you going to keep your word and treat me as an equal?"

The corner of his mouth ticked up. A week ago, he would've been mortified to have a female call him out in front of Bram and a near-stranger. In the present, he couldn't care less. "I might be able to swing it, provided you don't go off and do something daft by yourself."

Rafe took a step toward them. "I agree with the dragonman. Try to go off and take care of the Dragon Knights by yourself and I'll hunt you down."

Kai eyed Rafe and decided he and the human may get along after all. "If she does, I'll be right beside you."

Jane rolled her eyes. "Hello, I'm right here. I'm not sure if I should be irritated that you're planning my rescue before I've done anything or offended that you just assume I'll go off to take on the Dragon Knights all by myself."

"I just want to make sure you're safe, Jane," Kai murmured.

Before his human could reply, Bram did. "The idea about the knights is promising, but I want you two to come up with a more detailed plan before any of it is put into motion. I'm not about to risk the clan."

Kai grunted. "I would never put the clan in danger."

"Good," Bram replied. He looked to Rafe. "Before you leave Stonefire today, I want you to review all of the intelligence we have on the former Carlisle-based hunters. One of my Protectors, Zain, should have some new information this morning. Nikki can be your escort."

Rafe answered, "You mean my babysitter."

Bram smiled. "Call that to her face and see what happens. She's young, but strong and she can shift into a dragon. Don't forget that."

Rafe grunted and a small part of Kai wanted to see how Nikki handled the human.

But he trusted Nikki Gray to do her job. Besides, Kai needed to visit Sid, see about his injury, and strategize with Jane about the Dragon Knights.

His dragon grumbled, *If we're cleared for sex, then we're going to fuck Jane before strategizing.*

*We'll see, dragon. The clan matters, too.*

*The knights aren't our current threat. We're safe on Stonefire. They can wait a day.*

Kai tended to agree with his beast, but he wasn't going to get his hopes up. *Let's see what Dr. Sid says first.*

Kai looked to Bram. "Anything else? I need to visit the surgery."

Amusement danced in his clan leader's eyes. "I bet you do."

Evie smacked Bram. "Don't tease him."

Bram looked down at his mate. "Why not? I've already lost the bet. I may as well make the most of it."

Kai jumped in. "What bet?"

Evie shook her head. "Not now. Go to the surgery. We'll watch Rafe until Nikki shows up."

Jane snorted at Kai's side and Rafe glared at his sister. Grinning, Jane said to her brother, "I can't help it. The thought of anyone 'watching you' is hilarious. But, on the other hand, somewhat necessary. You get into far more trouble than me."

Rafe growled. "Not now, Jane. Shut it."

Jane shrugged. "Why not? I'm sure they've looked into your past. Kai here is quite thorough in his screenings."

His female was teasing him. Kai couldn't remember the last time someone had shared a private joke with him.

His dragon spoke up. *She is unafraid of us. She is perfect. Hurry, so we can claim her properly.*

Kai hugged Jane closer to his side. Ignoring Rafe's glare, Kai looked to Bram. "We'll contact you as soon as we have a rough plan."

"Aye, I know you will. Although tomorrow is fine. Since the knights aren't an immediate threat, there's no rush."

Kai knew his clan leader was hinting about Kai fucking Jane, but he wasn't going to acknowledge it. He wasn't a prude, but he also didn't need Rafe Hartley challenging him over his sister.

It may be the twenty-first century, but he had a feeling Rafe didn't care. Meeting Jane's brother had put her sass into perspective; she'd needed it to stand up to her brother.

His dragon growled. *Stop dawdling. Go to Sid's. I want our human.*

Kai looked to Rafe. "We'll be in touch." He paused, and then added, "Do what Nikki says or next time I'll be the one to watch over you."

Jane groaned at the same time Rafe narrowed his eyes and said, "Careful, dragonman. Don't dismiss me just because I'm human."

Before Kai could reply, Jane pushed against his side. "Let's go before you two start a growling contest."

Ignoring Bram and Evie's smiles, Kai let Jane lead him out of the room.

~~~

Once they were outside, Jane smacked Kai's good side. "You were antagonizing Rafe on purpose."

"He was doing the same."

She sighed. "I think once you two get past this I'm-more-alpha-than-you stage, you might actually get along."

"You say that as if it's a bad thing."

She raised her brows. "It is, because then you'll team up against me."

The corner of Kai's mouth ticked up. "If it keeps you out of trouble, then I'm all for it."

Rolling her eyes, Jane pointed in the direction of the surgery. "Start walking. I want to make sure everything's healing as it should."

"Yes, ma'am."

After a few strides, Jane looked up at Kai. "Sorry I didn't tell you about my source monitoring the Dragon Knights. I never brought them up because nothing of importance has surfaced recently. And before you ask, there hasn't been any chatter about me. I had no idea they had a reward for my capture."

"Not even I think you're daft enough to go into the heart of dragon-hater country with a price on your head. But one day, I will know everything about you, Jane Hartley. For now, I'll let this one slide."

"Let it slide, huh?"

His look turned heated. "You can make it up to me later."

She wanted to scold him, but the desire in his eyes warmed her skin. If Sid cleared him for sex, Kai would be doing much more than giving her a look like he would devour her. No, he'd devour her slowly and make her beg.

She was both irritated and aroused by that thought.

Clearing her throat, Jane forced the images away. The last thing she needed was for Kai to scent her arousal and then walk around like a smug idiot. "I'm sure you're holding out a secret or two from me, but those will have to wait. We need to think about the knights."

Kai was quiet for a second before he asked, "Are you sure about turning in your notice to the BBC?"

Her heart squeezed, just as it had done when she'd first said it. "Yes. They've been good to me over the last decade, but I think what I want to do will be too risky."

"Are you really going to make me ask you what you have planned?"

She flashed a grin. "Maybe. I like making you ask for things, especially since you much prefer to order people around."

"If I'm not careful, you'll probably start ordering everyone around for me."

"Of course. Whenever you're sick or injured—because, let's face it, you'll be injured again—I can help fill in."

"I'm not so sure my second-in-command, Aaron, would like that. You'll have to work it out with him."

"Well, I haven't met him yet, but give me time."

Kai chuckled. "You're pretty brave, for a human."

She raised an eyebrow. "I think I'm pretty brave even for a dragon-shifter."

When all Kai did was shake his head, Jane decided to stop teasing him for a little bit. They were drawing nearer to the surgery and she wanted him to hear her idea. She hadn't told anyone, not even her brother, and she wanted to share it with Kai first.

Jane nearly faltered at that thought. She'd only known him a few days. And yet, it was true—she wanted Kai to be the first to know about her plans. He wouldn't just smile and nod. If it was a crap idea, he'd say so. And she needed that.

Moving closer to Kai, she wrapped an arm around his waist. "Back to my idea, do you still want to hear it?"

"Yes."

She laughed. "Straight to the point as always." Kai grunted and she put up a hand. "Okay, okay. I want to do a series of audio and video podcasts centering around your clan. The audio reports would be for those who don't want to be recognized and we can even alter their voices, if need be. The video podcast would focus on certain aspects of dragon-shifter life and act as an introductory guide to understanding your kind. If Melanie Hall-MacLeod gives her blessing, I'd like to use her book as a starting point. After that, the possibilities are endless, especially if I can get Lochguard to participate, too."

"You've been thinking about this for a while."

"Yes, but none of my BBC producers wanted to commit to such a long series and I didn't want to stop after only three or six episodes. I want to create something that makes the listener or watcher feel a part of the clan. And, most importantly, I wanted everyone involved to feel like they were making a difference, too."

"I would have to approve your footage."

"Of course. The last thing I want to do is endanger Stonefire, especially since it might soon be my clan."

Kai remained quiet for a second and she worried she'd assumed too much too soon. Kai had asked her to stay, but nothing formal had been arranged. Were there some sort of protocols she had to go through first?

Before she could think too much more on the subject, Kai finally answered, "Both my dragon and I like that you think of Stonefire's safety. But putting that aside, I'm not sure why you went after the dragon hunters. Your 'Better Know a Dragon-shifter Clan' idea is far better."

She noted him brushing aside her statement about Stonefire becoming her clan and decided she would bring it up later. "Are you just saying that because you want to get into my pants?"

Amusement danced in Kai's eyes. "I don't think I need to butter you up to get into your pants." He lowered his voice. "All I need to do is kiss you and you'd start rubbing against me, Janey."

Remembering the last time she'd kissed Kai sent a rush of heat through her body. In the next second, the corner of Kai's mouth ticked up and approval flashed in his eyes.

She poked his side. "Behave or I'll tell Dr. Sid that you haven't been following orders. Then you'll have to spend all of your time with Ginny."

He growled. "You wouldn't dare."

Tilting her head, Jane smiled. "Wouldn't I? As I recall, you mentioned a war. I'm just trying to win."

Kai moved behind her before she could do more than blink and wrapped his muscled arm around her waist. The heat of his chest on her back, combined with his masculine scent, made her heart beat double-time.

Kai whispered, "I want you under me more than my next breath, Jane Hartley. And I will do whatever it takes to win if it means I can feel your tight, wet pussy around my dick."

Jane's breath hitched. She wanted the same thing, not that she'd let him know that just yet.

She swallowed before she replied, "Taking me before you're cleared will definitely bring down the wrath of Dr. Sid. Keep your dick in your pants for a little while longer, Kai Sutherland. Then we'll see."

Kai nuzzled her neck and nipped it lightly. "We're a little early for my appointment and I have ideas of how we can spend our extra time."

She turned her head. "So do I. You can feed me something. I'm starving."

Kai's pupils flashed to slits and back. "Bloody fantastic. You just had to mention you were hungry. For a human, you sure know how to get my damn dragon on your side."

Grinning, Jane patted Kai's cheek. "I need to keep my strength so I can keep up with you. If I need to get your dragon on my side to do it, then I will. Speaking of which, once you're better, I want to see you shift."

Kai grunted. "You've seen me in dragon form before."

"Only from a distance. I want to scratch behind your ears and pet your snout."

"It's not like I have a choice. My dragon is all but bursting to come out."

Jane turned and Kai loosened his hold so that she could face him. "Good. I've seen my fair share of the human half of you. I need to see what the dragon half is like."

"Does that mean you're tired of me already?"

After placing a gentle kiss on his lips, she murmured, "Not even close, dragonman."

He brushed her cheek. "Right, then let's get you a cup of tea and some food. You can tell me more about your Dragon Knight idea over breakfast."

Kai dropped his arm and Jane nearly reached out to take his hand. But before she could, he took her hand in his and tugged. "Follow me."

She tried to make her face stern, but amusement danced in Kai's eyes.

She'd master his neutral expression eventually, even if it killed her. "Since I have no bloody idea where we're going, I don't have a choice."

Kai tugged once more. "Then stop fighting me and let's go. If you waste much more time, you won't get to eat for a while."

"Fine."

Kai guided her toward one of the family restaurants on Stonefire and she followed. She needed to be careful or Kai might start assuming she'd follow his lead all of the time. As soon as she could, Jane was going to ask Bram, Evie, or one of the other people she knew on Stonefire to give her a guided tour.

Kai tugged her hand again and Jane picked up her pace. "For a supposed invalid, you're walking quite fast."

He flashed a smile over his shoulder. "You're nearly as tall as me and should be able to keep up. Stop dawdling."

Jane stuck out her tongue and Kai chuckled.

Damn the dragonman and his laughs. It was almost as if he knew they helped erase her irritation.

Determined not to let him win, Jane picked up her pace. She soon had Kai trying to keep up with her.

# Reawakening the Dragon

As they kept trying to outdo each other all the way to the restaurant, Jane forgot about the dragon hunters, the Dragon Knights, and her overprotective brother. In the moment, she was just a woman trying to best a dragonman.

And she was in it to win.

# CHAPTER THIRTEEN

Kai tapped his fingers against his thigh and glanced at the clock for the tenth time. He'd been waiting for nearly fifteen minutes in the examination room and Sid had yet to check in with him.

Normally, he was a patient man. Hell, he'd been willing to wait two years for a bloody female.

But Kai didn't like Jane being in the waiting room without someone to watch over her. After all, Stonefire did have a traitor the year before. Kai didn't think there were any in the clan presently, but with the threat of Dragon Knights looming over Jane's head, he wanted to be extra careful.

His beast spoke up. *She is safe in the waiting room. Leo at reception will watch over her.*

*My fifteen-year-old sister could probably take out Leo.*

*Don't be ridiculous. All of the clan members go through at least some basic training. He could handle your sister.*

*As if that's a comfort.*

His beast sighed. *There's also an alarm button at reception. Aaron will come if it's pressed.*

Kai grunted. He couldn't think of a single reason why Aaron wasn't good enough. *Since when are you the reasonable one?*

*Because I want to shift and have Jane pet me. Only Sid can tell us when we can do that again.*

# Reawakening the Dragon

*You keep banging on about Jane petting you. Next thing you know, you'll want to take her for a flight.*

*Of course. But that can wait until after we've fucked her.*

*So, the order of things are: have Jane pet you, shift back to human to fuck her, and then back to dragon to take her for a flight.*

*It's a grand plan, if I do say so myself.*

Kai sighed. He was going to have to talk to Jane about not feeding his dragon's ego.

His beast grunted, but the door opened before his dragon could say anything. Sid walked in and shut the door behind her. She studied him a second and then spoke up. "I don't know why you look so irritated. You know we're understaffed."

"I know."

Sid walked up to him. "Your human is safe and sound in the waiting room. Fifteen or twenty minutes apart won't kill you."

"It might."

Sid searched his eyes. "Is she your new true mate?"

"No."

"But you obviously care for her, and it's more than just being protective."

He frowned. "Since when are you a bloody psychologist? Just check my injury and let me know when I can shift again."

Sid tsked. "Order me around again and I'll make you wait a day."

Kai grunted. "My dragon is impatient and wants the human. He's driving me crazy." The second he said it, Kai regretted it. "Sid—"

She put up a hand. "Don't you dare coddle me, Kai. I'm doing a job I love and helping my clan. That's enough for me. If I couldn't stand hearing people talk about their inner dragons, I wouldn't be here. End of story."

Kai didn't even know what to say to that. As much as his beast annoyed him, he couldn't imagine living without his dragon's constant chatter inside his head.

He'd never had a problem before, of not referring to his dragon in Sid's presence unless she asked a direct question about his beast. Jane was causing all sorts of changes to his life. Kai only hoped the good would outweigh the bad.

His dragon chimed in. *She is good for us, full stop.*

Sid removed his sling and not-so-gently took off his bandages. Her poking and prodding helped Kai to shove his beast into the back of his mind and focus on the situation at hand. "Well?"

Leaning back to meet his eye, Sid answered, "It's healing well. I'll take the stitches out, but you'll need to perform a set of physical therapy exercises for a few days before you can shift, let alone fly."

She fell silent and Kai growled. "Are you really going to make me ask you?"

Crossing her arms over her chest, Sid shrugged. "I have no idea what you're talking about."

Bloody female. "I want to have sex."

"With me? Sorry, Kai, but you're not my type."

"Cassidy Jackson, now is not the time to play games with me."

She raised an eyebrow. "You're using my full name. If that's supposed to scare me, it's not working."

Sid turned, put on some gloves, and carried a tray over to him. Then the bloody female went to work at taking his stitches out.

After a few seconds, he finally decided Jane was worth Sid winning this round. "When can I have sex with my human?"

Sid peered up. "Your human, huh? That was fast."

"Cassidy."

Sid went back to his injury. "Fine. You won't be able to have the wild sex fest you're dreaming of until at least tomorrow." She paused, and then added, "But if you're lying on your back, I don't see the harm. Just be careful of your arm."

Kai's dragon broke out of his mental cage. *How many more minutes? After this, we're taking our human home and stripping her.*

*You heard what the doctor said.*

*That doesn't mean we can't have a little fun before Jane rides us.*

*Keep quiet until Sid's done and I might take some of your suggestions.*

*I could take control if I wanted to.*

*Don't start this again. In all our years together, you've yet to take control of me and keep it. Not even when Maggie rejected us did you take full control for more than a few minutes at a time.*

*Yes, but this time is different. Our human wants us as much as we want her.*

Not wanting to argue any longer, Kai shoved his beast back again and watched the second hand as it ticked around the clock. Five or ten minutes was going to seem like an eternity, especially when he could have Jane naked and screaming his name in twenty.

~~~

On the flight to Stonefire, Jane had lost her mobile phone somehow, so she couldn't check her email or go on the web. The magazine collection on the table was sparse and mostly about cooking or flying techniques. Since Jane couldn't fly, nor did she like cooking, she studied her surroundings.

Apart from the young dragon-shifter male at the reception desk, Jane was alone. The furnishings were old, but sturdy. Unlike the plastic chairs of human hospitals, Stonefire had wooden ones.

Given the muscles and size of the dragon-shifters, Jane couldn't blame them.

Even something as mundane as a waiting room gave her ideas for her podcast series. She wondered what dragon-shifter medicine actually entailed. Maybe Sid would be open to an interview.

One of the doors to the side of the reception desk opened and out walked Hudson Wells, one of the dragon-shifters she'd interviewed her first time on Stonefire. In his arms was his son, Elliott.

The dragonman smiled at something his son said and it was infectious. Considering the last time Jane had interviewed him, Hudson had been grieving hard about losing his mate, Charlie. Jane was happy to see the change.

Standing up, she waved and called out, "Hudson."

Hudson looked up and smiled. "Ms. Hartley."

Jane walked over to the dragonman. "I told you before to call me Jane."

"Jane then. Are you here to interview Dr. Sid?"

She wondered how much she should divulge, but decided since Kai had been open about his claim on her, she wouldn't hold back. "No, I'm waiting for Kai."

Hudson's pupils flashed to slits and then back. "Ah, I understand now."

"I wish you all would stop it with the super-senses. It's a bit unfair."

Hudson smiled. "Hey, we need every advantage we can take."

Hudson's son interjected, "I'm hungry, Daddy. You promised."

"Right, right, you want pancakes."

# Reawakening the Dragon

The little boy nodded enthusiastically. "I got my shot and didn't cry. You said dragons always keep their promises."

"So I did." Hudson gave Jane an apologetic look. "Sorry, Jane. This one is just starting to talk with his dragon and if I don't feed him, his little beastie will cause all sorts of trouble."

"No worries. I'll be around, so if you need to talk to someone, I'm here."

Elliott's pupils flashed to slits and stayed that way. "I'm hungry. Give me food."

Hudson peered into his little boy's eyes. "Even dragons need manners. What do you say?"

The boy grunted. "Please feed me."

"Better." Hudson shifted the boy in his arms. "Bye, Jane."

Jane waved. "See you around, Hudson." She tickled the little boy's side. "And behave for your father."

All Elliott said was, "Food."

Jane laughed as Hudson and his son left. Human and dragon-shifters boys might not be all that different after all.

She turned to go back to her seat when Kai came out the same door. Before she could say anything, Kai asked, "Why were you talking with Hudson Wells?"

She shrugged. "He's had a rough time. I just wanted to say hello."

Kai grunted. "But he's unattached."

Jane sighed. "Please tell me you're not going to order me not to talk to unattached men."

His pupils were slitted. "I'm thinking about it."

"Don't be daft. How about you tell me what Sid said instead? I see the sling is gone. That's a good sign."

Kai reached out his good arm and drew Jane against his body. "I can't have wild sex until tomorrow."

Jane raised an eyebrow. "I sense a 'but.'"

He leaned down and whispered into her ear. "But it's fine if I lay on my back and you ride me."

Despite her heart hammering in her chest, Jane couldn't help but say, "I've always wanted to ride a dragon-shifter."

Kai nipped her ear. "I am the only one you'll be riding, Janey." He nuzzled her cheek. "But first I'm going to strip you and make you come with my tongue."

Considering what Kai had done with his fingers, his words shot straight between her legs and her clit throbbed in anticipation. "Unless you're going to do that in full view of that bloke at reception, I think we should go."

"So my rather tall human is impatient. I'd say you're as much dragon-shifter as me."

Jane took his chin and turned his head until she could look into Kai's blue eyes. "Who wouldn't want to sleep with a clever, sexy man?"

Kai growled. "We have about five minutes before my dragon throws a fit and pushes to take you, no matter if we're in public or not. Start walking, human."

"Again with the ordering?"

His looked turned heated. "Oh, I think when you're naked and at my mercy, you won't mind it so much."

The thought of what Kai might do to her when she was naked sent a little thrill through her body. "You'd better live up to the hype, dragonman."

Kai gripped her backside possessively. "We can argue later." He slapped her arse. "Start walking."

He spun her around and kept a grip on her waist.

As her dragonman picked up his pace, Jane tried her best to keep up. Knowing Kai, he might toss her over his shoulder and not care about his injury.

And while she rather liked the idea of Kai whisking her off to some secret location and fucking her senseless, she didn't want to hurt him.

Half-running, Jane followed Kai's lead. Each step only made her heart beat faster and her skin grow warmer. Rumors said sex with a dragonman would change a woman's life forever.

Jane was ready to find out if it was merely a rumor or the truth.

# CHAPTER FOURTEEN

The instant after Kai shut the door to his cottage, he pulled Jane close and kissed her.

Stroking the inside of her mouth, he reveled in her taste, yet it wasn't enough. Kai wanted to feel Jane's soft, naked skin against his.

His dragon growled. *Now. I want her.*

For once, he agreed with his dragon.

Breaking the kiss, Kai lightly traced his way across her cheek with his lips until he reached her ear. He nibbled and licked a few times before he whispered, "Go upstairs, strip, and wait for me on my bed."

Jane pushed against his chest and he leaned back until he met her eyes. "Aren't you coming?"

"Not yet, Janey." He moved his hand to her breast and pinched her already hard nipple. "I have a surprise for you. But to give it to you, I need you to be naked."

She studied him and Kai tugged her nipple again. Jane let out a sound that wasn't quite a moan, and he smiled.

"So, you want to play that game, huh?" Jane asked.

His human laid a hand on his chest, and slowly stroked down his abdomen until she stopped at his waistband. As her light touch danced across his skin, he held his breath. Humans were rarely so bold.

# REAWAKENING THE DRAGON

He loved that Jane was different.

Undoing the button of his trousers, she moved her hand to just below the band of his boxers. His beast growled. *Yes, yes. Just a little more.*

Before Kai could reply, Jane took his dick in hand and squeezed lightly. Pleasure mixed with heat rushed through Kai's body and he groaned. "Janey."

Her voice was husky as she replied, "Unless your surprise is your cock tied in a bow, save it for later."

His dragon chimed in. *Just fuck her now. We can mete out our payback later.*

*No. I want her first time with me to erase any memory she has of other males. It must be special.*

Jane stroked up his dick and back down. Unable to concentrate enough to talk with both his beast and Jane, he shoved his dragon away and whispered, "No. Go upstairs, strip, and wait for me."

Running a finger up his cock, Jane traced circles on the tip. Each light caress against his sensitive skin chipped at his resolve.

His human was a bloody minx.

Taking a deep breath, Kai mustered every ounce of self-control he possessed and said, "Upstairs, Jane. This is your last chance; otherwise, I'll toss you over my shoulder and tie you to the bed."

The corner of her mouth ticked up. "Is that supposed to be a threat?"

*Bloody hell.* Jane was bolder than he'd imagined. She really was everything he wanted in a female. "It will be if I tie you and tease you for hours before I let you come."

"As much as I'd like to see you try, I want you too much to wait that long." Jane slowly removed her hand from his boxers, lightly scratching his cock as she went.

Kai nearly grabbed her wrist to guide her back, but remembered why he wanted to make their first time memorable, so he clenched his fingers instead.

Placing a hand on her hip, Jane tilted her head. "Your surprise had better be worth it, Kai. Otherwise, you're going to owe me one."

Unclenching his fingers, he reached out and cupped Jane's breast. As he squeezed and rubbed his palm against her hard nipple, he stated, "Oh, believe me. It'll be worth it." He squeezed her breast one more time. "Go, Janey. Unless you don't want to come harder than you ever have in your life."

The scent of Jane's arousal grew stronger. His human was nice and wet for him already.

Mischief mixed with heat danced in Jane's eyes. "I'll hold you to that. If you deliver, I might make you come harder than you ever have before too."

His beast snarled. *Stop talking and hurry up. I want her.*

Kai released his grip on her breast and stepped back. "Then get going. If you're not naked, then after I tie you up, I might have to rest some more before I feel up to sex."

Jane rolled her eyes. "As if you could hold back." Kai opened his mouth, but she beat him to it. "Just don't take too long. If you do, then I might just have to take care of myself."

With a smile, Jane turned and swayed her hips. Kai should say something to get in the last word, but he was entranced by his human's full arse.

His dragon spoke up again. *It will be hard not to take her from behind today.*

*I agree, dragon, I agree.*

As soon as Jane ascended the stairs, Kai shook his head to break the spell and headed into the kitchen. He needed to retrieve something before he could give Jane her surprise and finally claim his human completely.

~~~

Jane opened the door to Kai's bedroom. It was the first time she'd stepped foot inside it, but it was bare like her room, with just a bed, nightstand, clock, and lamp. Everything seemed bare in Kai's life.

Well, she hoped to change that.

Aware that Kai could enter at any moment, Jane stripped off her top and jeans. Despite her earlier bravado downstairs, she hesitated to shuck her bra and panties. It'd been a few years since a man had seen her completely naked.

But then she remembered it was Kai coming for her. She could have overgrown toenails and unshaven armpits and he'd still want her.

Tossing her bra and panties to the side, she crawled onto the bed.

While she was following Kai's orders, he'd left them vague. She would add her own spin to it.

Jane leaned against the headboard and gripped her elbows over her head, making her small breasts more prominent. Then she lay her feet flat on the bed and spread her legs wide.

For a split second, she felt silly. But then she pushed the feeling aside. In this position, she might be able to get Kai to drop his jaw again.

Her heart rate kicked up with each second that passed and her pussy throbbed. At this rate, Kai would merely have to brush her clit and she'd come.

Before she could think of a way to tone down her arousal so she could last longer, she heard footsteps echoing down the hallway. Two seconds later, Kai opened the door. The sight of him still in his trousers sent a rush of disappointment through her. She wanted to see all of him.

Kai stood in the doorway and stared at her exposed pussy. His gaze sent a rush of wetness between her thighs and his pupils turned to slits for a few seconds before changing back. His gaze moved up to her breasts. Even across the room, his attentions made her nipples harder.

When he finally met her eyes, the heat and yearning in his made her stomach flip.

Kai murmured, "You listened. That means I can reward you."

"You could reward me by taking off your clothes."

The corner of Kai's mouth ticked up. "Impatient, aren't you?"

"Mostly when it comes to you." Kai moved until he was standing at the foot of the bed. It was only then that she noticed his good arm was behind his back. "Where's my surprise?"

"Close your eyes first."

She gave him a skeptical look. "I'm not sure I should do that."

"Don't you trust me?"

She should say no and tell him it took time. Yet as she stared into his light blue eyes, she couldn't make herself say those words. Kai had protected her back in the alley in Gateshead, even with the threat of being shot. He'd also stood up to her brother as well as supported her plan to take her future into her own hands.

Despite every reason why she shouldn't, she trusted him.

Taking a deep breath, she closed her eyes and listened as Kai moved onto the bed. She could feel the heat of his body between her thighs, but he still hadn't touched her. She was about to ask him to hurry up when something cold and wet brushed across her nipple and she shivered.

Kai's husky voice filled her ears. "How does that feel? And don't just say it's bloody cold."

"But it is."

Something cold brushed across her other nipple and a small moan escaped her lips. Kai's voice replied, "Do you want more?"

She didn't hesitate. "Yes."

The coldness, which she figured was an ice cube, trailed down her belly before moving to her inner thighs. As the coolness inched closer to her pussy, Jane opened her legs wider. Kai chuckled. "Tell me what you want, Janey."

She could shoot off a barb, but her body was on fire. She wanted more of Kai's touch. Spreading her legs even further, she murmured, "Touch me here."

Kai remained silent. Five seconds passed, and then ten. Finally the cold, wet object touched her swollen flesh and she drew in a breath.

Her dragonman then moved it up to just above her clit and went down the other side. "Kai."

"Hm? What do you want, my tall human?"

Jane's clit throbbed so hard she nearly whimpered. "Touch me. I want to feel your heat."

The bed shifted under her and she was tempted to open her eyes. Kai's voice ordered, "Keep your eyes closed."

Hoping her silence would finally persuade him to give her an orgasm, Jane kept her eyelids firmly shut.

Her heart thundered in her ears as she waited. Never in her life had a man been able to draw out this kind of anticipation. She couldn't wait to see what Kai came up with once he was healed.

Something hot, wet, and soft thrust into her pussy and Jane leaned her head back. His tongue swirled inside before licking her slit and tracing the skin around her clit in slow circles.

He repeated the actions of plunging, licking, and tracing, but he never touched her sensitive bundle of nerves. "Kai."

Even to her own ears his name sounded like a plea.

Kai didn't move from lapping her pussy, but the ice cube brushed against her clit and she moaned. The contrast of Kai's heat with the ice was a strange sensation; even the icy caress set her skin on fire. She had always wondered what alternating the heat and cold would feel like.

However, she lost her train of thought as Kai removed the ice and flicked his tongue against her clit. His heat was almost burning after the coolness of the ice. Each pass of his wet flesh against hers made her breasts ache and the pressure build.

She opened her mouth to ask for more when Kai slowed his movements on her clit. She cried out in frustration, but then he traced the lips of her pussy with the ice cube and she bucked her hips. "Kai."

In response, her dragonman stopped his attentions and brushed her clit again with the ice. The sudden cold brought her that much closer to the edge. However, she wanted, no needed Kai's mouth on her again.

Afraid he might pull away completely and leave her panting for more, the bastard, she threaded her fingers through his hair. She wasn't letting him up until he made her come.

Kai sucked her clit deeper and bit gently. Jane dug her fingernails into her dragonman's scalp and he nibbled some more.

She was close.

Pressing against his head, she ordered him to finish it. Kai growled as he thrust two fingers into her pussy. He bit her clit hard and she cried out as pleasure shot through her body. With each spasm she dug her nails into Kai's scalp a little more.

When she finally came down from her high, Kai removed his fingers and his head lifted from between her legs. He murmured, "Look at me."

Jane opened her eyes to see Kai's slitted pupils and his eyes full of desire. "Hi, dragonman."

He growled. "Not 'hi.' I want a thank you."

She smiled. "Whatever for?"

Kai brushed against her sensitive clit and Jane cried out. Kai grunted. "For devouring you with my mouth."

"Maybe later."

She noticed how his pupils remained slitted as he answered, "When I'm well, you have payback coming."

"I look forward to it." Jane sat up and ran her hand down Kai's chest. "But will it be from man or dragon?"

Kai trapped her hand with his. "Both."

Her heart skipped a beat at the thought of his beast being unleashed. According to rumors, a dragon in charge would not only be rough, but had a whole hell of a lot more stamina than the human half.

Just imagining a long, rough encounter made her ache between her legs.

Kai's nostrils flared. "What are you thinking about?"

"Your cock."

"That's only part of the truth."

She traced Kai's nipple with her free hand. "Do you want to keep talking or do you want me to ride your dick like there's no tomorrow?"

He captured her other hand and tugged her closer. "You will tell me every little detail later." He leaned forward and took her bottom lip between his teeth before releasing it. "For now, I want to feel your tight pussy gripping my dick as you scream my name."

Jane leaned forward until her nipples brushed Kai's chest. "I never thought I'd have to tell you this, but you need to stop talking." She moved back to her heels, but before she could say anything else, Kai leaned forward and sucked her nipple deep.

As he caressed her tight bud, Jane's pussy pulsed, demanding more. With great effort, Jane placed a hand on Kai's head and pushed back. He released her nipple with a pop.

She shivered at the heat in his eyes, but stayed strong. She needed much more than his mouth. Only his cock could ease the pounding between her legs.

Jane motioned toward the bed with her head. "On your back, Kai, or I leave the room."

~~~

Kai had temporarily allowed his dragon to take charge, but the instant Jane ordered him on his back, Kai pushed his way to the front of his mind again. *It's my turn, dragon.*

*I wasn't done.*

*Too bad. The first fuck is mine.*

Before his beast could reply, Kai tossed him into a mental prison. Running his hand up and down Jane's inner thighs, he replied, "I can scent how much you want me, Janey. Your words are nothing but an empty threat.

She raised her brows. "Are they now?"

She moved toward the edge of the bed. With a growl, Kai reached out and pulled Jane up against his body. The feel of her naked skin flush against his made him want to claim her all the more. "I don't think so, human. Kiss me first, Janey, and I'll do what you say."

"I'm not sure what to think of that order."

Kai took a possessive hold of her backside. "Just bloody kiss me, woman."

Jane shook her head. "You're so bossy and demanding."

Kai closed the distance between his lips and Jane's, leaving only an inch of space. "But you like it."

Before she could reply, Kai took her mouth.

Jane cried out in a mixture of surprise and desire. He took advantage by plunging his tongue into her hot, sweet mouth.

His human groaned as she met him stroke for stroke, their teeth clashing in the process. He would never get enough of his female's taste.

His dragon roared inside his head as his beast clawed against his prison. If Kai didn't get inside Jane soon, his beast might manage to break free and take control. And he wasn't having it.

Breaking the kiss, Jane's breath was hot against his lips when he said, "Now, you can have me."

He released Jane and carefully laid down on his back. With Jane's breasts jutting out over him, he reached out and pinched her nipple. "I'm waiting."

Jane narrowed her eyes for a split second before they filled with mischief. "No matter what I do, keep your hands on the bed until I say so."

He growled, "Don't play games with me right now, Jane. My dragon is close to breaking free."

"Then contain him."

"And if I don't?"

She straddled his thighs and placed her hands on his hips. "Then your dragon will be the first to have me."

"No fucking way that's happening."

"Good." She moved a hand to his balls and cupped him. "Are you ready?"

As she massaged him, it took everything he had to concentrate. "Jane, I've been waiting my whole life for you. I'm more than ready."

Something unreadable flashed in Jane's eyes, but it was gone in the next second. "Then let's test your self-control."

In the next heartbeat, Jane's hot mouth engulfed his cock.

He groaned as he clutched the sheets in his fingers. Not touching his human was going to be the most difficult test of his life.

~~~

Taking Kai into her mouth was the distraction she needed. All of her attention was focused on his long, thick length.

Since she couldn't take all of him and Jane didn't know the first thing about tricks to swallow and draw him deeper, she moved her hand from his balls to the base of cock. Squeezing tightly, she moved up and then down, twirling her tongue along the way. When she finally licked his tip, she tasted his saltiness.

She groaned and Kai bucked his hips slightly. Jane looked up to meet Kai's eyes as she licked down his cock.

Even though his eyes were flashing, Kai never made a sound.

Bloody stubborn dragonman.

She squeezed her fingers tighter as she moved. When she lightly scraped his dick with her teeth, Kai finally groaned.

The second he did, she trailed her tongue up his cock and released him with a long, slow lick. Sitting up, she took in Kai's clenched hands in the bed sheets before meeting his flashing eyes. The hunger in them made her shiver.

# Reawakening the Dragon

Kai snarled, "Why did you stop?"

A stranger might be afraid of the frustration in Kai's voice, but she knew he would never hurt her.

Jane tilted her head. "I'm not ready for you to come just yet. I have more teasing to do."

He clutched the sheets tighter. "You're testing my patience, Jane."

"Well, it's a good thing you can't take control because of the doctor's orders." She rubbed up and down Kai's thighs, loving the roughness of his leg hair under her palms. "Come to think of it, I'll save some of my teasing for when you're well. It'll be that much sweeter." Kai narrowed his eyes, but Jane spoke again before he could. "But before I can ride you, I need a condom."

Kai didn't so much as hesitate and nodded toward the nightstand at his bed.

Opening the drawer, she took one out and rolled it slowly down his long length. She loved that he was prepared and didn't try to dissuade her from using one with an idiotic excuse. She'd learned over the last few months just how much dragon-shifters treasured children, but deep in her gut, she knew Kai wouldn't press her until she was ready.

Pushing aside her serious thoughts, she finished with a flourish and crawled up Kai's body until she lay on top of him, with his cock pressing against her stomach. Tracing his brow, she murmured, "Are you ready for me, dragonman?"

"Almost. Let me touch you with my hands."

Bopping his nose with her finger, she smiled. "I kind of like being temporarily in control."

"Jane."

She laughed. "I know how hard it must be for you." She winked. "In more ways than one."

"Janey."

After pressing a gentle kiss to his lips, she answered, "Touch me, Kai, and set me on fire."

Kai's large, rough hands moved to her arse and squeezed. "When I'm cleared, I'm going to enjoy pounding into you from behind and feeling this soft arse against me."

"Me, too. So don't do anything to piss me off."

"Idle threats, Jane."

She opened her mouth, but Kai moved a hand to her head and brought her lips to his. As he explored her mouth, his fingers found her pussy. He teased her opening, making her wetter.

Desperate for more than a whisper of touch, Jane moved with him and managed to take his fingers deeper.

Kai pulled away and ordered, "Fuck me, Jane. I want you. Now."

"So bossy."

He slapped her arse in response and the slight sting shot straight between her legs.

Deciding her dragonman had enough, Jane slowly rose up and positioned herself above Kai's cock. Never breaking eye contact, she lowered herself inch by inch until he was in to the hilt.

*Bloody hell.* Kai was big.

Her dragonman growled as he rubbed her backside in slow circles. "So tight and wet, and for me. It will always be for me, Jane. Understand?"

"We'll see."

He grabbed her hips. "You're mine."

The dominance and truth in Kai's words squeezed her heart. No man had ever wanted her to this degree before.

She moved forward and back, and Kai growled some more. Stilling for a second, Jane whispered, "More like you're mine."

# Reawakening the Dragon

Kai's eyes flashed and he guided her hips. "Then ride me, Jane. I want you to claim what's yours."

Her heart skipped a beat at his words. But Jane was done talking for the moment. It was time for action.

Moving her hips, Jane created a steady pace. Kai's dick reached deep and the delicious fullness created friction that hit her in all the right places.

Kai guided her hips and moved faster, pulling her forward and slamming her back. Only because she had her hands on his chest did she keep upright.

Even as the sound of flesh slapping against flesh mixed with her moans, Kai never broke eye contact. The heat of his blue eyes combined with their flashing pupils made her wonder what it would feel like to be at Kai's mercy when he was healthy and whole.

Then Kai smacked her backside and kept her hips forward. She tried moving, but his grip was like steel.

His voice was husky as ordered, "Don't think about anything else but this."

He slammed her down in one quick motioned and Jane cried out. "Kai."

"My human likes it rough."

Kai repeated his actions, but this time raised his hips at the last moment. Pleasure flashed in her eyes. "You're going to kill me."

He kept her on top of him and rotated his lower body. His hard dick hit her G-spot and Jane clutched the hairs on Kai's chest.

He murmured, "Just wait, Janey. This is me holding back."

After slapping her arse, he roamed up her side to her breasts. Tugging one of her nipples, he murmured, "Move."

She should argue about how it was her turn to be in control, but Jane decided to just fuck it. She was close, so she moved her hips.

As she increased her pace, Kai continued to roll and pinch her nipple. Just the one, and her other ached for his touch. Kai slapped her bum again and then moved his other hand to her lonely breast. As he lightly twisted both nipples at the same time, Jane lowered her head.

Kai dropped his hands and she cried out, "Don't stop."

"Look at me."

Slowly, she raised her head. The second she met his gaze, Kai lightly brushed her clit. "I want you to come for me, Janey."

She opened her mouth to tell him he couldn't just order for it to happen, but then he tweaked her sensitive bundle of nerves. When he did it again, lights flashed across her eyes as her orgasm hit her hard.

When her pussy gripped and released Kai's dick, he moved his hands to her hips again and moved her forward and back. "You're mine, Janey." He claimed her with a hard piston. "Don't ever forget that." And again. "Mine."

He increased the tempo. Each long, hard thrust increased her pleasure to the point it was nearly too much. A mixture of pleasure and pain, Jane barely noticed when Kai cried out and stilled.

Eventually, Kai moved his hands from her hips to her back and pressed down gently. Too boneless to protest, Jane curled on top of Kai's chest and he engulfed her in his strong arms.

The sound of his heartbeat combined with his masculine scent filling her nose relaxed her even further.

For whatever reason, laying in Kai's arms made her feel safe and cared for. It was almost as if it was where she had always belonged.

# REAWAKENING THE DRAGON

An image of her waking up in the arms of her dragonman when she was old and gray popped into her head. Given it had only been a few days, the thought should terrify her. Yet as she snuggled into his chest, Jane thought it might not be a bad thing.

True, there were still issues between them, especially when it came to ensuring Kai was over his true mate. But if they could work them out, she might've found a strong man who wasn't afraid to stand up to her.

In other words, Jane might have found her perfect match.

~~~

Kai laid his cheek on the top of Jane's head and breathed in her scent. The combination of her long body on top of his, and the heat of her pussy around his dick relaxed him in a way he hadn't felt since before meeting Maggie.

There might not be a frenzy, but he didn't care. His dragon's instinct had been wrong eleven years ago. Jane would be his.

His beast's sleepy voice filled his mind. *I can't control the frenzy, either. Don't blame me. Besides, who cares? We have Jane.*

Stroking the soft and slightly damp skin of her back, Kai answered, *It's a bit soon to have her, if we can ever have her.*

*If we lose her, it will be your fault.*

*Just shut it and go to sleep.*

*And miss seeing Jane's flushed face again? I don't think so.*

*Then just be quiet.*

With a harrumph, his dragon faded into the back of his mind.

Kai had never been chatty, but for once, he wished he were. He wanted to know everything about his human, but didn't have the foggiest idea of how to ask her without issuing an order.

211

His dragon snorted, but thankfully remained silent afterward.

Content to stroke up and down Jane's back, several minutes passed until Jane's voice filled the room. "I do care about the dragon-shifters, you know." She looked up. "And not just because you're good in bed."

"Good, am I?"

She playfully slapped his chest. "I'm trying to work up the nerve to tell you something about my past and you want me to feed your ego."

Both man and beast perked up. "You can tell me anything, Janey. I'm pretty good at keeping secrets."

She smiled and rubbed her hand back and forth across his pecs. "Yes, but only because you utter the bare minimum."

Moving his hand to her bum, he squeezed. "Except for you. I don't know if it's your years of being a reporter or your pretty eyes, but I like talking with you."

She snorted. "You don't have to sound as if that's a bad thing."

Giving her backside a light tap, he asked, "What were you going to tell me?"

Jane looked back to his chest and traced circles with her forefinger. It was the first time she'd shown any lack of confidence and he didn't like it. "Jane, tell me."

She met his eyes once more. "Again with the orders." Kai merely raised his brows and she sighed. "Since I have a feeling you won't feed me again until I tell you, I should just spit it out."

Kai remained silent despite his dragon pacing back and forth in his mind, concerned about feeding their human. *If she's hungry, we should find food.*

*She'll last a little bit longer. Aren't you curious about her secret?*

His beast paused and finally replied, *I do like secrets.*

212

# Reawakening the Dragon

*Good. Then hush.*

Kai's silence was finally rewarded when Jane spoke again. "It was my first exciting assignment. After a few years of reporting on things such as dangerous weeds for children or senior citizen art shows, I was more than ready to investigate an arson. My boss at the time said it was a test—if I could handle the story, I would move up from local inconveniences and events to crime.

"Back then, I thought crime was where I wanted to be, so I dug in and went to work." Jane laid her head on her hands and continued, "I did what I would do with any story and reached out to my police contacts, interviewed witnesses, and eventually discovered the two men suspected of the crime as well as a third person of interest.

"I tracked down the person of interest first. He was determined to clear his name and so he agreed to do an interview.

"Fast forward two days and my story was in the newspaper. The story did well and my boss promoted me. It should've been a fantastic day."

Kai's voice was quiet when he asked, "So what went wrong?"

Jane closed her eyes a second and then opened them again. "While everything the suspect, Tom Smith, had told me was true, I didn't provide the whole context."

"How did that slip past your editors? Or were you working for a tabloid?"

Jane shook her head. "It wasn't a tabloid, but it was a smaller newspaper with a limited number of staff. Our fact checkers were overworked and some things slipped through from time to time. And my story was one of them."

He rubbed Jane's lower back. "What exactly did you say and what happened as a result?"

"Tom had told me about how he picked up his two friends from the nightclub and drove them to a local train station to catch the last southbound train for the night. Since they were students at the University of Manchester with him, he just assumed they were going home for the break and thought nothing of it. He had no idea his friends had just committed arson."

Kai interjected, "But arson itself isn't that bad of a crime, compared to others."

"That's true, but two of the injured died the next day and it became a homicide case."

"Right, so what did you leave out and why does it still linger with you?"

Her brows furrowed. "How did you know that?"

"Jane, it's my job to notice changes in behavior. Ever since you got the idea to tell me about this story, you've lost most of your confidence. That tells me something happened and it left a lasting impression on you. So tell me what it is."

When she didn't even try to argue back, Kai knew he was right. "Well, I mentioned Tom knowing the suspects and driving them to the train station. However, I didn't quite mention that he had no idea what was going on. My conscience ate at me and I forced a correction two days later. But by then, the damage had been done. Everyone accused Tom of being a part of the crime. He lost his part-time job and eventually dropped out of uni. He couldn't take the stares and accusations."

Kai frowned. "No one bothered to read the retraction, I take it. But the bigger question is whether he ever was convicted or not."

"Tom was deemed not guilty and cleared of any charges. However, it was all because of me that Tom's life went off track. I tried to hunt him down, talk to his employer, and make things right. But while I was trying to do that, Tom committed suicide."

"Jane."

Jane rolled off him and sat up. Hugging her chest, she continued, "It took me years to get past that, but I vowed that I would never misdirect the public again. With my new work ethic, I switched jobs and worked on fluff pieces again. When my next shot came, I took it. But never again did I not disclose the full truth and distort the narrative to fit my goals."

Kai wanted to hug his human close, but sensed Jane didn't want it quite yet. "That's why you were so upset when I accused you of using the dragon-shifters only to further your career and that you didn't give a shit."

She bobbed her head. "Helping the dragon-shifters was risky, but I knew I could help make a difference. Telling the truth would do all dragon-shifters good. In some small way, I thought it might help make up for ruining someone else's life."

Kai sat up slowly and reached out a hand to touch her bicep. "You have helped."

"Not nearly enough."

He grunted. "I agree. You need to do more."

Jane unfolded her arms and leaned forward. "If you're ordering me to work harder, that's not what I need right now."

"Wrong. It's exactly what you need." Kai cupped Jane's cheek firmly and leaned closer. "I think your podcast idea from earlier is brilliant and only you can pull it off." He pressed his forehead against Jane's. "So you'd better stick around long enough to see it through."

Jane raised an eyebrow. "So you can make those decisions now, huh, instead of Bram about who gets to stay or not?"

He shrugged his good shoulder, knowing it might stir her fire even more. He'd do anything to keep her from doubting herself again. "If I recommend you, then Bram won't think twice about letting you stay."

There was a question in Jane's eyes. Instead of asking it, she scooted over to Kai and leaned against his chest. "We'll see. I think my first real test will be luring the Dragon Knights to a specific location so you can deal with them. The combined Lochguard and DDA attack last month helped to thin out their numbers, but one more major takedown should do it. At least, in the UK. I wish there was a way to help the other clans around the world, too."

He laid his head on top of Jane's. "Clans are territorial. Hell, I can't remember the last time we even talked with any of the clans on the Continent, let alone America."

"That's going to change, I think."

He snorted. "Oh, really? Are you a psychic now, too?"

She pulled back and looked up at him. "I would almost think you're teasing me."

The corner of his mouth ticked up. "Kai Sutherland doesn't have a sense of humor. That's what everyone says."

"I think he does. It's just a bit rusty."

She tickled his good side and a bark of laughter escaped before he could stop it. Jane removed her hand and grinned. "That laugh sounded pretty rusty, too. I'm going to have to coax it out of you some more."

"I have a better idea."

He flipped Jane onto her back and tickled her side. As her laughter rang out, he couldn't help smiling.

Then she kicked him in the balls and pain shot through his body. "Bloody hell, woman, are you trying to make me a eunuch?"

Jane's eyes were bright and she put on a look of fake innocence. "I can't control my legs when you tickle me. It's your own fault."

Ignoring the dull pain in his balls, Kai removed his condom, tossed it aside, and then laid on top of Jane. "Then we'll just have to make sure you're restrained."

"Don't you dare, Kai."

As he tickled her again, he enjoyed the feel of her body wiggling under his. Only because his dick was still soft from Jane's kick did he not put on another condom and take her again.

Instead, he switched to caressing her side and nibbling her neck. His female started to relax and he murmured, "You're going to ride me again as an apology, Jane. But first, I'm going to make you come again."

"Kai, you just can't—"

He shut her up with a kiss. Jane melted as he devoured the inside of her mouth. Raising his hips, she moved her legs to wrap around his waist.

The time for talking was over. Kai was ready to play.

# CHAPTER FIFTEEN

Ten days later, Jane stood on the edge of one of the dragon landing areas and watched as her dragonman performed a series of dives, twirls, and escape maneuvers in the air. Bram, Dr. Sid, and Aaron, Kai's second-in-command, were at her side.

To Jane, Kai looked to be in full fighting-force again. But she wasn't a dragon-shifter, so she glanced at Bram and Sid. Their faces were unreadable as always, so she looked to Aaron.

While she was still getting to know the dragonman, Aaron Caruso was one of the more approachable clan members she'd met so far. He always had a smile and liked to tease everyone. Of course, there had to be more to him than he allowed Jane to see.

Still, Kai trusted Aaron despite the fact the dragonman had only recently returned from living abroad with his mother for a few years. If Kai trusted him, then so would she.

Before she could ask her question, Aaron looked over at her and raised his brows. "Is it killing you yet, not knowing whether he's cleared to fly again for missions?"

Jane frowned. "What do you think?"

Aaron grinned. "I think you can wonder a bit longer."

Bram grunted. "Aaron, what do you think will happen if I tell Kai you're flirting with his female?"

Aaron looked innocent. "What are you talking about? I would never do that."

# Reawakening the Dragon

Bram murmured, "Remind me to strangle my cousin for bringing you back from Italy. You should've stayed there."

Aaron shrugged. "Mum said she missed the rain. Not that I understand how that's possible."

Jane knew their stay in Italy had had something to do with Aaron's mother, but she hadn't found out what it was just yet.

Still, her curiosity about Aaron would have to wait. Jane spoke up. "How much longer are we going to watch Kai?"

Sid answered, "I need to test his stamina. So probably another twenty minutes."

Jane resisted a sigh. She had a million things to do for both her and Kai's plan for the Dragon Knights as well as for her podcast pitch scheduled next week with Bram, Evie, and Melanie.

Yet as she watched Kai's golden dragon move through the sky, she knew her place was here, supporting him. Her tasks could wait twenty minutes. She would never be able to concentrate if she walked away anyway.

She was about to ask another question when Nikki jogged up to where they were standing. The dragonwoman wasn't even breathing hard as she said, "Sorry I'm late. The human male was being a pain in my arse again."

Bram glanced to Nikki. "Regardless of his arsehole status, how is Rafe's monitoring going?"

Nikki shrugged. "Same as before. The former Carlisle-based hunters have settled near Birmingham. Rafe still thinks it's partly so the hunters can focus on both our clan and Skyhunter's without stretching their resources too thin."

Bram shook his head. "I would try to warn the southern clan, but Skyhunter is unstable right now. Until there's a new clan leader, I don't think they'll listen to anything I have to say, let alone work with us against a common enemy."

Nikki nodded. "I know. But at least we're aware of their general location. Rafe's working on a more precise set of coordinates. His gut says they've split into two or three camps."

Kai dove down toward them and only pulled up when he was fifteen feet from the ground. The whoosh of the wind sent Jane's hair every which way. Once Kai was back in the air, Bram stated, "We still have time to find out more information. Rafe, Finn, and I have expanded our reach via our contacts. If there is even a whisper of trouble, I'll know about it."

Aaron answered, "Add in the extra security—both in terms of dragonman- and woman-power and security alarms and cameras—and it's going to be bloody difficult for anyone to slip through like when they took Evie and little Murray."

Bram met Aaron's gaze. "Let's hope so. I'm not about to be too cocky. There's always someone worming their way into one clan or another. Lochguard has the additional threat of clan deserters. If Finn needs our help, he has it."

Aaron grunted. "I still need to meet the Scottish bastard."

"He has a pregnant mate and is trying to heal the divide in his clan. He has better things to do than challenge you to who can out-alpha and out-charm each other." Bram looked up to Kai in the air. "For now, I want to take care of the easier threat—the Dragon Knights."

Sid spoke up. "I'm not going to rush this, Bram. I need to test Kai's limits or it could cost Kai his life."

"No one's rushing you, Sid. I just hope he's ready," Bram murmured.

Every one fell silent as they watched the huge golden dragon in the sky test out his wings.

~~~

# Reawakening the Dragon

Kai stretched his wings and beat them faster until he nearly reached the clouds. Then he dove back down and twirled off to the side.

Normally, he loved flying more than anything. But he had yet to take Jane up into the air. If he was cleared, he would find a time as soon as possible to bring her.

His dragon spoke up. *We're fine. Not tired, our muscles don't hurt. I don't know why Sid makes such a fuss.*

*It's her job to make a fuss. How many times have we had to pester younger Protectors until they admit the full truth of their injuries?*

*Maybe. But we're different. If we lie, then we could put the whole clan in danger.*

*Just a little longer. Think of Jane. She's watching us and I know you want to impress her.*

*Jane. Yes, she must see how skilled we are.*

As his beast concentrated on impressing their female, it gave Kai time to remember the way she looked when she woke up with her hair mussed and her eyes heavy with sleep. Or, how her lips parted when she came before screaming his name.

But his favorite was when fire flashed in her eyes as she argued with him.

The past week and a half had been a blur of planning, talking, and fucking. He'd told his female more about his mother and little sister, Delia, than anyone else alive. He knew she wanted to meet them, but Jane hadn't pressed the issue yet.

She would eventually. Family was important to Jane and she thought he should visit his mum and Delia more often.

His dragon pulled them up from another roll maneuver just before they would hit one of the mountains. Kai grunted. *That was close. You're acting like a reckless teenager.*

*The difference is that I know what I'm doing.*

221

His beast had just started to ascend when Bram gave the signal for Kai to land.

Even as his dragon began their descent, he grumbled, *I have so many more moves to show Jane.*

*We have plenty of time for that later.*

*She still hasn't said if she's staying or not.*

*Jane wants to prove herself first. Give it time.*

His beast growled. *I don't want to risk losing her.*

Kai paused and then replied, *I don't, either. But she needs to do this. Be patient.*

With a huff, his dragon concentrated on slowing down their speed and gently landing on the ground. As soon as his wings stopped beating, Jane raced straight for him.

She stopped just in front of him and raised her brows. "Well? Aren't you going to give me a dragon cuddle?"

Only because dragons couldn't roll their eyes did Kai not do it.

Still, he lowered his head and Jane hugged his snout as he wrapped his tail gently around his human.

His dragon chimed in. *I love dragon cuddles.*

*You would think she'd choose a different name.*

*Why? It's to the point.*

*Because it's "cute" and not very dragon-like.*

*I'm the dragon half and I say it is dragon-like. We should make it an official term*

Thankfully, Jane lifted her head and patted his snout, which shut up his beast. She demanded, "That wasn't so hard, was it?" He huffed and her hair blew out behind her. Jane grinned. "I'm going to interpret that as you want another one."

She had just hugged his snout again when Bram's amused voice filled the clearing. "As much as I love watching Kai give you dragon cuddles, we need him to shift back."

# REAWAKENING THE DRAGON

Jane kept her hand on his snout but turned her body toward Bram's. "Tell Sid and Nikki to look the other way."

Bram was trying hard not to smile. Kai's dragon chimed in. *She is possessive and loves to give cuddles. There is no way I'm letting her go.*

Nikki's voice rang out, and it sounded as if she were trying not to laugh. "We've turned around, Jane."

Jane nodded and looked back to Kai. "Now you can shift."

He grunted. Sometimes it was hard to be in dragon form and not be able to talk.

Once Jane was at a safe distance, Kai imagined his talons shrinking into hands and feet, his tail merging into his back, and his snout changing into his human face.

Before Bram could say anything, Kai strode up to Jane and whispered into her ear, "I'm getting you back later for the dragon cuddles. I thought we'd agreed you wouldn't say that in front of others."

Jane raised an eyebrow. "You stated I wouldn't do it. I never agreed."

He moved his hand to her arse and squeezed. "I'll deal with your payback later." Kai looked to Bram. "Well?"

To his credit, Bram didn't laugh. "Sid needs to ask you a few questions." Bram looked to Jane. "Can she come over now?"

Jane motioned toward Kai. "Give him the blanket."

Bram did laugh as he handed Kai an old, woolen blanket. Wrapping it around his waist, the material made him want to itch. "You could've brought something nicer."

Bram grinned. "And miss you scratching yourself? I think not."

Jane ignored them and shouted, "Dr. Sid, would you come over?"

As the doctor made her way over, Kai tried holding the material away from his body, but it didn't help. He gave a glance to Jane indicating that he wanted to speak with her later. His female merely shrugged.

His dragon laughed. *If you haven't learned by now that your glares don't work on her, then you're a lost cause.*

*I have to do something.*

*Withhold sex. When she starts begging for our cock, then you can negotiate a few things.*

*As if you could last, dragon.*

Sid's voice cut through his conversation with his beast. "I made my observations, but first I want to hear a report on your flight."

Kai shrugged a shoulder. "Everything felt as it should. Nothing was tight or painful. In all honesty, I've never felt better."

Sid studied him a second before she replied, "Judging from your flight and maneuvers, I think you're healed. If you're lying to me, Kai Sutherland, it'll be your own damn fault that you're injured again, or worse."

"I'm telling the truth, Sid," Kai stated as he wrapped an arm around Jane.

Sid glanced to Jane and back to him. "Since getting yourself killed means being separated from your female forever, I think you're telling the truth." Sid looked to Bram. "He's your problem now."

"Aye, I know. Thanks, Sid," Bram answered.

With a nod, Sid walked off in the direction of her surgery.

To some the action might seem cold, but Kai knew it was never easy for her to watch a dragon-shifter fly around in dragon form. The sight only reminded Sid of what she could never have again.

Bram spoke up. "I'll contact the DDA to let them know the plan is still set for tomorrow. You and Aaron need to ensure our Protectors are ready to go."

"And Lochguard?" Kai asked.

"Aye, they're ready too. Although Finn's being a bit paranoid about his pregnant mate and doesn't want to allow his land to be vulnerable. Still, ten extra dragons will make a difference."

Jane chimed in. "Who knows, maybe next time, we can have my brother and a few other humans help us."

Hearing Jane say "us" warmed Kai's heart. "We'll see."

Bram slapped his bicep. "We'll have one final meeting this evening. But for now, I'll let you get things in motion and spend a little time with your female. It'll help calm your dragon for tomorrow."

Kai hugged Jane tighter and she leaned more into his side. "Thanks, Bram."

As Stonefire's leader left, Nikki came up to them. "I can double-check the supplies and go over the plan again with the Protectors if you want to take Jane for a quick flight."

Jane answered, "No, we'll do that later. When he takes me up, I don't want to rush it."

Kai turned to Jane and brushed her cheek with his forefinger. "It's moments like these when I forget how you drive me mad most of the time."

Jane grinned. "Despite your views to the contrary, I know when to hold back."

Nikki cleared her throat. "While you two get your kissing out of the way, I'll head back with Aaron to central command. Come when you're ready."

As Nikki walked off, Kai stated, "She's grown up."

"Probably because she's had to deal with my brother."

Kai sensed that Nikki was hiding something from him about Rafe Hartley, but he'd been so busy planning the attack on the Dragon Knights and healing that he hadn't had a chance to talk with her about it.

His dragon spoke up. *She's a grown dragonwoman. She'll talk when she's ready. We did.*

Ignoring his beast, Kai waved goodbye to Aaron and then looked down to Jane. "Sid cleared me."

Jane tilted her head. "And?"

With a growl, he pulled her up against his front and lowered his head until his lips were less than an inch away from hers. "I want to claim my prize."

"You're not quite yet to twenty points and if you expect me to give you bonus points for being fully recovered, then you don't know me at all."

"I think your counting skills need a little work." Jane opened her mouth to argue, but Kai beat her to it. "But I'll agree to wait for now. However, I'm going to claim what's mine."

She batted her eyelashes in a dramatic fashion. "And what would that be?"

"You."

And he kissed her.

~~~

The second Kai's lips met hers, Jane's body burned for much more. She wanted to feel his hands on her skin and his cock inside her.

Kai threaded his fingers through her hair and explored her mouth slowly. No matter how many times he'd kissed her over the last two weeks, she never thought it was enough. His taste and heat were addictive.

# Reawakening the Dragon

Kai gently tugged her head back and broke the kiss. She frowned. "Why did you stop? That's unlike you."

He murmured, "Because if I keep kissing you, I'll take you here on the landing area in front of everyone. And no one deserves to see your naked body except for me."

Jane tilted her head. "You deserve it, huh? I would think it's a privilege."

He squeezed her waist. "Bloody woman, can you not challenge me for once? I was being chivalrous."

"If I know you at all, that's crap. You're probably going to propose taking me to that hidden field you keep talking about and I'm supposed to be grateful for your thoughtfulness."

Kai blinked. "I'm not sure I like how well you're getting to know me."

Jane grinned. "Someone has to keep you on your toes. That's one of my jobs on Stonefire. Bram and Evie said so."

Her dragonman grunted. "I think I need to chat with Bram about minding his own business."

She ran her fingers through Kai's chest hair and his tension eased a fraction. "It's good because it means they care about you."

He grunted. "Forget Bram and Evie. I want to know if you'll let me take you in a field." Kai nuzzled her cheek and she melted against him. "It's going to be too cold soon to do it."

"It's already too cold. October in northern England isn't exactly tropical and I'm only human." She moved until she could see Kai's eyes. "But I do have a proposal."

"You and your bloody proposals."

She raised her brows. "Hey, if you want to take me naked outside before June next year, then you might want to listen."

Kai's pupils flashed to slits and back, and Jane smiled wide. Whenever Kai's dragon was on her side, she tended to win.

And judging by Kai's irritated look, his dragon wanted to hear Jane's proposal. "Well? Are you ready to listen?"

"You already know the answer to that."

"I do, but it's amusing to hear how your dragon likes me better."

"Not better. He just does whatever it takes to get inside of you."

Jane looped her hands behind Kai's neck. "Well, my proposal is this—come back alive from the Dragon Knights' attack and—"

"Done."

She tilted her head. "I wasn't finished."

Kai's hands moved to her bum and he pressed her against his lower body. It took everything she had to ignore the hardness of his dick or she might give in and let him take her in the freezing wind.

Her dragonman whispered, "I'll agree to anything if I can take you outside any way I want."

The huskiness of his voice sent a rush of warmth through her body and she nearly forgot her idea. But then she checked herself. "Good. Because you just agreed to come back alive to me and go visit your mother and sister on Snowridge before that happens."

Kai frowned. "What?"

She poked his chest. "For a head Protector, you should know better than to agree to something without hearing all of the details."

He grunted. "I was distracted by your hard nipples pressing into my chest."

"That doesn't matter. Will you agree? If so, we can take a mini-holiday somewhere warm and you can do whatever you want to me for twenty-four hours."

Kai fell silent and Jane wondered if she had pressed him too hard.

Yet Kai had mentioned taking Jane to Snowridge several times over the last few days. It wasn't as if she was demanding it out of the blue. She just knew he'd put it off indefinitely if given the chance.

And Jane couldn't allow that. Things were good between her and Kai, but there was something she needed to do before she decided to stay on Stonefire or not.

Jane wanted to meet Maggie Jones.

She trusted the human half of Kai with her heart, but his dragon's instinct was something else. It was best to see if his dragon had truly moved on or not because Jane was falling for her growly dragonman. She might not survive the rejection if Maggie Jones showed up in three years' time single again and wanting Kai. Even if the man was over her, the dragon might demand their true mate.

And since mate-claim frenzies always resulted in pregnancy, Kai would have no choice but to take Maggie as his mate. He wasn't the type of dragonman to abandon his children, no matter the circumstances of their birth.

Kai finally answered, "Provided everything is safe here, then yes, I agree to your proposal. But with one condition."

Relief coursed through her body. Kai's response had made her decision about staying on Stonefire that much easier. "What condition?"

He hugged her tightly. "You let me tie you to my bed for the next hour without complaint."

"There are more important things to be doing right now. Tomorrow is a big day and could determine the future of our clan."

"Our clan is ready and can spare me an hour."

"Thirty minutes."

"Forty-five."

Jane nodded. "Done. But your forty-five minutes start now."

With a growl, Kai released his hold on her, dropped the blanket around his waist, and tossed her over his shoulder.

Jane squeaked. "What the hell are you doing?"

He lightly slapped her backside. "Shush. You agreed to forty-five minutes and I'm using it how I see fit. Part of that includes me getting you back home as soon as possible. Carrying you is the fastest way."

She tried to be outraged at his behavior, but as her dragonman caressed her arse and wetness rushed between her legs, she forgot why she was outraged. After all, it wasn't as if she were naked.

With another light tap on her bum, Kai ran toward their cottage. Everyone gaped as they made their way and Jane couldn't help but laugh. Kai was destroying his stony, badass image and didn't seem to care.

Yes, her dragonman had come a long way from issuing orders in Newcastle.

The second Kai stepped foot inside his bedroom inside his cottage, he tossed her on the bed and covered her body with his. As he kissed her, Jane forgot about everything but the man above her.

# CHAPTER SIXTEEN

The next day, Kai beat his wings as he glanced over his golden shoulder to check on his team. All ten dragons were in a V-formation behind him, creating a rainbow of colors in blue, green, purple, red, black, and gold.

Turning his head back around, he focused on their target in the distance. He'd soon know if Jane's contact had been successful in leaking Stonefire's "training location" to the Dragon Knights.

His beast spoke up. *They had better be there. I want to take care of these bastards once and for all.*

*Me, too, dragon.*

*Good. Then make this quick. The longer we're away, the more our female will worry.*

Kai signaled with his wing and put his team on high alert. It was showtime.

Kai barreled to the side and the dragons behind him alternated in dropping to the left and right before beating their wings and heading straight toward the ground. The objective was for each dragon to pick up a log or boulder, simulating a rescue mission. With any luck, the knights would be waiting in the nearby forest.

Of course, what the knights didn't know was that Aaron and his team were also in the forest in their human forms, waiting to pounce.

Since Kai always joined in his team's drills, he dove toward a fallen log near the edge of the forest. The knights might try to attack him, but if it gave away their position, the pain would be worth it.

He swooped down, snagged the hunk of wood with his talons and flew back up. As he hovered in place about five hundred feet in the air, he watched as one by one the rest of his team seized their intended targets and returned to their respective places in formation.

When all ten beasts were back in position, Kai scrutinized the tree line. Yet nothing emerged from the forest or shot into the air.

His dragon spoke up again. *If they're clever, they'll wait until the dragons are tired and then attack.*

*You have a point.*

*Our female must be wearing off on you because you never used to mention when I was right.*

*Shut it, dragon. I need to concentrate.*

With a huff, his beast fell silent and Kai roared out the code for his team to do an attack drill.

Each of the ten dragons dove down and released their logs and boulders against an exposed rock face. Wood splintered and rocks broke into pieces, but there still wasn't any sign of the knights.

Since Kai believed in Jane, he spent the next twenty minutes putting his team through one drill after another. When their reaction times slowed and their wings started missing beats, Kai knew they needed to rest.

# REAWAKENING THE DRAGON

Guiding them to a nearby lake, it hit him—the best place to attacks a team of dragons would be when they were tired and playing in the water.

For once Kai wished he could communicate beyond wing and leg signals. But since that was all he had, he fisted his back talon and then touched it to his other back talon, which meant everyone should follow his lead.

As they made their way toward the lake, Kai only hoped Aaron understood his message.

~~~

Nikki watched as Kai took his team of dragons through a basic set of training maneuvers. Her job was to radio the Department of Dragon Affairs when Kai signaled it was time for them to capture the Dragon Knights.

Despite the cool October air, Nikki's hand gripping the two-way radio was sweaty. If the Dragon Knights had somehow gotten word of their plan, Jane would be devastated. Kai's female took things nearly as seriously as her male.

And Nikki wanted Jane to stay on Stonefire. Not just for Kai, but for the clan as well. The female had grand ideas of how to help the dragon-shifters. If Jane paired up with Melanie and Evie, the trio of humans would become unstoppable.

Her dragon chimed in. *Stop fretting. Kai is ready for any situation, not just the easy ones.*

*I know that, but it's been nearly twenty minutes. Something should've happened by now, unless Jane's contact is unreliable.*

Then Kai and his team turned away from the open field surrounded by trees and changed directions. From experience, Nikki knew there was a lake nearby. But would Kai really take them away from the leaked location?

Her dragon growled. *Look.*

Sure enough, Kai touched his back talons together, which meant to follow. Even if the knights had cracked the dragon signals, they wouldn't think anything of the order.

Yet Nikki's gut told her the order was for her, Aaron, and the others too.

Looking around, she spotted Aaron about ten feet away. Careful to move without making a sound, Nikki approached Stonefire's second-in-command. Aaron frowned, but she motioned for him to lean down. When his ear was in front of her mouth, she whispered, "We should follow him."

Nikki moved her head and Aaron whispered back, "The plan is to stay here. Unless you received a different order from Bram or the DDA, we should stay in position."

Nikki replied, "I mean no disrespect, Aaron, but I've been working with Kai for nearly two years. He wants us to follow. There's a lake nearby. The dragons are tired and need a rest. If the knights are aware of dragon training patterns, they'll know to wait until the dragons rest at the lake before they attack."

Aaron moved to study her, his brown eyes scrutinizing her own. Finally he moved back to her ear and whispered, "Take two others with you and follow him. I have a spare two-way radio in my pack and can call the DDA if need be."

With a nod, Nikki moved through the forest, tapping Seb and another Protector, Brenna, to follow her. Since Nikki had seniority, they obeyed without question.

They moved as quickly as they could without making much noise. A car engine turned over in the distance. Meeting Seb and then Brenna's eyes, she mouthed, "Dragon Knights."

They had no hope of catching them on foot, but Nikki wasn't about to give up. She'd trained in this forest for years and knew every shortcut they could take to reach the lake.

# REAWAKENING THE DRAGON

As she blazed a path, Nikki only hoped they could make it in time. Kai might be skilled, but without DDA support, Kai and his team could be taken if the knights had any sort of weaponry.

Picking up her pace, Nikki pushed away her doubts. If there was an attack, Kai would hold off until help arrived. She would radio the DDA now, but a false alert might damage the tentative trust Stonefire had earned with the agency.

No, Nikki needed to be 100 percent certain the knights were near the lake, so she pushed herself harder. The dragon hunters had bested her once and Nikki wasn't about to allow the Dragon Knights to win.

~~~

Kai stood on a rock at the edge of the lake and kept one eye on his team and his other eye on the trees. Even though the ten dragons on his team were all well-trained and seasoned fighters, he still didn't like putting them in danger. If the knights had a gun that could shoot electrical blasts, they could all be taken out in a matter of seconds.

His beast grunted. *Stop worrying. You're not acting like yourself.*

Kai was tempted to brush off his dragon's words, but decided to tell the truth. *Our possible future with Jane is riding on the success of this mission.*

*She will stay.*

He paused and added, *She'd better. After having her fire and sass in our life, I don't want to go back to the way it was.*

*At least you're admitting it now. That's progress.*

*Bloody dragon. Do you have to throw everything back in my face?*

*Of course. Otherwise you'll get too cocky.*

Before Kai could reply, an engine in the distance caught his attention. Motioning for his team leader to take charge, Kai jumped into the air and beat his wings until he had a clear view of the surroundings.

One road wound through the forest to the lake. Yet the road was empty.

The engine noise drew nearer.

Scanning the lake, Kai didn't see any boats, either. That only left one possibility—the knights could be riding dirt bikes along the edge of the forest, out of sight.

Just as he began to descend, a shot fired from the trees at his team below. While dragonhide was tough, armor piercing bullets could cause a lot of damage.

He glanced down and saw his team leader, Quinn, giving orders. Trusting Quinn, Kai swooped toward the road and landed.

With no bikes, cars, or men nearby, he imagined his legs and forearms shifting back into limbs, his snout shrinking into his nose, and his wings merging with his back. The second he was in human form, Kai dashed toward the trees and headed in the direction of the sounds of gunfire.

Due to years of training, Kai didn't so much as flinch at the rocks and sticks under his bare feet. The hard part was not running full tilt so that he could retain the element of surprise.

Even if they saw him land in the distance, they had no idea he'd shifted and was in the forest.

The sound of guns drew nearer until Kai could make out some light-colored t-shirts. For all their planning, the Dragon Knights weren't soldiers and had overlooked camouflage.

A dragon's cry roared out, but Kai pushed aside his worry. If he didn't take down or distract the shooters, more dragons would be injured.

Kai jumped and took hold of the branch above before swinging his body up. Crouched on the branch, he took in the position of the three shooters. They were close enough together that he could easily take them, provided they didn't shoot him down first.

His dragon snorted. *They don't stand a chance against us.*

Swiftly yet silently, Kai flung himself toward the nearest shooter and tackled him to the ground. Taking the strangely shaped gun out of the human's hand, he flung it behind him. With a punch to the back of the head, the male went still.

Another tried to tackle him, but Kai smacked the back of his head into the man's nose. The human cried out and Kai took the split-second advantage to use the momentum of his body to toss the man in front of him. The human crashed into the tree with an audible crack. He didn't get up.

The last shooter fired and Kai dove to the side, undeterred by the scratches from the debris on the forest floor. With a growl, he jumped to a crouch. From behind a tree, he peeked around the corner. The human shot at him, and Kai moved back to safety.

Even though he was naked and hiding behind a tree, he would think of something.

Just as he calculated if he had enough space to shift into a dragon or not, a purple dragon crashed through the trees from above and grabbed the human with her talons. The dragon tossed the human against a tree and he fell silent.

Kai nodded at Nikki in dragon form and then motioned up for her to fly back to the others.

Crouching low, Nikki jumped high into the air and just managed to clear the treetops so she could flap her wings enough to rise into the sky.

He brushed off the dirt from his chest and thighs as he confiscated all the weapons he could find. Two of the humans were dead, so he ripped a strip off one's t-shirt and secured the remaining knight's hands behind his back.

The sound of helicopters drew near. It was most likely the DDA, come to smoke out the knights from the forest.

Kai retrieved the three strange-looking guns and ran back toward the road. He had no idea what the DDA would use to contain the knights and he sure as hell wasn't going to stick around to find out.

Running as fast as he could, Kai weaved through the trees and under forest. The second he hit the road, he lay down the guns and imagined his wings extending from his back, his fingers growing into talons, and his face turning into a snout and ears.

The helicopters were nearly overhead when he plucked the guns up with his back talons and jumped into the air. By the time he was three hundred feet above the road, the DDA helicopters began dropping canisters that left behind a trail of smoke as they fell.

Not wanting to inhale the chemicals, Kai flapped his wings and headed back to his team. The knights might be the DDA's problem now, but at least one of his dragons were hurt. Kai needed to take care of them.

Only once he ensured everyone's safety could he return to Stonefire, and to Jane.

~~~

Inside the Protectors' central command building, Jane paced back and forth, clenching and releasing her fingers. The wait was killing her.

She trusted the source who had leaked the information to the Dragon Knights, but there were a million reasons why the knights might dismiss it. For all she knew, Kai and his team would find nothing. Not only that, her actions might've destroyed the tentative trust between Stonefire and the Department of Dragon Affairs.

She paced harder.

Bram's voice interrupted her thoughts. "If you wear a hole in the rug, then you're going to have to replace it, lass."

Jane stopped in her tracks and frowned. "How can you be so calm?"

Bram shrugged. "I have bigger things to worry about. Besides, I trust Kai with not only my life, but my son and Evie's as well. If the Dragon Knights show up, he'll take care of them. He's one of the best Protectors in the world."

Jane clenched her fingers again. "You have to say that, but it's not helping."

Bram opened his mouth to reply, but Evie hung up her phone call and interrupted him. "Arabella wants a video conference."

Jane asked, "Care to share a little bit more information about why?"

Evie raised an eyebrow. "Someone's a tad bit testy." Evie looked to Bram. "There is no doubt, Bram. I now have naming rights to our baby."

There was a twinkle in Bram's eyes. "We'll see, love, we'll see."

Jane let out a sigh. "What are you talking about? Is everything all right? What does Arabella know?"

Evie looked back to Jane. "We'll find out together."

Jane growled, but nodded. "Fine."

Bram chuckled. "You're starting to sound like Kai." Jane glared and Bram put up his hands. "All right, all right." He looked toward the Protectors' IT specialist, Nathan. "Patch Arabella through."

The young dragonman nodded and Arabella MacLeod's scarred face appeared on the big screen TV on the wall. Her dark brown eyes darted around the room before going back to Bram's. "You sure you want the reporter to hear this?"

Jane opened her mouth, but Bram beat her to it. "Jane is one of us now. I trust her not to leak confidential information."

Under normal circumstances, Jane would feel grateful and tell Bram thanks. However, her man was out fighting against who knew what kind of weaponry, so Jane barked out, "Just tell us what you know, Arabella."

Arabella raised her brows, but looked away from Jane to Bram who shrugged. "She's worried about Kai."

Arabella nodded. "That I can understand. Normally, I'd tease her about Mr. Talkative, but I'm not sure how much longer I can hold back my news."

Evie sighed. "Just tell us then, Ara."

Arabella replied, "Whoever was masking the IP addresses of the Dragon Knights was smart, but me, Ian, and Emma are smarter."

Bram asked, "So you managed to track them down?"

"Yes," Arabella answered. "Well, at least most of them. No doubt a few of them realized they were being hacked and went into hiding. But I have the DDA and local police tracking the lower downs."

Jane jumped in. "So, not all of them are taken care of, then?"

Arabella frowned. "I'd say about 75 percent of them, but the DDA can give a more final number later. It's still the vast majority of knights."

Jane took a step toward the TV. "I sense a 'however.'"

Arabella leaned back in her chair. "If we don't find the leaders, they can always find more recruits, grow their numbers, and attack again. The next time we go after them, we need to strike the leadership."

Jane murmured, "Kill the brain and the body dies."

Arabella nodded. "Right."

Bram hugged Evie to his side. "Can you convince Finn to allow you, Ian, and Emma to work on tracking the leadership?"

Finn was Arabella's mate and Lochguard's clan leader.

Arabella raised a brow. "I don't need him to 'allow' me to do anything. I'll just do it and make it up to him later."

Evie jumped in. "Just make sure to keep me in the loop so I can approach the DDA again if we need it."

"Of course," Arabella answered.

While Jane was glad there would be fewer Dragon Knights out and about to terrorize the dragon-shifters, she was still worried about the other battle. "Did the DDA pass on any updates on Kai and his team?"

Arabella shook her head. "Not yet." The dragonwoman looked over to her side and back to the screen. "I need to go and talk with the DDA liaison. I'll let you know if I find out anything else."

Bram answered, "Thanks, Ara."

With a nod, Arabella severed the connection and the screen went black.

Bram met Jane's eye. "As long as the leaders of the knights are still around, you need to be careful, Jane."

"You're starting to sound like Kai," Jane bit out.

"I'll let that slide because you're worried about Kai."

Evie lightly smacked Bram's side. "Leave her alone. You'd act exactly the same way if you were waiting for me." Evie smiled at Jane. "I know you're worried, but Kai is the best there is. Did you want some tea whilst you wait?"

Jane just prevented herself from snapping at Evie. The woman didn't deserve her rudeness. "No. I just need to move or I'll go crazy."

As Jane started pacing, Bram's voice filled the room. "Trust in Kai, Jane. There's no need to worry. It won't help."

Jane stopped and narrowed her eyes at Bram. "Yes, I'm sure you'll heed that advice without question whenever Evie goes into labor."

Fear flashed in Bram's eyes and he growled. "Don't even joke about that. Childbirth is riskier."

Jane raised her brows. "Sorry, Bram. But for me, it's the same thing. Kai may not come back."

Evie rubbed her pregnant belly. "Stop being daft, you two. Death could happen to anyone in a heartbeat. As I've told Bram, use your energy to worry about something else. Say, like how to mend peace with Clans Skyhunter and Snowridge."

Bram brushed Evie's cheek. "And what did I tell you? Deliver me a baby and come out of it safe and sound, and I'll do whatever you like."

As Jane watched the love shining in both Bram and Evie's eyes, her heart squeezed. She wanted to find her own happy ending, but she was afraid to hope.

She wanted to stay on Stonefire with Kai, but there was still the matter of his true mate. For all she knew, even if Kai survived the current battle, he still might be ripped from her side if Maggie Jones showed up out of the blue and kissed him.

*Get a grip, Jane. Just like Evie said, worrying isn't going to accomplish anything.*

It was easier said than done, but Jane took a deep breath to help clear her mind. After a second, she cleared her throat. Bram and Evie looked at her. "Maybe if you gave me a task, it would help distract me from imagining every worst-case scenario."

Bram continued to caress Evie's cheek as he talked. "You could always pitch your podcast idea now instead of next week."

"I don't have any of my materials, notes, or even Melanie here to help. That will have to wait," Jane answered.

"Then, I don't know, you could show us a dance?" Bram asked.

Evie smacked him in the side. "Don't be silly. You could always tell her embarrassing stories about Kai."

"Aye, I could," Bram replied. "But I'd rather not have him telling you embarrassing ones about me."

Evie studied her mate. "I will get it out of your later."

Just as Bram opened his mouth, Evie's mobile phone rang again and Jane nearly sighed. As much as she was starting to like Bram and Evie, the last thing Jane needed was the glow of love that she may never have.

Evie's face remained neutral as she talked and Jane waited with bated breath. *Please let Kai be okay, please.*

Evie said, "Okay," and hung up the phone. Then she looked at Jane and smiled. "It's done. There are a few injuries, but your dragonman is alive and well."

She let out a breath. "Good. Then I get to scold him when he gets back for scaring me."

Evie and Bram grinned, but it was Bram who replied, "Maybe kiss him first, lass. He deserves it."

"Maybe. It depends how injured he is."

Bram chuckled and Evie added, "Your source did his job. Thank you, Jane, for helping us eradicate one of the pains in our arses."

Jane shook her head. "Don't thank me. Part of the reason I set it all up was to save my own skin."

Bram studied her a second before his deep voice filled the room again. "You're as bad as Kai when it comes to taking a bloody compliment. Can't you just say thank you like a normal person?"

Jane shifted her feet. She had never handled compliments well and decided to change the subject. "Kai and the others will probably be back soon. Shouldn't we go to the main landing area and wait?"

Bram put out a hand and Evie took it. "Then let's go. The sooner we get you out of here, the sooner we can save the carpet from your pacing."

Not waiting for Bram and Evie, Jane walked out of the room, down the hall, and out the front door of the central command building. As soon as her feet hit the grass, she all but ran toward the landing area. Hearing Kai was okay and seeing it for herself were two very different things.

She needed to hug her dragonman close. Only then would her heart rate slow and her stomach settle.

As the sight of dragons appeared in the distance, Jane decided to screw it and ran all the way to the landing area.

~~~

Kai glanced behind him to the road below, but didn't see the car being used to transport the injured back to Stonefire. In total, there were three injured, one of which required immediate medical attention.

Everyone had survived and he was grateful for that because it wasn't always the case in his line of work.

His dragon spoke up. *Hurry. Our female is waiting for us.*

Despite the adrenaline fading from his system, Kai beat his wings faster. He'd never had a female to claim after a mission before. He didn't know how other dragon-shifters felt, but all Kai could think about was hugging Jane close and kissing the living

244

shit out of her. Stripping her naked and taking her slowly would have to wait until later. But for the moment, a kiss would do.

His dragon grunted. *Make sure to tell her she's staying with us.*

*We'll see, dragon, we'll see.*

*Why hesitate? She's proven her worth to the clan and she already gave up her human job. Stonefire is where she belongs.*

*It's her choice. I can't force her.*

His beast huffed. *In the old days, males could order their females around.*

*Hm, and what fun would that be?*

His dragon sulked and focused on flying.

Kai smiled. He was winning more and more over his beast these days. If nothing else, he should keep Jane around just to irritate his dragon.

As the peaks marking Stonefire's northern-most border came into focus, he signaled the lightly injured toward the landing area reserved for dragons needing medical attention. Kai and the remaining five dragons headed toward the main landing area in the center of Stonefire.

On the final approach, Kai scanned the small figures on the ground until his eyes locked onto a dark-haired female standing next to Bram and Evie. Even from several hundred feet in the air, he would know Jane Hartley anywhere.

*Ours.*

Agreeing with his dragon, Kai slowed down the beat of his wings and gently lowered himself into the landing area. The second his feet touch the ground, he imagined his body shrinking back into his six-foot-three human frame.

He'd barely taken two steps when Jane jumped into his arms. Kai hugged his female tightly and murmured, "Hello."

Looking up, Jane frowned. "Hello is not nearly enough. What happened? Were you hurt at all? Where's the rest of your team?"

Kai chuckled. "Inquisitive one, aren't you?"

She lightly slapped his chest. "Stop stalling. You know I don't like being left in the dark."

He cupped her face and strummed his thumb on her cheek. Jane's tension eased a fraction and he answered, "We won. I'm fine. The others are with Sid."

"Kai Sutherland, we need to work on your elaboration skills."

He grinned. "Maybe."

Jane smiled and shook her head. "Sometimes I wonder why I want to stay with you at all."

Both man and beast stopped breathing. After a few seconds, Kai found his voice again. "So you're staying?"

Running her hands up his chest and resting them on the back of his neck, she leaned her body against his. "Provided I can find work here and survive meeting your family on Snowridge, then I'm probably staying."

"I don't like the 'probably' part of your sentence."

"We can discuss my reasons for it when we're alone, but not before," Jane stated

Kai nuzzled Jane's cheek. "Whatever your doubts, I will erase them."

"I hope so, dragonman, I really do," she murmured.

His beast growled. *Kiss her. Let everyone know she's ours.*

Not needing any further encouragement, Kai hugged Jane close and kissed her.

Oblivious to the others watching, he moved his hands to Jane's arse and squeezed before stroking his tongue into her mouth. Just tasting his sweet female helped to calm his heart and wash away some of his fatigue from the battle.

When his female groaned, the vibration sent a shot of lust straight to his dick.

His beast spoke up. *Not here. I don't want the others to see her.*

His dragon's words were the equivalent of someone pouring ice water over his head. Kai broke the kiss and Jane whispered, "Why did you stop?"

Kai cleared his throat and kept his voice low. "I'm naked and a good portion of the clan are here, watching us."

Jane tilted her head. "What was it that you told me in the beginning? Oh, that's right. Clothing is a human concern. Dragon-shifters don't care about such things."

He gently slapped her bum. "It matters when it's my female."

"I'm yours, huh? I don't remember anyone asking."

Kai growled. "You didn't give me a bloody chance, woman. You jumped me as soon as I was human again."

Jane rubbed her lower body against his and Kai sucked in a breath. Jane's voice was husky as she replied, "I can walk away right now if you want to try this again."

His beast growled. *She teases us. I don't like it.*

*Yes you do. Stop lying.*

After a second, his dragon added, *Yes, I do. But we still should take our female somewhere private.*

*I'm going to try, dragon, but Bram will want details.*

*Then keep Jane close so we can have her as soon as possible.*

*I will never let her go.*

Jane moved a hand to his face. "Are you done talking with your dragon? I still need an answer."

Lowering his head, he nipped her bottom lip and murmured, "For a human, you're demanding."

She nipped him back. "I rather have to be if I want to keep up with you."

Kai was about to kiss her again when a male cleared his throat and broke the spell. Kai snarled as he looked up to see Bram. "Everyone's fine. Aaron can give you the report. I'm busy."

Bram chuckled. "I see that, Kai. If you're not careful, you'll be walking home with a hard cock."

Jane nuzzled his chest and it helped calm Kai. As he held Jane in his arms, Kai answered Bram, "The DDA can tell Evie the specifics of the capture near the lake. Much like they did on Lochguard's border, they smoked the human knights out of the forest with special tear-gas canisters."

Jane touched Kai's jaw. "I wish that was the end of it."

Kai frowned down at Jane. "What are you talking about?"

Jane filled him in on Arabella's report and he grunted. "We'll just have to up our security and ensure you never leave Stonefire without an escort."

Jane opened her mouth, but Bram beat her to the reply. "He's right, Jane. If they ever find out you were the reason we set them up to be captured, they'll be out for your blood."

Kai hugged Jane tighter against his body. "I will protect her."

Bram clapped Kai's bicep. "Aye, I know you will, Kai." His clan leader motioned with his head. "Enjoy Jane for a little while and then come debrief me the rest."

Jane spoke up. "Is anyone going to ask me?"

The corner of Kai's mouth ticked up. "No. Your next hour is mine."

His human tilted her head. "And I suppose we'll spend that hour touring the clan's lands?"

Kai growled. "No. You're going to spend it in my bed."

# Reawakening the Dragon

Even though Jane's eyes flashed with heat, she tried to frown. "How about if you shout it to the wind? I don't think the dragon-shifters on the other side of the landing area heard you."

Kai raised his voice. "Jane Hartley, I'm taking you home, stripping you, and plan to make you scream."

Jane's cheeks flushed pink. "Stop it."

Bram laughed and Evie walked over to join them. "What's so funny?"

Hugging Evie to his side, Bram shook his head. "Nothing, love. I'll explain it later." Bram met Kai's eyes again. "Go, but keep your mobile phone nearby. I'll talk to Aaron and the others, but if I need to reach you, you'd better bloody well pick up. I don't care what you're doing. Understand?"

Kai grunted. "Fine."

Evie jumped in. "I would almost say you're pouting Kai."

Jane lifted her head and looked to Evie. "He does it all the time with me. It really destroys the badass image he has going on."

Since Jane and Evie would conspire against him until it grew dark and the moon rose, Kai adjusted his grip and lifted Jane over his shoulder.

His female squeaked. "I thought we talked about this."

"That's the problem. Too much talking." He lifted a hand. "Bye Bram. Evie."

As Kai raced toward his cottage, he ignored the people staring or Jane's protests over his shoulder. He wanted his female and he wanted her now.

# CHAPTER SEVENTEEN

After about thirty seconds, Jane stopped protesting and tried to think of how she'd get her revenge on Kai. Each step he jogged jarred his shoulder against her stomach. He had payback coming his way.

But since she couldn't do anything about it until he put her down, Jane reveled in the feel of Kai's hard muscles under her body and took a deep inhalation of his musky male scent.

Her dragonman had come home safe and sound.

Seeing Kai shift into a human had sent a rush of relief through her body. In that second, she knew her place was with Kai at Stonefire. Not just because of her feelings for her dragonman, but she could also do the most good for the British dragon-shifters by working with Bram, Evie, and Melanie.

Hell, Jane could do more than help Stonefire. She could probably improve the status quo for dragon-shifters the world over. No reporter had the access and resources Jane would have on Stonefire.

There was only one thing preventing her from telling Kai she'd stay forever.

While she was pretty confident Kai would repair relations with his mother and sister over time, Jane needed to give Kai the chance to choose his future. If he still wanted a chance with his true mate, Maggie, then Jane would let him go. After all, a dragon-shifter's true mate was supposed to be their best chance at happiness.

Not that Jane liked that idea one bit. Digging her nails into Kai's back, she fought the urge to scream, "Mine."

For better or worse, Kai was rubbing off on her.

Before she spent too much more time thinking of her future, Kai opened the door to his cottage. Once they were through, he slammed it shut and dashed up the stairs. In the blink of an eye, Jane was facedown on his bed.

"Kai, what are you—"

The dragonman tore off her top and trousers, tossing the scraps of fabric on the floor as he went. Before Jane could do more than blink, her bra and underwear were also shredded and tossed to the ground.

Jane found her voice. "Hey, that was my best bra."

Kai tugged off one trainer and then the other before removing her socks. "You can get another one."

"That's not the point."

Kai ran his warm, rough hands up the back of her thighs. "They are just things. You are important. Whatever you wear doesn't matter."

At the combination of his touch and his words, Jane softened a fraction. "That's a start, but I need something else as way of an apology."

Her dragonman rubbed her buttocks in slow circles. Without realizing it, she opened her thighs and Kai chuckled. "Your body tells me what I need to do."

One hand stilled and slowly moved between her thighs. As he played with her slit, Jane couldn't help but moan. "Someday, your magical fingers aren't going to work on me."

"Not if I have anything to say about it."

He thrust his finger into her pussy and Jane wiggled her hips. His finger wasn't nearly enough.

Yet Kai took his time removing and plunging into her heat. Clenching the sheets in her fingers, Jane gritted out, "I should be the one teasing you."

Kai ran his other hand up to her lower back and pressed down. "Not until I've taken you from behind."

She was about to protest when he removed his fingers and hand. In the next second, Kai lifted her hips and teased her opening with his cock. "Have you been on birth control long enough to go without a condom?"

"Yes. Just hurry up already."

He rubbed through her wetness again. "Maybe I should make you beg."

"Kai Sutherland, if you don't—"

He thrust into her pussy and Jane rested her forehead on the bed. She had a feeling he'd keep interrupting her and surprising her until they were eighty.

Remaining still, Kai rubbed her back, her shoulders, and reached around for her breast. The contact brought her back to the present and she wiggled her hips. When Kai sucked in a breath, she smiled. "I've heard rumors about post-battle hard-ons. You're not going to last long if I keep this up." She moved her lower body again.

He hissed, "Bloody female," and then pinched her nipple.

Jane arched her back at the pleasure mixed with pain. "Kai."

Tweaking her again, he retreated and then slammed hard into her. Even after nearly two weeks of sex with her dragonman, she knew she would never tire of feeling his long, thick dick inside of her.

# Reawakening the Dragon

Kai released her breasts and took hold of her hips so she couldn't move. But as the seconds ticked by and he didn't do anything, Jane knew what was coming. She growled out, "I'm not going to beg."

Without a word, Kai moved a hand around and lightly brushed her clit. "Just ask me nicely."

Another light brush and Jane nearly screamed, both from frustration and pleasure.

Deciding she would have her turn with Kai next, she turned her voice sweet and answered, "Please."

~~~

Kai was holding on by a thread. Between the post-battle high and his dragon wanting to fuck Jane until she couldn't walk, he would come too soon if he wasn't careful.

His beast huffed. *She is wet and ready. Stop with the games. Take what is ours.*

As Jane's feminine scent surrounded him, Kai wanted his human more than his next breath. He'd just have to draw on every iota of self-control he possessed to hold out a little longer. Jane needed to come before him. Always.

His dragon growled. *We can last. I will help. Just start moving.*

Jane saying please broke his restraint and Kai held her hips in place as he pounded in and out of her tight, wet pussy.

It was the first time he'd felt her gripping his dick without a condom and it was hot, warm, and snug. In other words, it was bloody perfect.

He'd never tire of her. Jane was his and his alone. He needed to tell her.

Possessiveness coursed through his body and he growled. "Mine, Jane. You're mine."

He increased his pace and Jane raised her hips in answer. He loved how her sass melted away when he was inside of her.

Well, mostly melted away.

He pounded harder and the sound of flesh on flesh filled the room. Even with Kai guiding Jane's hips, his female arched her back, unafraid to tell him what she wanted.

He moved a hand to around her abdomen and lifted Jane's upper body. Moving his leg slightly in front of hers, he took her from a different angle.

Jane moaned as she leaned against his chest.

His dragon snarled. *Make her scream.*

Ignoring his beast, Kai roamed up her ribcage and gripped her breast possessively. Jane's pointy nipple pressed against his palm. Rubbing in slow circles with his hand, Jane raised her hand to his head behind her and gripped his hair. "Kai. You know what I like. Do it."

Kai grunted and lowered his head to Jane's neck. He bit her where her neck met her shoulder and then soothed his bite with his tongue. "Later, I'm going to do the same to your breasts."

He nuzzled her neck and Jane murmured, "Mm, yes."

The pressure building at Kai's spine told him he needed to hurry if he wanted Jane to come before him. He whispered, "I'll torture you more later," before releasing her breast.

As he rubbed down her abdomen, he finally reached her clit. Brushing it lightly with his forefinger, Jane moaned.

Kai continued to rub her nub in circles, increasing both the pace of his fingers and the thrust of his cock.

His balls slapped against her flesh, bringing his own orgasm closer. But Kai gritted his teeth. Jane needed to come first.

More than that, he needed her. She was their life. He needed to brand his female and convince her to stay.

# Reawakening the Dragon

Rubbing her clit in short, rough strokes, Jane screamed. Kai never stopped moving as she gripped and released his dick. Only when she started to soften did he place a possessive hand over her lower belly and give a few more rough thrusts before stilling. As he screamed her name, each spurt of semen wracked his body anew as pleasure shot through his body.

Never before had he felt as if he'd die from an orgasm. Only Jane could do this to him.

When he could finally string two thoughts together again, he knew he should hold his female close and talk.

But the urge to take her again was strong. His dragon roared. *She is our mate. Take her.*

*She needs a rest.*

*No, Fuck her. Now. She's ours.*

Kai's confusion gave his dragon an opportunity to seize control of his mind. Before Kai could push his beast back, his dragon forced them to pull out of Jane, flip her over, and restrain her hands over her head. "Mine."

There was no fear in Jane's eyes, only curiosity. "Hello, dragon. Can I have Kai back?"

"No. You're mine."

Kai attempted to push his beast back, but for once, his bloody dragon was too strong.

If he didn't do something, his dragon would be fucking Jane instead of him. While the practice wasn't unusual with dragon-shifters, Jane had no idea what she was getting into.

Finally, Jane opened her legs and said, "This should be interesting."

Kai's dragon roared out loud and plunged their cock into Jane's pussy. As his beast pistoned their hips so hard that Jane's breasts jiggled and the bed moved, Kai took a step back and tried to think of why his dragon was acting so possessive. There was no urgency to impregnate Jane, which came with the mate-claim frenzy. Nor did his semen send Jane into an orgasm like it did with true mates.

Maybe there was something else in between.

Then his dragon blasted a roar inside their head and Kai couldn't concentrate. The need to brand Jane with their scent and make her come blocked out everything else.

His dragon released Jane's hands and pushed her legs wider. They were nearly there. A few more seconds and they'd come.

~~~

Jane could barely think straight as Kai's dragon took her roughly. She was still sensitive from her orgasm a few minutes before and each hard stroke of Kai's cock inside of her sent her a little closer to the edge.

As she stared into Kai's slitted pupils, she decided having his dragon in charge wasn't that bad. Would Kai be upset if she asked to share sometimes?

Then Kai-slash-dragon pressed against her clit and she screamed. A pleasure that was nearly too much, hovering near the point of pain, rushed through her body. And yet her dragonman never ceased his movements.

She was still orgasming when Kai's dragon roared, "Mine," as he came. This time, she felt each hot spurt of semen.

When Kai finally collapsed on top of her, she loved the weight of his body on hers. As she traced a finger along the ridge of his spine, she really hoped she could experience this every day. She wanted Kai for her own.

Not just because he was great in bed, which was true. Jane loved his emerging humor, his stubbornness, and his dedication to those he cared about.

She was falling hard for him.

Yet she refused to examine her feelings until she knew she could keep him.

Kai's rough voice filled her ear. "You alive, Janey?"

"So, you're back, huh?"

Kai rolled to his back and dragged Jane onto his chest. Placing his finger under her chin, he raised her head until she met his eyes. "Are you okay? Did my dragon scare you?"

She smiled. "No. It was…different. But in a good way."

"If you say he's better, I will tie you to this bed and change your mind."

Grinning, she tilted her head. "You still don't have enough points to claim me that way yet."

"Only because you cheat."

"What? Me? A cheater? No, never."

Kai grunted. "You're such a cheater."

In the next second, he tickled her side and Jane couldn't stop laughing. After nearly two weeks, Kai knew her most ticklish spot was just under her armpit.

He didn't hold back.

She kicked him in the shin a few times and he finally stopped. Nuzzling her cheek, he murmured, "You may be a cheater, but you're my cheater."

Jane melted at his words, but the niggling fear from earlier crept back into her mind. It must've shown on her face because Kai's voice turned dominant. "Tell me why you will only 'probably stay' with me, Janey. Something's bothering you and I don't like it."

"You could ask, you know."

He hugged her tighter against his body. "Don't try to distract me. Whatever it is, you can tell me."

Jane rarely hesitated, but she did in that second. As much as she wanted to know the truth, Kai's answer could instantly rip away the happiness she'd found with her dragonman.

Kai grunted. "Tell me, Jane. I'm not allowing you out of this bed until you do."

She pushed past her fear and spit out, "It's about Maggie Jones."

Kai's voice softened. "What about her?"

Jane picked at Kai's chest hair before she answered, "I'm not your true mate, Kai. I understand that your dragon's instincts are strong. If you want her, then tell me now. Because if she shows up a few years down the line wanting you and the frenzy takes over, it will break my heart."

"Look at me, Jane Hartley." She obeyed. Kai's gaze was fierce as he continued, "It's true that a frenzy can overcome a weaker dragon-shifter and they lose the ability to control their lives. But I am not weak-willed. You may have noticed my stubbornness." Jane smiled at that and Kai traced her cheek. "I don't want Maggie Jones. Hell, I don't think my dragon even wants her anymore." He traced her brow. "All we want is you, Jane. You're clever, stubborn, and more beautiful than any female I've ever seen. I'm stronger with you at my side and while I won't admit it to anyone else, I'm a better male because of you. You brought laughter back into my life when I thought I'd never have it." He laid his forehead against hers. "I love you, Jane Hartley. Will you stay with me forever?"

Jane's eyes teared up. "You say all of that with such conviction. I'm not sure I can say no."

Kai growled. "That's still not an answer, Janey."

Jane raised a hand to Kai's cheek and whispered, "I bloody love you, too, so I guess that means I don't have a choice."

Kai growled and flipped her onto her back. "Tell me you want to stay."

"Kai Sutherland, I want to stay. You and Stonefire are my future."

"Good answer," he murmured before he kissed her and showed just how much he loved her.

# CHAPTER EIGHTEEN

A few hours later, Kai squeezed Jane's hand in his as they approached Bram's cottage. "I still say we should've just talked with Bram over the phone."

Jane squeezed back. "You of all people should appreciate a face-to-face conversation. There's so much we can learn from Bram's facial expressions."

Kai grunted and looked down at Jane. "Remind me why I love you again."

She grinned and his heart skipped a beat. "Because you can't scare me and I don't put up with your crap."

Kai's dragon grunted. *Why did you let her convince us to do this? If you had allowed me to be in charge, I would've found other ways to persuade her to stay home.*

*It's hard to say no to her. You know that.*

*We're going to work on that soon. I can keep her in line.*

Kai snorted inside his head. *I'd like to see that.*

Jane's voice interrupted his conversation with his dragon. "What is your dragon going on about now?"

Kai paused and tugged Jane's hand until she crashed against his body. "It doesn't matter. Just give me a kiss to shut him up."

"You're going to try to order me around until I'm ninety years old, aren't you?"

The corner of his mouth ticked up. "Probably. But I have other ways of getting what I want."

Jane opened her mouth, but Kai cut her off with a slow, lingering kiss. He was about to wrap an arm around Jane's waist and hold her tightly when Bram's voice boomed out. "I believe your hour was up quite some time ago, Kai."

Kai broke the kiss and murmured, "As if an hour is enough time to spend with my female."

Bram spoke as if Kai had shouted it across the way. "You and Jane are the ones who wanted to see me, so hurry up. Evie's feet are killing her and I'd like to massage them before much longer."

Kai shook his head, gave Jane one last kiss, and turned to face his clan leader. "You've changed, Bram."

Bram smiled. "Aye, and for the best. Much like yourself."

Jane tugged Kai's hand. "In the amount of time you've been teasing him, we could've received answers already. Let's go."

Kai followed Jane's lead, but soon he was in front and tugging her along. They reached the front door and Bram stepped to the side as he motioned toward the living room. "We'll talk in there."

Kai guided Jane into the living room. Nodding to Evie, who sat in the armchair, Kai plopped onto the couch and tugged Jane into his lap. She landed with a squeak. "What are you doing?"

He hugged her tightly. "I want to hold the female I love in my lap. It's not a crime."

Jane tried to frown but ended up smiling. "There's that hidden romantic side again."

Kai merely grunted and Jane laughed. However, before he could say anything in response, Evie's voice caught his attention. "I knew it. See, Bram? Kai and Jane are in love. Kai even mentioned it. There's no way you can't say I didn't win the bet. I now have full naming rights to our unborn child."

Bram sighed. "Aye, you do. Just don't name our baby Gladys or Jethro."

Mischief danced in Evie's eyes. "Oh, I'm sure I can do worse."

Bram shook his head before sitting on the arm of the chair and taking a possessive hold of Evie's shoulders. "We can argue about it later. Kai and Jane requested a meeting, so let's hear what they have to say."

Kai laid his chin on Jane's shoulder and met his clan leader in the eye. "Jane wants to stay."

Jane wiggled in his lap. No doubt she was tempting him with her full bum against his cock. "Let me translate Kai-speak for you. Kai has asked me to be his mate and I've said yes. The question is twofold. One, will you allow it? And two, will the DDA allow it?"

As Bram's eyes darted between Kai and Jane, Kai's heart rate kicked up. There were very few situations that made Kai nervous or anxious. Only because he held Jane's body close and was surrounded by her scent did Kai not jump up, tug Bram up by his shirt, and demand an answer.

Taking a deep inhalation of Jane's scent, Kai waited for Bram to decide his future.

~~~

Jane clutched Kai's arms around her waist. Being surrounded by his hard chest and delicious heat helped keep her nerves calm. She knew Bram was only half-responsible for her ability to live on Stonefire with Kai, but it was the important half. No doubt, Evie could work her magic with the DDA.

But if Bram said no or told Jane to leave, she wouldn't have a choice.

Kai had offered to follow her wherever she went earlier, but she couldn't allow him to leave Stonefire. He was the clan's best chance at a secure future.

Bram grinned and Jane's stomach stopped churning. "Of course my answer is yes. Jane can stay. I just like to make Kai sweat it a little since I rarely have the chance."

Kai growled. "That's not bloody funny, Bram."

"I thought it was hilarious. But it was a test of sorts."

Jane frowned. "What sort of test?"

Bram motioned toward them. "Watching the two of you hold onto to each other for support tells me volumes about your feelings for each other. Saying you love someone is grand, but actions speak the truth of a strong bond. The two of you belong together."

Jane relaxed against Kai's chest and her dragonman nuzzled her cheek as he asked, "What about the DDA?"

Evie waved a hand in dismissal. "I asked them about it last week. The special license is waiting in Bram's study."

Jane jumped in. "You knew before we even did?"

Evie smiled. "Of course. I have the best track record when it comes to guessing future mates."

Bram grunted. "Only when you see them together. You've been dead wrong about Sid so far."

Evie met her mate's eyes. "She's hard to read, but I'll crack her yet."

Jane cleared her throat. "As much as I'd love for Sid to find happiness, maybe one of you could collect the special license and give it to us?" Kai squeezed his arms around her waist and she rubbed his forearms as she added, "I just want to make sure you don't change your mind."

Bram stood. "Impatient, are you?"

"Yes," Kai and Jane said in unison.

Bram chuckled and exited the room. Evie looked to them and tilted her head. "I somehow can't see Kai wanting a grand mating ceremony in front of the clan, but if you two want one, maybe you can delay it a bit."

Kai growled. "I want everyone to know Jane is mine."

Jane patted his arm. "Calm down, boy. Let Evie finish."

Kai growled again but remained silent. Evie placed her hand over her pregnant belly. "Once you two sign the license, you'll be legally mated. However, if I know Jane at all, she'd like to use her mating ceremony as an opportunity to help the dragon-shifters' cause."

Jane raised her brows. "If I remember right, you did the same."

"Yes, but it was only for a handful of reporters."

"Not me," Jane added.

Evie grinned. "No, but you won the best scoop in the end."

Kai muttered, "Do I get a say in this?"

Jane turned her head to meet his eye. "Don't you want your mum and sister to be there, too? It will take some time to garner permission from Snowridge. It's just a ceremony. You're already mine, dragonman."

Bram entered and handed Jane a piece of paper. Written on it were the words, "Special Mating License." In black ink were hers and Kai's names.

Her hand shook a little and her eyes grew wet. Kai moved one hand to cover hers and he whispered, "No second thoughts allowed, Janey. There's no bloody way I'm letting you leave."

"As if you could prevent me from doing anything."

Kai's eyes turned concerned. "Then what's wrong?"

Jane gave a weak smile. "I'm not having second thoughts. I'm just happy and trying not to cry."

Kai kissed her cheek. "You're strong, Janey. Go ahead and cry if you like. I'll always be there to hold you close."

Jane's throat closed up. "Kai."

Her dragonman plucked the license from her hand and tossed it to the side. Then he half-turned her body toward him and he cupped her cheek. "I once thought I'd never love again. But you brought both man and beast back to life with your sassy attitude and heated looks. You could grow two heads and I'd still love you. Never hold back with me, Jane Hartley. Never."

Jane nodded as a tear trailed down her cheek. Kai gently brushed it away and she sat up a little taller. "Then kiss me, Kai Sutherland, and make me so happy tears roll down my cheeks."

Kai frowned. "I don't want you to cry if you're happy."

Jane laughed and lightly tapped Kai's cheek. "Then how about we go home and you make me happy in other ways. I think you like screaming, if I remember right."

Jane ignored Bram's chuckle, but Kai glared at Stonefire's leader before looking back to Jane. "Let's go home. And I'm impatient, so I'm carrying you."

"Don't you—"

Kai stood up with Jane in his arms. "This way is faster."

Jane clutched her arms around Kai's neck not a second too soon. Her dragonman was running out of Bram's house and toward their own within seconds.

Laying her head over his heart, she listened to the steady rhythm and couldn't help but smile. Kai was hers as much as she was his. And there was no bloody way she was giving him up. Even if Maggie Jones showed up, Jane believed Kai would choose Jane over the Welsh dragonwoman. Bram's words about actions speaking volumes were true. Kai would always hold her close and never let her go.

Not even a dragon's bloody instinct was going to change that.

# EPILOGUE

*Three weeks later*

Jane eyed the seven-foot wide and four-foot tall basket with large metal ring handles and then back to Kai standing beside her. "Have any of those rings given out before? They're only attached to the basket with a few scraps of fabric."

The corner of Kai's mouth ticked up. "That's excuse number fifteen as to why you don't want to go up for a flight. You're running out of excuses."

She straightened her shoulders. "I'm not making up excuses. I'm trying to ensure quality control."

Kai crossed his arms over his chest. "I don't bloody care what you call it. If you want to meet my sister, mum, and stepfather, then you need to get into that damn basket."

"I still don't understand why we can't drive."

"They live in the mountains near Snowdonia National Park in Wales. It's extremely difficult to drive there. Flying is easier."

"Ah, but driving isn't impossible."

Kai sighed. "You're the one who wants to go. I'm content to have them come here."

Jane eyed the basket again. The trip was much more than Kai getting to see his family, and she knew it. Bram and Evie were pinning their hopes on the visit going well. If it did, it opened up further talks of alliances and cooperation.

Jane refusing to crawl into the basket would be extremely selfish.

Looking up at Kai, she reached out and placed a hand on his chest. "You promise to catch me if the basket falls?"

He placed his hand over hers and grunted. "It won't bloody happen. But if it does, I will always catch you, Jane. Even if it means breaking every bone in my body."

She smiled. "You're turning into quite the romantic. Are you still the strong, fierce Protector I first met in Newcastle?"

"Of course." He tugged her close. "Even a soldier can have a soft spot for his mate."

"I'm not your mate, yet."

Kai's pupils flashed to slits and back. "Only because you haven't decided on a date yet."

She placed a gentle kiss on his lips and murmured, "Be patient, Kai. The best things are worth waiting for."

His look turned heated and Jane knew if she didn't run to the basket in the next ten seconds, their trip would be postponed yet again.

She pushed against Kai's chest and he reluctantly let her go. Walking toward the basket, she said over her shoulder, "Aren't you coming? We don't want to keep your mum and sister waiting."

Kai merely shook his head as he shucked his clothes and tossed them into the basket. "If we're late, it's your fault, not mine."

Jane paused and then leaned against the woven basket. "I thought that a dragon in love bent over backwards for his or her mate."

"You're not officially my mate, yet." Kai smiled. "Regardless of what that scrap of paper says, you need to wear my name on your arm and claim me in front of the clan to truly make it official."

Jane stuck out her tongue and then replied, "You might've won this round, but I'm still ahead."

Kai walked a little further away to give him room to shift. "Only because you cheat."

"Hey, it's not my fault you lost five points for punching my brother in the face."

Kai grunted. "He started it."

She placed a hand on her hip. "Still, you promised not to hit him. You could've pinned him with one of your special moves instead."

"He scolded you for 'shacking up with a dragonman' and then yelled at me for defiling his sister. He was the idiot who punched me. He learned his lesson in the end."

Jane still remembered Rafe's black eye from the video conference a few days later. "Just be glad he hasn't withdrawn his help in tracking the hunters."

"For all his faults, Rafe cares about your safety. He'll do whatever it takes to ensure it." Kai gestured toward the basket. "Now, stop stalling and get into the bloody basket."

Before Jane could reply, wings grew from Kai's back, his nose elongated into a snout, and his arms and legs stretched into longer limbs with talons.

It may have been a cloudy November day, but Kai's golden hide shined even in the dim light.

He was beautiful.

Kai squatted before jumping into the air. A few beats of his wings later and he hovered in place to the left of where she was standing.

Taking her cue, Jane climbed into the basket and rearranged his clothes on the floor. After she picked up the thermal blanket she needed to keep warm, she shouted, "I'm ready."

Kai bobbed his head before slowly lowering over the basket. Wrapping herself in the blanket to help keep out the wind from his wings, Jane sat down on the floor so she wouldn't have to watch the ground speed past below her. She'd survived the flight with Nikki because Jane had been concentrating on Kai's injuries. She didn't have anything to distract her this time.

She swore amusement danced in Kai's eyes before he delicately gripped the rings in his talons.

As her bastard dragonman lurched into the air with more force than was necessary, Jane closed her eyes and shrank into her blanket. He'd done that on purpose and she'd get him back later.

For the moment, Jane focused on staying warm and keeping her eyes closed.

The ride was smoother than she'd imagined, but the air whooshing above her in combination with the beating of Kai's wings reminded her they were several hundred if not thousands of feet up in the air.

Humming a popular song she'd heard on the radio, Jane shifted her mind into reporter mode and ran through everything she wanted to find out about not just Kai's family, but Clan Snowridge as well. Bram and Evie were counting on her and Kai and she wasn't about to let them down. Not just because Bram had approved her podcast idea, but also because Stonefire was her home and she would do whatever it took to make it a safe place for all.

# REAWAKENING THE DRAGON

~~~

Kai looked down for the fiftieth time, but Jane was still huddled inside her blanket.

Leave it to him to have a mate who didn't enjoy flying.

His dragon spoke up. *She will. Give it time.*

*Says the beast who wants to do a sharp dive and then pull up again. It's fun.*

*Not to Jane.*

His dragon huffed and concentrated on flying. Without his mate or dragon to talk to, his mind fell back on the upcoming meeting on Snowridge.

It'd been a few years since he'd seen his mum and sister. Mostly because of his cowardice, but also because of the terse relations between the two clans.

Yet the scare of the Dragon Knights and news of Stonefire and Lochguard's alliance had reached the ears of the Snowridge leader, Rhydian, who saw an opportunity.

Since Kai's job was security, he'd leave politics to the likes of Bram. If something could be salvaged, Bram would do it.

All Kai needed to do was not piss anyone off.

Oh, and avoid Maggie.

His beast chimed in again. *Who cares? We have Jane. She is ours.*

*I know and I will drug you unconscious if that's what it takes to keep Jane over Maggie.*

*The frenzy pull lessens with time. Nothing will take me away from Jane.*

At his dragon's confident tone, Kai's nervousness eased a fraction. *Good, because I don't think I could live without her.*

*Neither could I.*

271

Content with his beast's answer, Kai enjoyed the majestic mountains below. They were nearing Snowdonia National Park and would soon be at Snowridge.

Unlike Stonefire and Lochguard, most of Snowridge's clan members lived inside the mountains. The scarce flat land was used for landing areas, the main hall, and for livestock.

Kai spotted the main landing area on the edge of Snowridge and slowed his descent. With Jane's life at stake, he needed to be extra careful. Miscalculating the distance of a sharp rock face could injure his fragile human.

His dragon snorted. *Fragile indeed.*

Ignoring his dragon, Kai worked with his beast to slowly lower the basket to the ground. Once Jane was safe and sound on solid land again, he scanned the area out of habit.

His mother and sister stood in human form at the far edge of the landing area.

The sight of his sister Delia all grown up squeezed his heart. She was fifteen years old and nearly as tall as him, if he had to guess. Her previously long, brown hair was short, though. He wondered if there was a reason she cut it.

Jane's voice drifted up to his ears. "Kai."

Looking away from his sister, Kai moved a few feet over and landed. Imagining his body shrinking back into a human, Kai stood on his two feet again just as a wind blew across the landing area. Even though dragons could survive the cold longer than humans, he still shivered. "Bloody Welsh winds."

Jane arrived at his side and tossed her blanket over his shoulders. "There. Now you won't shiver as you greet your mother."

"I could hold back even without the blanket."

# Reawakening the Dragon

Jane rolled her eyes and thrust his clothes into his arms. "For maybe another thirty seconds. But I rather like you in a warm, pink color. Blue doesn't suit you."

At the mention of turning blue because of the cold, Kai scrutinized Jane's face, but apart from being a little paler than usual, she looked fine. "How are you feeling? Do you need to lie down?"

"I'm fine. If this is how you act now, I hate to see what happens if we ever decide to have a child."

Since Kai and Jane had a lot to accomplish over the next few years, it wasn't the right time for a child just yet. However, the thought of one day having a little one warmed Kai's heart.

Before Kai could reply, his mum's voice cut in, "Stop fretting over the girl, Kai Wilbur Sutherland and give your mum a hug."

Jane's voice was full of laughter as she echoed, "Wilbur?"

Ignoring his mate, Kai turned toward his mother, who already had her arms open. With a sigh, he lowered the blanket to his waist and walked into them. "Hello, Mum."

His mother hugged him tightly. "It's been too long, Kai." She pulled back and her green eyes searched his before she smiled. "But I'm glad you're happy this time."

Delia spoke up. "Hey, Kai."

As his mum released him from her hug, he looked over at his sister, who had her thumbs tucked into her jeans. For a variety of reasons, Kai and Delia had never spent much time together after he joined the army. He missed hoisting his baby sister onto his shoulders and mimicking a flying dragon.

He'd let too many years slip away.

Jane came up to his side and her actions broke through his memories. Hugging his female, he nodded toward his mum and sister. "Jane Hartley, may I introduce my mum, Lily Owens, and

273

my sister, Delia Owens. Mum and Delia, this is my female, Jane Hartley."

Delia's eyes lit up. "You're the reporter we saw on TV, who interviewed Melanie Hall-MacLeod and the others."

Jane smiled. "Yes, that's me."

Delia looked back to Kai. "You didn't tell me your female was famous." His sister moved to Jane's other side, threaded her arm through Jane's, and tugged. "You made me want to be a reporter. We don't have a lot of them inside the dragon clans, but I think that could change. Would you let me pick your brain? I have so many questions."

Kai grunted. "We just arrived. Give Jane some time to recover."

Jane raised an eyebrow. "As I said before, I'm fine." She looked to Delia with a smile. "And I'd love to chat, as long as it's indoors and I can have a cuppa."

Delia nodded. "We have all kinds of tea. Come, I'll take you to our quarters." Delia looked up at Kai. "You can keep Mum company."

Before Kai could do more than blink, Delia had pulled Jane along and was chatting her ear off. Delia definitely took after their mum and his stepdad, both of whom never stopped talking.

His mum touched his bicep. "You'll deny it with your dying breath, but you're probably cold. Let's get inside and you can tell me all about how you met Jane Hartley."

He shrugged. "Nothing special. We crossed paths tracking down some dragon hunters."

"Is that sarcasm I hear? I never thought I'd hear it again."

Staring at his mother's face with its slight wrinkles around the eyes and mouth as well as her graying blonde hair, it hit him just how long it'd been since he really talked with his mother.

"You should thank Jane, although I wouldn't mention it to her directly. It might get to her head and inflate her ego."

His mum chuckled. "Sounds like someone I know." She looped her arms around his waist. "Come, Kai. I want to get to know your female better. I have plenty of embarrassing stories to tell."

"Mum."

She grinned. "Your mate's a reporter. She could probably find them all out anyway. Besides, giving her a few stories will put me in her good graces. That way, we can team up against you later on."

He grunted, but then smiled. As he walked with his mum toward her home, the part of Kai that had missed his family faded away. Thanks to a stubborn, reckless female walking into his life, Kai had not only had found love again, but he also had his mum and sister.

His dragon spoke up. *One day, we will have our own family. I will never let Jane go.*

There was still a lingering worry about seeing his true mate.

But a few minutes later, Kai spotted a dark-haired female peeking around a rock at him.

It was Maggie Jones.

Yet as he watched the timid female, there was no desire to rush over and win her. And he had zero interest in kissing her.

Not even his dragon did more than blink.

His beast huffed. *I told you. I only want Jane.*

He waved at Maggie, but she turned and ran away.

A female like that would never be the right fit for Kai. Maybe a dragon's instinct wasn't always right.

His dragon chimed in again. *We all have a say in our future. We were lucky and had a second chance.*

His mum scrutinized his face. "Are you all right, Kai?"

Squeezing his mum's shoulder, he answered, "Never better, Mum. Now, let's hurry. I want out of this bloody cold."

"More like you want to cuddle your female."

He grunted. "Dragon-shifter males don't cuddle."

His mum laughed. "Keep telling yourself that, Kai. Maybe one day it will actually come true."

As he mum chatted about recent events in the clan, Kai picked up their pace. His mum was right—he wanted to cuddle his female and never let her go.

Dear Reader:

Thanks for reading Kai and Jane's story. Like all of my heroes and heroines, they'll show up again in future books! The next Stonefire Dragons story is a novella about Bram and Evie having their baby and is called *Loved by the Dragon*. After that, it will be Nikki and Rafe's story, *Surrendering to the Dragon*. (And don't worry, I have many more stories to tell after that!)

If you liked this story then you may enjoy my Asylums for Magical Threats series. Turn the page for a synopsis and excerpt from the first book in the series, *Blaze of Secrets*.

With Gratitude,
Jessie Donovan

# *Blaze of Secrets*
## (Asylums for Magical Threats #1)

After discovering she has elemental fire magic as a teenager, Kiarra Melini spends the next fifteen years inside a magical prison. While there, she undergoes a series of experiments that lead to a dangerous secret. If she lives, all magic will be destroyed. If she dies, magic has a chance to survive. Just as she makes her choice, a strange man breaks into cell, throws her over his shoulder, and carries her right out of the prison.

To rescue his brother, Jaxton Ward barters with his boss to rescue one other inmate--a woman he's never met before. His job is to get in, nab her and his brother, and get out. However, once he returns to his safe house, his boss has other ideas. Jaxton is ordered to train the woman and help her become part of the anti-magical prison organization he belongs to.

Working together, Kiarra and Jaxton discover a secret much bigger than their growing attraction to each other. Can they evade the prison retrieval team long enough to help save magic? Or, will they take Kiarra back to prison and end any chance of happiness for them both?

**Excerpt from *Blaze of Secrets*:**

# CHAPTER ONE

*First-born* Feiru *children are dangerous. At the age of magical maturity they will permanently move into compounds established for both their and the public's protection. These compounds will be known as the Asylums for Magical Threats (hereafter abbreviated as "AMT").*
　　　—Addendum, Article III of the *Feiru* Five Laws, July 1953

*Present Day*

　　　Jaxton Ward kept his gaze focused on the nearing mountain ledge ahead of him. If he looked down at the chasm below his feet, he might feel sick, and since his current mission was quite possibly the most important one of his life, he needed to focus all of his energy on succeeding.

　　　After all, if things went according to plan, Jaxton would finally see his brother again.

　　　He and his team of three men were balanced on a sheet of rock five thousand feet in the air. To a human, it would look like they were flying. However, any Feiru would know they were traveling via elemental wind magic.

　　　Darius, the elemental wind first-born on his team, guided them the final few feet to the mountain ledge. As soon as the sheet of rock touched solid ground, Jaxton and his team moved into position.

The mountain under their feet was actually one of the most secure AMT compounds in the world. Getting in was going to be difficult, but getting out was going to take a bloody miracle, especially since he'd had to barter with his boss for the location of his brother. In exchange, he had promised to rescue not just Garrett, but one other unknown first-born as well.

Taka, the elemental earth first-born of Jaxton's team, signaled he was ready. He nodded for Taka to begin.

As Taka reached a hand to the north, the direction of elemental earth magic, the solid rock of the mountain moved. With each inch that cleared to form a tunnel, Jaxton's heart rate kicked up. Jaxton was the reason his brother had been imprisoned inside the mountain for the last five years and he wasn"t sure if his brother had ever forgiven him.

Even if they survived the insurmountable odds, located Garrett, and broke into his prison cell, his brother might not agree to go with them. Considering the rumors of hellish treatment inside the AMT compounds, his brother's hatred would be justified.

Once the tunnel was big enough for them to enter, Jaxton pushed aside his doubts. No matter what his brother might think of him, Jaxton would rescue him, even it if took drugging Garrett unconscious to do so.

Taking out his Glock, he flicked off the safety. Jaxton was the only one on the team without elemental magic, but he could take care of himself.

He moved to the entrance of the tunnel, looked over his shoulder at his men, and nodded. After each man nodded, signaling they were ready, he took out his pocket flashlight, switched it on, and jogged down the smooth tunnel that would lead them to the inner corridors of the AMT compound.

# Reawakening the Dragon

If his information was correct, the AMT staff would be attending a site-wide meeting for the next hour. That gave Jaxton and his team a short window of opportunity to get in, nab the two inmates, and get back out again.

He only hoped everything went according to plan.

*~*~*

Kiarra Melini stared at the small homemade shiv in her hand and wondered for the thousandth time if she could go through with it.

She had spent the last few weeks racking her brain, trying to come up with an alternative plan to save the other prisoners of the AMT without having to harm anyone. Yet despite her best efforts, she'd come up empty-handed.

To protect the lives of the other first-borns inside the AMT, Kiarra would kill for the first and last time.

Not that she wanted to do it, given the choice. But after overhearing a conversation between two AMT researchers a few weeks ago, she knew the AMT would never again be safe for any of the first-borns while she remained alive.

The outside world might have chosen to forget about the existence of the first-born prisoners, but that didn't make them any less important. Kiarra was the only one who cared, and she would go down fighting trying to protect them.

Even if it meant killing herself to do so.

She took a deep breath and gripped the handle of her blade tighter until the plastic of the old hairbrush dug into her skin. Just as she was about to raise her arm to strike, her body shook. Kiarra closed her eyes and breathed in and out until she calmed down enough to stop shaking. Ending her life, noble as her reasons may be, was a lot harder than she'd imagined.

Mostly because she was afraid to die.

But her window of opportunity was closing fast; the AMT-wide meeting would end in less than an hour. After that, she would have to wait a whole other month before she could try again, and who knew how many more first-borns would suffer because of her cowardice.

Maybe, if she recalled the conversation between the two researchers, the one which forebode the future harsh realities of the other AMT prisoners, she'd muster enough nerve to do what needed to be done.

It was worth a shot, so Kiarra closed her eyes and recalled the conversation that had changed the course of her life forever.

Strapped to a cold metal examination table, Kiarra kept her eyes closed and forced herself to stay preternaturally still. The slightest movement would alert the researchers in the room that she was conscious again. She couldn't let that happen, not if she wanted to find out the reason why the researchers had increased her examination visits and blood draws over the past two weeks.

Most AMT prisoners wouldn't think twice about it, since they'd been conditioned not to ask questions, but Kiarra had gone through something similar before. The last time her visits had increased with the same frequency, the AMT researchers had stolen her elemental magic.

Since then, no matter how many times she reached to the south—the direction of elemental fire—she felt nothing. No tingling warmth, no comforting flame. She was no different from a non-first-born, yet she was still a prisoner, unable to see the sky or feel a breeze, and forced to live in constant fear of what the guards or researchers might do to her.

Of how they might punish her.

Dark memories invaded her mind. However, when the female researcher in the room spoke again, it snapped Kiarra back to the present. The woman's words might tell her more about her future, provided she had one after her treatment.

She listened with every cell in her body and steeled herself not to react.

"Interesting," the female researcher said. "Out of the ten teenagers, nine of them still can't use their elemental magic, just like F-839. Dr. Adams was right—her blood was the key to getting the Null Formula to work."

It took all of Kiarra's control not to draw in a breath. Her serial number was F-839, and all of the extra blood draws finally made sense—the AMT was using her blood to try and eradicate elemental magic.

The male researcher spoke up. "They're going to start a new, larger test group in a few weeks and see if they can stop the first-borns from going insane and/or committing suicide. If we don"t get the insanity rate below ten percent, then we'll never be able to implement this planet-wide."

"Don't worry, we'll get there. We have a few million first-borns to burn through to get it right."

Kiarra opened her eyes and embraced the guilt she felt every time she thought about what had happened to those poor first-born teenagers.

Because of her blood, not only had five teenagers already gone insane, but their insanity was driving an untold number of them to suicide.

And the researchers wanted to repeat the process with a larger group.

She couldn't let that happen.

They needed her blood, drawn and injected within hours, as a type of catalyst for the Null Formula to work. If they didn't have access to her blood, they wouldn't be able to conduct any more tests.

There was a chance the researchers might find another catalyst within a few weeks or months, but it was a risk she was willing to take. Stopping the tests, even for a few months, would prevent more people from going insane or committing suicide.

Kiarra needed to die.

*I can do this. Think of the others.* Taking a deep breath, she tightened her grip around the shiv's handle and whispered, "Please let this work,'"" before raising the blade with a steady hand and plunging it into the top half of her forearm.

Kiarra sucked in a breath as a searing pain shot up her arm. To prevent herself from making any more noise, she bit her lip. Despite the AMT-wide staff meeting, a guard would come to investigate her cell if she screamed.

*You can do this, Kiarra. Finish it.* With her next inhalation, she pulled the blade a fraction more down toward her wrist. This time she bit her lip hard enough she could taste iron on her tongue.

While her brain screamed for her to stop, she ignored it and gripped the handle of the blade until it bit into her palm. Only when her heart stopped beating would the other first-borns be safe—at least from her.

An image of a little girl crying, reaching out her arms and screaming Kiarra's name, came unbidden into her mind, but she forced it aside. Her sister had abandoned her, just like the rest of her family. Her death wouldn't cause anyone sadness or pain. Rather, through death, she would finally have a purpose.

This was it. On the next inhalation, she moved the blade a fraction. But before she could finish the job, the door of her cell slid open.

Kiarra looked up and saw a tall man, dressed head to toe in black, standing in her doorway and pointing a gun straight at her.

Shit. She'd been discovered.

---

Want to read the rest?
*Blaze of Secrets* is available in paperback

*For exclusive content and updates, sign up for my newsletter at: http://www.jessiedonovan.com*

# AUTHOR'S NOTE

I hope you enjoyed Kai and Jane's story. Believe it or not, theirs has been the hardest one for me to write so far. Probably because they're both stubborn and exhausting. However, with some time, I may write a follow-up story for them (after I write the one for Finn and Arabella).

As always, I have a lot of people to thank for making this book a reality. First and foremost is my editor Becky Johnson of Hot Tree Editing, who never hesitates to tell me when I'm being lazy. I also want to give a shout out to my beta readers—Iliana, Donna, and Alyson—who help give my stories the final polish they need to shine. These ladies help me for free and I'm incredibly grateful for their input.

If you don't know my cover artist by now, Clarissa Yeo of Yocla Designs, then you should! She is amazing and I love her work. She's done all of my covers and helped to create the brand that is Jessie Donovan. I owe her a lot.

Lastly, my readers and fans are awesome. Whether you merely read all of my books or are active in my Fan Group on Facebook, I treasure all of you because you make writing full-time a reality. Thank you!

After this book, the series is splitting into two. Stonefire will continue to have books released, but I'm also writing about Clan

Lochguard in the Scottish Highlands. The first Lochguard book is *The Dragon's Dilemma* and it's available now. After that, the next Stonefire book will be *Loved by the Dragon*, which is Evie and Bram's follow-up novella. To keep abreast of all of my new releases, make sure to join my newsletter at:

http://www.jessiedonovan.com/newsletter.

# About the Author

Jessie Donovan wrote her first story at age five, and after discovering *The Dragonriders of Pern* series by Anne McCaffrey in junior high, she realized people actually wanted to read stories like those floating around inside her head. From there on out, she was determined to tap into her over-active imagination and write a book someday.

After living abroad for five years and earning degrees in Japanese, Anthropology, and Secondary Education, she buckled down and finally wrote her first full-length book. While that story will never see the light of day, it laid the world-building groundwork of what would become her debut paranormal romance, *Blaze of Secrets*.

Jessie loves to interact with readers, and when not traipsing around some foreign country on a shoestring or reading a book, can often be found on Facebook. Check out her pages below:

http://www.facebook.com/JessieDonovanAuthor

And don't forget to sign-up for her newsletter to receive sneak peeks and inside information. You can sign-up on her website:

http:///www.jessiedonovan.com

Made in the USA
San Bernardino, CA
18 May 2017